D1035406

THE DAISY CHAIN

Recent Titles by Sally Stewart from Severn House

CASTLES IN SPAIN
CURLEW ISLAND
FLOODTIDE
LOST AND FOUND
MOOD INDIGO
POSTCARDS FROM A STRANGER

THE DAISY CHAIN

Sally Stewart

This first world edition published in Great Britain 2001 by
SEVERN HOUSE PUBLISHERS LTD of
9–15 High Street, Sutton, Surrey SM1 1DF.
This first world edition published in the USA 2002 by
SEVERN HOUSE PUBLISHERS INC of
595 Madison Avenue, New York, N.Y. 10022.

British Library Cataloguing in Publication Data

Stewart, Sally
The Daisy chain
1. Gascony (France) – Social life and customs – 20th century – Fiction
I. Title
823.9′14 [F]

ISBN 0-7278-5794-0

Except where actual historical events and characters are being described for the storyline of this novel, all situations in this publication are fictitious and any resemblance to living persons is purely coincidental.

Typeset by Palimpsest Book Production Ltd.,
Polmont, Stirlingshire, Scotland.
Printed and bound in Great Britain by
MPG Books Ltd., Bodmin, Cornwall.

One

A rich, full life required contrasts – the more extreme the better, people liked to say. Robert Ashton paid little heed to them as a rule, being a man who chose to work out his own opinions. But he couldn't deny that the difference in the journey he was making now from his first arrival in this place eight years ago was as poignant as anything he could remember. Then, he'd been an airman on the run after being shot down over Northern France and, with the Channel ports in German hands, there'd been only one way to go – down towards Spain. Often hungry, mostly frightened, he'd finally survived that journey. He hadn't been back since. Now, in this year of comparative grace, 1950, France might be shabby still, and poor, but he could drive through it unchallenged and unafraid. The grey Wehrmacht uniforms had disappeared, and so, thank God, had the miasma of humiliation and defeat.

One day he'd repeat that first journey, to find the people who'd been brave enough to help him, but for the moment he had a more limited objective and a more urgent need. His search would begin in Auch, ancient capital of what, despite newer names thought up by bureaucrats in Paris, the inhabitants still insisted on calling Gascony. When he'd stumbled into it on a November afternoon in 1942 it had seemed to be the despairing end to his attempt to evade capture; instead, it had been only the beginning of a brief interlude he'd never forgotten.

He had no address now to guide him, only a remembered name engraved on a doctor's brass plate, and a recollection, fever-heightened at the time, of a tree-lined square lying in the shadow of a vast church. That, at least, was easy enough to find – the Cathedral of Sainte Marie dominated both the city and the river Gers that flowed through it. He found that he remembered something else as well – the monumental staircase that led up to the church. Inching his way up those bloody steps had taken the last of his strength, but the church doors at the top had been firmly locked: no refuge there from the Vichy police and the German soldiers patrolling the streets. They'd have picked him up soon enough if a woman hadn't found him first and refused to leave him there. With her arm holding him up, he'd staggered the hundred yards to her front door and collapsed inside the door.

The square behind the cathedral looked different now. Instead of being bare the plane-trees were springing into vivid leaf. But the pleasant, dignified houses struck no chord in his memory – which had it been? They all looked alike. He'd almost completed a circuit of the square when the sign he needed sprang out at him – a professional man's plate beside a shabby green door. The name wasn't the one he remembered but he knocked anyway, suddenly convinced that the house seemed familiar.

A stranger opened the door, and her expression didn't change even when he apologised courteously for troubling her. He'd come to the wrong address, she said at once; Dr Morisot, the present owner, was away and she knew of no other doctor or his wife. Her accent was hard to follow but her attitude was not. Robert Ashton supposed that his own speech might identify him to her as a Parisian, and to a true-born Gascon, therefore, he would seem an unwelcome foreigner from the north. To these people the rest of France was a different country.

'I've come from London,' he explained quickly to make matters clear. 'Dr Mayer and his wife saved my life during the war. Perhaps you at least knew them then if you were here?'

He thought she debated whether to reply or close the door; either way, London seemed quite as bad as Paris in her view. Then to his surprise, she answered him.

'I wasn't here; I lived twenty kilometres away, waiting for my husband to get himself killed, spying for the British. He finally managed it; that's why I have to work for Dr Morisot.'

He could feel the anger that still burned in her – for herself, more probably, than for the fool she thought her husband had been. 'Then you lost a brave man, Madame; I'm very sorry,' he answered quietly.

She shrugged the sympathy aside, but something in his manner seemed finally to lessen her hostility. 'I've not heard mention of the Mayers, but that isn't surprising. People prefer not to talk about what happened in the war. You could ask in the cathedral – one of the priests might know.'

He tried to thank her but she was already closing the door, and he turned away, trying not to feel discouraged. Her reaction was what he might have expected, of course. The men and women of the secret networks had been heroic, God knew, but they'd often brought harsh reprisals on their fellow-citizens; steering a perilous course between collaboration and resistance had been as much as most people could manage.

The cathedral doors were open this time, but instead of going in search of a priest he was momentarily held transfixed by the blaze of colour that poured down from the tall windows encircling the apse behind the high altar. On glass painted crimson, violet, blue and gold the story of the Nativity and the Crucifixion was still being told, as vividly now as the day a medieval master-craftsman had begun his task. Finally jolted out of wonder by the sight of a priest emerging from the choir, Robert again explained his purpose there but this time with a half-rueful apology.

'I'm clutching at straws, I'm afraid. My guess, Father, is

that you were still at a theological college when I met the Mayers in 1942!'

'In fact I was about to leave school – but in Toulouse, not here,' the young priest admitted. 'Nevertheless it happens that I *can* add something to your story. Come with me, Monsieur.'

Together they walked the length of the nave and stopped at a small chapel almost beside the door Robert had come in by. Sunlight glowed through stained-glass here as well, but the window was very small and its beautiful simplicity was entirely modern. An engraved plaque beneath dedicated it to the memory of Dr Alain Mayer and his wife Marguerite, put to death in Auschwitz in 1943.

The two men stared at it in silence, one of them struggling under the onslaught of emotions that he reckoned his godly companion would be bound to condemn. Clerics were obliged nowadays only to use words like forgiveness and love. Anyone who called himself a Christian wasn't supposed to hate his enemies or rage against what they'd done – that was the vengeful fire and brimstone stuff of an Old Testament he was meant to have outgrown by now. With a huge effort Robert mastered himself enough to speak quietly.

'The Mayers died for helping men like me – their lives in exchange for ours. They were such good, useful people that I wonder if the sacrifice was worth it.'

The young man beside him hesitated for a moment. He knew what his superiors would say: a veil had to be drawn over the past if wounds were ever to be healed; but wasn't it also a priest's duty to give comfort where he could?

'Their death had little if anything to do with you,' he finally insisted. 'They were rounded up with others who weren't found . . . acceptable. Dr Mayer's grandparents had been Alsatian Jews who settled in Auch before the First World War.'

'How do you know that? You said you weren't here,' Robert pointed out hoarsely.

'Their daughter told my predecessor when she made us a gift of the window. If she'd had her way the inscription would have said something else – that her parents had been killed by the Germans but first betrayed by some of their fellow Frenchmen. The authorities refused permission for that and she had to accept their ruling in the end, but my colleague remembered her because she had been so angry.'

Robert nodded, easily able to believe what the priest said. Jeanne Mayer would have been a good hater of her parents' enemies; not for her the tactful lie that concealed treachery. But she'd been up against more than the authorities. Hadn't the woman he'd spoken to in the square confirmed that everyone preferred to hide what had happened in the war? Five years into so-called peace, the ghosts of the past were still haunting the country, and perhaps he'd been over-optimistic about its recovery.

After a moment or two he turned away from the little window, unable to bear the contrast between its glowing beauty and the hideousness of what it commemorated. 'I came to find Jeanne Mayer, Father, as well as her parents. Can you tell me where she is?'

He thought he was half-prepared for the priest to shake his head, just as the man was doing now. Instinct had insisted all along that tracking Jeanne down wouldn't be easy; he had so little to go on, as well as so little idea of whether she would want to be found or not.

'I regret I can't help you, Monsieur,' he heard the priest say. 'Dr Mayer's daughter came here, of course, but she didn't live in Auch, so I was told. She certainly hasn't been back since I was appointed two years ago.'

Robert looked at the earnest young man in front of him, seeing instead the shadowy pictures that filled his mind's eye. 'How well do you know this part of Gascony?' he asked abruptly. 'You see, Dr Mayer couldn't keep me hidden in Auch – it was too dangerous when searches were being made all the time. I was taken instead to Marguerite's old home –

the farm where Jeanne had already been sent to live with her grandparents.'

'You never knew who they were?' the priest asked curiously, 'didn't even know where you'd been taken?'

'To begin with I was too ill to care. They expected me to die, I think, but I gradually got better. Even then I wasn't allowed out of doors, and it was made clear that I was to ask nothing about them. What I didn't know I couldn't give away if I was caught when I was fit enough to start travelling again.'

'It must have been a strange interlude,' the priest suggested rather helplessly.

His companion's faint smile acknowledged the understatement. 'Strange enough – I lived in a hayloft above the barn! The roof was a rustic masterpiece of beams and rafters and I'd spend hours trying to work out how artisans with the simplest of tools had ever managed to create it. There were peep-holes in the walls – enough to give me glimpses of the valley around the farm and the village that crested a neighbouring hill like a horse's mane. It seemed only to consist of a single street of houses, but there was a church, and a tall tower at one end – what I took to be the remains of an old fortress.' Robert Ashton stared at the priest's calm face, resisting a sudden, shocking urge to disturb its blandness by shouting at him. 'Doesn't that suggest *something* to you . . . a high village with a very noticeable tower?'

The young man lifted his shoulders in a faint shrug. 'Gascony is full of such old settlements, Monsieur – *bastides* we call them. They're relics of the days when this countryside was continually being fought over, not only by ourselves but by your countrymen as well!' He smiled at the idea, then brushed the smile aside for fear of having been tactless. 'Wait here a moment, please. There's an electrician working in the cathedral; he may know the environs of the city better than I do.'

Left alone, Robert turned round to face the little window

again. He wouldn't think of Jeanne; better to remember the couple it commemorated – a brave and clever doctor and his equally brave wife. Had they at least been allowed to die together in the bestial inhumanity of that concentration camp? He couldn't even permit himself the comfort of thinking so. By then they'd become simply numbers to their gaolers, not human beings at all. He knelt quickly at the altar-rail, wondering what chaotic prayer he could offer up that a tolerant God Almighty might make sense of. Then, as he stood up again, the priest came scurrying back towards him.

'The man has made a suggestion, Monsieur, and I should have thought of it myself. What you described sounds like the Donjon at Bassoues. It's something of a landmark in these parts, not easily missed from the surrounding valleys. At any event, it's a start, *n'est-ce-pas*?'

Robert thanked him and agreed that it was. About to leave, one more question framed itself on his lips.

'You were still a schoolboy at the beginning of the war but you must have learned about the horrors of it, perhaps even witnessed some of them. How do you reconcile those memories with your faith in a loving God?'

The priest paused a moment, then shook his head. 'I don't try – I only ask His forgiveness for them,' he answered simply. 'Now, I must leave you and attend to my duties. I hope you find what you are looking for, Monsieur.'

He smiled and walked away, leaving Robert to consider an answer that should have been expected. 'Forgive us our trespasses as we forgive them who trespass against us.' How many times had he mindlessly chanted that at school and RAF services? The truth was that he would never be able to forgive the people who'd reduced Jeanne's parents to nameless bodies in a mass grave. Much more, it went against all justice, all humanity, that *she* should be asked to do so.

The Hotel Aramis sounded more swashbucklingly jolly than

it proved to be. He spent an uncomfortable night in one of its gloomy bedrooms, wrestling with a bolster pillow presumably stuffed with bricks, but sleep wouldn't have come anyway. His mind was full of memories stirred up by the previous day, and ahead of him was the prospect, however faint, of finding Jeanne Mayer.

It was a relief to hear the neighbourhood church clock strike seven, and then repeat the process, according to French custom. He went downstairs to the cold dining-room shared the evening before with a handful of commercial travellers. This morning, empty of guests, it looked no more cheerful, and the waitress was unsmiling when she brought his breakfast. Still, the coffee was unexpectedly good, and the crisp, freshly baked bread a reminder of one of the pleasures of being back in France. He said so to the girl and wondered why she stared at him. With his fair hair she'd taken him for a German at first glance; now she thought she was sure where he came from.

'We don't see many Anglais here,' she announced, rather truculently. 'I expect they prefer to go down to the Mediterranean.'

'They aren't able to go anywhere much at all at the moment,' he felt obliged to point out. 'It's difficult to take money abroad, unless we have business to attend to.'

'Still, England wasn't occupied,' the waitress insisted. 'Things must be better than they are here. *We* still suffer, Monsieur.'

The English, she made it clear, hadn't suffered at all, and it was also clear that nothing he said would change her view of history. But he was irritated enough to answer her.

'Leaving aside the war itself, we still endure food rationing and the scarcity of everything we used to take for granted,' he pointed out firmly. 'Shall we agree that we're *all* still suffering, even though the worst is over?'

Her hands sketched an apology, grudgingly. 'Well, we aren't told now what's happening over there. During the war we listened in to the BBC – we weren't supposed to, of course, but people did. Funny, really, when a lot of them scarcely knew where London was. I expect you think we're still just as backward now.'

She seemed intent on finding his attitude something else to resent but the telephone out in the hall began to ring and she had to go and answer it. By the time he was ready to leave she hadn't reappeared, and he took away with him the renewed impression of wounds festering just below the surface. The priest yesterday hadn't been hostile, but all his other conversations had had this same edginess about them. Identified as English, he was being made to feel unwelcome; but a sadder fact was the mistrust he sensed between one Frenchman and another. Even the ending of the war hadn't brought an end to the suffering, because although collaborators had been punished, more often than not justifiably, there'd been vendettas as well, and the cruel settling of old scores that had nothing to do with the years of German occupation. The French seemed no more sure of themselves than of their erstwhile allies.

Setting off on his journey again, he had no idea how this would affect his arrival at the farm he was looking for; but if, assuming that he found it at all, there was to be no welcome offered to the Anglais, it would be just like the first time. They'd taken him in and refused to let him die, but only out of sheer Gascon stubbornness and pride, not because they thought anything of the English. Marguerite's brother had been at pains to make that clear, and so had her daughter, to begin with.

Two

Once the outskirts of Auch were left behind, the drive became beautiful. Those bird's eye glimpses from the hayloft hadn't prepared him for the loveliness of gently rolling hills, lush valleys cultivated or richly wooded, and countless streams born in the foothills of the Pyrenees all hurrying to find small rivers to flow into.

This far south the spring was already well advanced. The vineyards on the higher slopes were a froth of bright, fresh green, and beside every old stone farmhouse was an orchard fountaining blossom into the soft April sky. He could see why Gascony had been fought over for so long. Those medieval English kings could scarcely have been blamed for wanting to make a grab at it.

He was travelling south-westwards and each time the road crested a hill the clear air gave him skyline glimpses of the mountains blocking the way into Spain. Every hilltop seemed to have a fortress settlement clinging to it, well placed to observe where its next attack might be coming from. The villages were linked by small, hidden lanes that must have defeated even their most recent invaders. No wonder the wartime resistance here had been so determined and so successful.

Thinking of these things kept him from admitting that he was probably on a fool's errand. If Bassoues turned out not to be the place he dimly remembered, which of a dozen other hilltop villages was he to try next? And if beginner's luck *was* smiling on him and he got out of the car and walked smack into the very girl whose unfading image had brought him there, what idiocy would he stammer out . . . 'Just passing by, my dear Jeanne . . . no harm in looking you up, I hope?'

The mere thought of it made his hands clammy on the wheel and his heartbeat uneven. He'd have to do better than that, because Jeanne herself most certainly would. She'd be a poised woman of twenty-six now, but even in those days of stress and danger he'd never seen the girl she'd been then falter or lose her head.

However uncertain he was of what to do or say, the village was directly ahead of him. He must park the car and saunter along the street – the picture of a phlegmatic Englishman come to do the not very extensive sights of Bassoues. He could see the famous Donjon on the right-hand side of the road, and further along something else that he was sure he recognised – a church whose stone bell-tower was topped by a slate steeple that sat on it like a small and inappropriate hat.

Almost in front of it was a covered market whose great beamed roof straddled the main street, and he didn't know whether to be glad or sorry that he'd arrived on what was obviously market-day. Aproned farmers' wives, too busy to notice him, were selling eggs and early vegetables, and the special delicacies of the region – terrine of duck, and foie gras, and delicious Agen prunes steeped in Armagnac. Their menfolk were content to shake hands with each other as if they hadn't met for weeks, and make a great deal of noise. They stared curiously at the stranger, identifying him as not one of themselves, but preferring to be wary of a man they didn't know. Once he stopped with his heart in his mouth, but when the girl turned away from a stall he could see that only her cropped dark hair had made her seem familiar.

Rather to his surprise, the door of the Donjon was open. For the payment of a franc or two he could climb the stairs inside and emerge on to a platform that showed him the entire countryside. From his hayloft the tower had surely risen to the right of the village; so, with the road running westwards, it followed that the farm had been in the valley to the south. He could see several clusters of buildings scattered in that direction; it was a simple matter of calling at each of them in turn.

The first, when he found his way to it, was a disappointment. The once-sturdy half-timbered farmhouse must have been quietly falling into ruin for years. Its nearest neighbour *was* still a working farm but he'd have remembered the copse of tall trees it hid behind, and in any case they blocked out all sight of the tower. The next looked so feasible that he got out of the car and walked towards an open door. But a dog leapt out at him, snarling and eager to attack, and he was thankful when a man appeared and called it to order.

'I don't know you. Why are you here?'

The question aimed at him was harsh and didn't encourage him to confess the reason for his visit. About to apologise for trespassing and walk away, he tried one despairing question of his own.

'I don't suppose you happen to know someone who went by the name of "Cheval" during the war? I think he farmed not far from here.'

It produced an effect; he could have sworn to that. The man in front of him might think he'd given nothing away, but his knuckles had whitened on the stick he was gripping, and he couldn't quite sound unconcerned.

'Stupid sort of name, but I've never heard of it. You'd better clear off now; my dog doesn't like English strangers and no more do I.'

The unmannerliness of it, combined with a growing sense of futility, stung Robert into a sharpness of his own. 'Don't worry, Monsieur; I'm going. Perhaps *you* don't like my accent either, but I doubt if you're young enough to have had a father who spied for the British during the war. I wonder what *your* reason is for hating us?'

The man spat on the ground – a gesture that seemed more shocking than actual violence would have done. 'The

British led us into the war, and then ran away. Is that reason enough?'

'It would be if it were true,' Robert agreed. 'It *isn't* true, but I don't suppose you want to hear about that.'

He managed a faint smile that he hoped would be more irritating than rudeness would have been; then walked back to where he'd left the car. The farmer was still watching him as he drove away, perhaps wondering why the unknown Englishman should be looking for someone he'd pretended not to know.

The little incident had been unpleasant, but in an odd sort of way it had done him good. He'd find what he was looking for even if he drove about the damned district all day; but he'd do it simply to keep a promise he'd made to himself, not because he now had much hope that any good would come of it. Then, as usual when ignored, Fate suddenly decided to relent. Before he'd covered another half a dozen kilometres a neat sign beside a gateway read '*Ferme Darroze, propriété privée*', and he knew he'd seen it before. The name, glimpsed so briefly, hadn't registered enough to be recalled until now, but a car's dim sidelights *had* picked it out the night Alain Mayer had brought him here.

He parked the car by the side of the road, certain without knowing why that this time he wanted to arrive on foot. He walked on the grass verge that bordered the lane leading to the farm while in the meadow alongside it gentle-faced, cream-coloured cattle raised their heads to stare at him. He could even remember what they were called – 'Blondes d'Aquitaine' – and the lovely name suited them. There wasn't any doubt about it now. This *was* where Jeanne Mayer and a man he'd known only as 'Cheval' had taken care of him.

He could see people working among the vines on the land that sloped up towards another line of hills. Immediately in front of him was a long, low, stone-built house. Outbuildings clustered round the cattle-yard on one side; beyond it was the barn – *his* barn, he called it in his mind – the front of it set back in the usual Gascon way under a deep, beautifully beamed overhang.

He stood still for a moment, overwhelmed by the memories that flooded over him. The weeks he'd spent here amounted to a fraction of his thirty-odd years, but in terms of emotion experienced – more then than ever before or since – he wouldn't be able to forget them. He'd come empty-handed; what he *should* have done, he now realised, was to bring gifts from England. But the thought made him suddenly grin; he might have been an adolescent again, about to be looked over by his sweetheart's family for the first time!

That was how Pierre Darroze saw him – a tall, fair-haired man smiling at some thought of his own – until he saw who it was that walked towards him out of the barn. There was a little silence while Gascon and Englishman recognised one another, measuring the changes eight years of war and peace had made.

'We didn't ever expect to see you back,' Pierre said at last. He didn't smile or close the gap between them to shake hands, and the lack of welcome was clear, but not the reason for it. Should the visit have been made sooner, or not at all? Robert didn't know, but a glimmer of humour insisted that there had been something wrong with the legend foisted on the world by Alexandre Dumas. D'Artagnan and his rollicking musketeers could never have been based on taciturn men like this one in front of him.

'I would have come sooner but it's hard for us to travel abroad,' he explained quietly. 'A business trip to Bordeaux gave me the chance I'd been waiting for since the war's end.'

Darroze thrust both hands into the pockets of his shabby trousers. 'You weren't supposed to have known where to find us.'

'I didn't know; had to begin by looking for the Mayers' house in Auch. I found the memorial window in the cathedral instead. There's nothing I can find to say to you about the loss of your sister and brother-in-law.'

The man in front of him lifted thick shoulders in a gesture that forbade sympathy, but for the moment he seemed uncertain what to do next. While he made up his mind, Robert looked at him more carefully. 'Cheval' had been a good *nom de guerre* for this tough, strong-featured man. His dark hair was flecked with silver now, and years of hard outdoor work combined with wartime stress and danger had etched deep lines in his face, making him look older than he was. He'd been a good Resistance leader – resolute, clever and brave. He was probably a successful farmer too, but there was still an air of wary alertness about him that seemed inappropriate in the peaceful setting of his home. Perhaps it had become a habit he couldn't lose; but left to him the conversation might founder altogether on the subjects he seemed disinclined to talk about.

'I hope your parents are alive and well,' Robert said tentatively, feeling his way towards the question that really mattered.

'A little older than you remember them, but my father still insists on running the vineyards. He's there now, convinced the men won't tie in the new vines properly unless he watches them.' There was a slight hesitation before Darroze went on. 'My mother is in good health but . . . but mentally not quite herself. She doesn't accept Marguerite's death – thinks my sister will walk in any day. We don't try to make her face the truth any longer.' His voice sounded unsteady for a moment but he got it under control again. 'That's why I don't invite you into the house; she'd get upset if she remembered you.'

Instead he pointed to a small office partitioned off from the rest of the barn, and new since Robert's memory of it. 'We could drink a glass of wine together here before you leave.'

His meaning was easy to understand: he was offering a small gesture of hospitality, but no invitation to linger on *propriété* that was very much *privée*. Inside the room he poured wine and pushed it across the table with something nearly approaching a smile.

'*Santé*, Mr Ashton! You see, I even remember your name!'

'And I never knew yours,' Robert pointed out, 'although I did hear a code-name mentioned once or twice.'

'I'm Pierre Darroze again now, son of André.' With the information came a little bow, and then a question. 'Did you make it back to England? We never used to hear what happened to the people we passed along the line.'

'Yes – with one or two adventures on the way, we got down to the coast. An RNVR boat masquerading as a fishing smack picked us up. It took us to Gibraltar and we were flown home from there.' He took a gulp of wine which didn't help the dryness in his mouth, and spoke again more abruptly than he meant to. 'I came to thank you, of course, for taking care of me. I owe my life to your sister and brother-in-law and the shelter I was given here. But I also need to know about Jeanne. The priest I spoke to in the cathedral said she'd never been back – is she still here?'

He knew what the answer was going to be, but something in the dark, watchful face opposite him made him suddenly cry out. 'They can't have got her as well – she provided her parents' memorial.'

Pierre Darroze shook his head. 'They might easily have done – once Marguerite and Alain were seized she ran mad risks; anything to defy the Germans. But she was still alive when the war ended. She'd married a friend of mine by then, one of the old Resistance group. They live with their son in a small town not very far away. Her husband is Mayor there, and the head of the farm co-operative.'

The sudden volley of information came to an end but Robert found nothing to say. He couldn't imagine now why, eight years on, he should have expected anything else. Any man she met would probably have wanted to marry Jeanne Mayer. There was no reason on God's earth why she should have waited for a chance-met Englishman to come back and track her down.

'Is she happy?' he finally asked, aware of a silence that had lasted too long. Pierre's expression made him add something more. 'It isn't a stupid question. She never bothered to hide what she was feeling, so you ought to know, one way or the other.'

'People change.' The answer came slowly. 'Jeanne is no longer an eighteen-year-old girl living on the wartime drugs of excitement and danger. As far as I know she's happy enough.' Pierre filled his guest's glass before he spoke again. 'I'm not going to tell you where she is. That would be pointless. The past is over and done with.'

A note of utter finality was in his voice, making it useless to persist, because nothing would persuade him to change his mind. What he knew of the past, or what he thought he knew, was enough, he believed, to repel an intrusion that could only do more harm than good. And he was right, God damn him. Jeanne was married to his friend; Robert Ashton could do nothing but accept the fact.

'I can't make you tell me where she is,' Robert said slowly, 'but perhaps you'll at least explain to her that I finally managed to come back.'

The man opposite him answered with a gesture of his head – agreement or refusal? It was impossible to know. Then he bestirred himself to change the conversation. 'I suppose you went back to your squadron when you got back to England?'

'Only briefly,' Robert replied. 'I wangled a transfer out of Fighter Command into the unit that flew Lysanders, carrying agents and supplies here to circuits like yours. Each trip I made I hoped to find you and Jeanne waiting at the landing-field, but I never did. I couldn't be sure you'd even survived.'

The anguish of those disappointments echoed in his voice and Pierre Darroze responded to it in his own way. 'They were strange times we lived through,' he muttered, after another glance at his visitor's withdrawn face. 'Unreal times, although that's not how they seemed then. They're over and best forgotten; thank God we can lead normal lives now.'

Robert drained the last of his wine, reminded that a farmer's normal life was a busy one. But there was still one thing to say. 'You speak of the past as being over and done with. I wonder if it is. Before I found this place I called at another farm a few kilometres away. An ill-tempered man and his even more unpleasant dog warned me off, but when I mentioned the only fact I had – your old wartime name – I'm certain he recognised it. It seemed to make him still more anxious to see the back of me.'

Pierre Darroze gave one of his expressive shrugs. 'All right, we *aren't* quite back to normal. People suffered because of our activities during the war; we haven't always been forgiven, I'm afraid.'

He watched his visitor stand up to leave and at last offered the handshake that so far hadn't been forthcoming.

'Thank you for this visit. I don't suppose we shall meet again, so I'll say now what should be said. It's not our way to admit the fact but the truth is that we had a great deal to thank the Anglo-Saxons for. We're still not very ready to acknowledge it, I'm afraid.'

Robert's taut face suddenly broke into a smile. 'Don't strain yourself – General de Gaulle has taught us not to expect too much in the way of gratitude! Now I'd better push off and let you get on with your work. Remember me to your parents, or not – as you think best.'

He hesitated, wondering still whether a message for Jeanne might be refused, but walked out with nothing more said. What was there to say, in any case, that wouldn't now have been – in the word Darroze had used – quite pointless?

On the long drive back to Bordeaux he kept telling himself that he'd done what he'd set out to do. An unfinished episode that had weighed on him for years had been completed and now he could get on with his life. A faint dream could at last be allowed to die in the cold, bright light of knowing that Jeanne Mayer was another man's wife and the mother of their child. Released from the time-warp he'd been trapped in like a fly in amber, he was free to go home and take a wife himself. The girl he had in mind to marry bore no resemblance at all to the unpredictable, small, brave, obstinate creature he had known as Pierre Darroze's niece. Christine wouldn't rail like a termagant one moment and dress his wounds the next, would never both madden and delight him, but so much the better for that. They would do what normal people did – live together in reasonable affection and harmony, and be grateful to God for that.

William Harcourt, Christine's uncle and his own guide, mentor and friend since they'd worked together during the latter part of the war, was waiting for him in the bar of their Bordeaux hotel. As usual, William had found someone to enjoy a conversation with but, at the sight of Robert, he went over to join him.

'We were right about this, dear boy,' he said happily, pointing to the wine in his glass. 'Already it's better than I thought, and in a year or two we'll have something remarkable to offer to the few clients who are worthy of it.'

The comment was typical. Only the chosen ones, Robert knew, would be allowed a sniff at it, much less be given the chance to buy. William didn't believe in casting pearls before swine, especially when pearls were still in such short supply. A new, post-war generation of wine-fanciers had to be educated and he was doing his best; but a real 'find' – a small vineyard that other shippers hadn't had the luck or wit to stumble on – was something to keep for his most discriminating customers.

'So the trip has been worthwhile,' Robert suggested, smiling at him.

'A trip to France is *always* worthwhile, but this has been especially useful. It was high time you met my old friends here, and I'm glad to know that they obviously liked you.'

William took another sip of wine, nodded to confirm his opinion of it, and then glanced at his companion. 'How did your own search go – at least, I assume it *was* a search that you set out on?'

His round, pink face looked grave for once, as if without being told he understood that the day had been important. But there was a great deal that William Harcourt understood, Robert reflected. He might look like everyone's idea of Mr Pickwick, and be known in London simply as a well-placed connoisseur with connections that every other shipper envied. But what wasn't public knowledge was the service he'd rendered France during the war. It had earned him the ribbon of the Légion d'honneur, an award that Charles de Gaulle hadn't ever made lightly.

William stared at his companion a moment longer, then spoke again. 'Forget my question, Robert – whatever you went looking for was something too personal to share.'

'I'd like to tell you about it all the same,' the answer finally came. 'I wanted to find the family I was rescued by during the war. My starting-point was Auch, where a woman called Marguerite Mayer risked her own life to save me. She and her husband took me to her parents' farm where her daughter, Jeanne, and her brother nursed me back to health. They didn't do that for love of the English, but only so that I could get back to fighting the Germans.'

'You managed to find all these people again?' William prompted gently.

'By no means. Marguerite and Alain Mayer died in Auschwitz. Their daughter had married and left the farm. Her grandparents *were* still there, but I wasn't invited to meet them. I saw only Marguerite's brother, Pierre Darroze, and he was no more cordial than in the days when I'd known him simply by his Resistance code-name, Cheval.'

'At least he could tell you where to find Jeanne,' William ventured.

'He chose not to,' Robert said briefly, 'and only brought

himself to admit as I was leaving what I was beginning to doubt. We *had* been comrades during the war, fighting the same monstrous enemy.'

The bitter sadness in his voice made William hesitate, but at last he found something to say. 'You can't give up on the *Entente Cordiale*, even if we and the French do find it all too easy to misunderstand and even mistrust each other. They blame us as much as we blame them when things go wrong; I'm afraid it comes more naturally than blaming ourselves. But Europe needs us both . . . always has done.' He pondered his next question carefully before he put it into words. 'Is that the end of your connection with the Darroze family?'

'Oh, I think so. Pierre's message was clear enough: forget the past; but if that's too difficult, at least bury it out of sight where it can't embarrass or disturb us. I expect the message was right, but going back to the farm was something I've always known I had to do.'

He'd had to know especially, William thought, what had happened to Jeanne, the girl who'd married and left the farm. William wished he could ask what *this* had meant to his friend, but Robert's controlled face defeated him. Instead, he risked a different question that might also seem too personal.

'Not my business, of course, but with the past safely tucked away, does the future involve my niece?'

'Yes – if Christine agrees,' Robert admitted. He offered his friend an apologetic smile. 'She might have got tired of waiting for me to sort myself out, and I couldn't blame her if she had.'

'*Most* unlikely,' Mr Pickwick advised him, restored to cheerfulness again. 'We Harcourts are a tenacious lot, and you've been her hero since I first took you home to meet an impressionable teenager!' He patted Robert's hand in a small, affectionate gesture. 'I'm very glad – it's what I always hoped would happen, even though I tried hard not to interfere.' He nearly added that their visit to France had now been everything they could have hoped for; but he remembered the discoveries Robert had made and said instead that there was time for a snack supper before they boarded the night train for Paris and the ferry home.

The wagon-lit was comfortable and Robert usually enjoyed night journeys on trains. The changing rhythm of the wheels, the disembodied voices in the darkness calling out station names whenever the great engine hauling them along hissed to a standstill . . . these were reminders of schoolboy travel with his mother before the war. But tonight there was no pleasant half-way state between daydream and sleep. His mind was wide awake but, commanded to think about the future, refused to let go of the past.

He still shied away from thinking of his mother's death in one of the first air-raids on London, but from then on memory ran clearly. He'd been luckier than most fighter-pilots and survived; then, after his escape to England, night-flying for F Section of the SOE, he'd had the great good fortune to meet William Harcourt. But for William he'd probably be dinning French irregular verbs into unwilling schoolboys by now. But for William he wouldn't have met beautiful, bright Christine, whose adolescent hero-worship of her uncle's protégé had grown into something much more adult and permanent.

With her image clear in his mind, he could get a grip on the future. If the train wheels lulled him to sleep it was likely the dream he'd relived so often might come again, but it would be for the last time. With the past decently interred, he could begin to look forward at last, not back.

Three

It *was* the same dream, or the same half-conscious re-enactment of a story that he'd never felt inclined to share with anyone else. Perhaps that was why it had remained so vivid; nothing had been leached away by repeated telling.

It had always begun in the same way – he was back in the cockpit of his Hurricane again, aware of having been hit. The fragile thing was doomed, and somehow he must get out. The dream never showed him how that was managed; he only remembered the relief of finding himself floating down through the cool air. The silk mushroom that had opened out above his head looked strangely beautiful and the silent drift to earth was peaceful after the bedlam that had gone before.

The afternoon was damp and dull – visibility, therefore, mercifully poor – but there was time to wonder who might be watching this unscheduled arrival. Then a different alarm . . . was he going to miss the copse he could see beneath him, or end up stranded in a tree? He thudded to the ground just missing the trees, but the undergrowth fringing the wood concealed different hazards. His left foot twisted agonisingly on a hidden piece of stone, and his right leg connected with a wire fence also unseen. For a few moments he could do nothing but sit doubled up on the ground until his mind began to clear. He must first rid himself of the parachute, then find somewhere to hide.

It was a struggle to release the harness but at last he was free of it and able to bundle up the silk. He crawled with it into the shelter of the trees that had now become something to be thankful for, and tried to take stock of his situation. Beyond feeling sure he'd crossed the French border before being hit, he had little idea of where he was. But the walk back to England was going to be long and he was scarcely equipped for it. His pockets contained a compass, a small torch, a slab of probably half-melted chocolate, and – his mother's gift of long ago – a paper-bound anthology of the sonnets of William Shakespeare.

The outlook was so bleak that he forced himself to concentrate on his immediate problems: a damaged foot, and a uniform that would identify him to the first German soldier he met. He also felt unbearably lonely, but when his hand touched the blood that was seeping through his torn trouser-leg, at least it brought a ray of hope. The wire that had caused it suggested farmed land, and when the dim light faded he might, by crawling along beside it, find a shed to shelter in for the night.

He set out when it was almost dark and came sooner than he expected to a whole huddle of buildings – surely the farm itself. There was no sign of life, no glimmer of light from shuttered windows. Upright now, he limped towards the looming outline of what he thankfully made out to be a Dutch barn – no locked doors, and countless bales of straw to hide behind. He risked the torch for a moment to select one as a bed, then collapsed on to it. One last effort eased the boot off his tortured foot – and then he could lie back on the straw. The morning would be time enough to consider what chance he had of doing anything but giving himself up.

A lantern shining in his face brought him awake. Behind it he could make out a man's dark shape, and beyond that the very faint beginning of the autumn dawn. The light moved over him and lingered on his tell-tale flying boots and jacket. No lie would have helped him even if he could have thought of one.

'You're the pilot whose plane crashed yesterday. Are you English?' At least the sharp question was voiced by a Frenchman, not a German trying to speak a foreign language.

'Yes, I'm English. I hope the plane chose an empty field to land in, and did your crops no damage.'

'You don't sound English – your French is too good.'

The strong inference that he wasn't what he claimed to be was very irritating but he answered patiently. 'My name is Robert Ashton. When the war broke out I was studying languages at Oxford – French and German.' He pulled on one boot, trying to decide what to do with the other one – carry it, or somehow cram his swollen foot inside? 'If you'll be kind enough to forget that I was here, I'll . . . I'll get on my way.'

'You might get as far as my house,' the man behind the lantern pointed out, 'not much further. You'd better come now before it gets light.'

Robert heaved himself upright and hopped behind his host across the farmyard. He was led into a large, dimly lit kitchen whose only illumination came from a log-fire burning in an ancient range. A woman putting out bowls and plates on the table gave no greeting as a stranger limped in, but she didn't look surprised.

'*Il est Anglais, Madeleine*,' the man explained. '*Il me comprend bien; aussi, il est un peu blessé*.'

It was so pithy a summing-up that Robert was forced to smile. The woman watching him registered the charm it lent to his tired, unshaven face, but still only spoke to her husband.

'*Il faut changer les vêtements, n'est-ce-pas? Je vais chercher quelque chose*.'

The farmer nodded and she left the room; then he turned to Robert again. 'I'm not a vet, but I'm used to treating animals. You'd better let me look at your foot.'

His large hands were unexpectedly gentle but the examination turned the patient's face chalk-white and clammy with sweat.

'Not broken, I think, but you've probably torn some ligaments. I can strap it up, but not till the swelling's gone down. It needs rest if it is to mend properly.' He shrugged the idea aside as being unrealistic in the circumstances and turned his attention to Robert's leg. When the dirt and dried blood had been swabbed away he smeared the wound with disinfectant ointment and bandaged it as neatly as any professional nurse could have done. There was a knock at the door and his wife returned with an armful of clothes which he took from her.

'You can wash at the sink,' he said to Robert, 'then get into these. Leave off anything that's got an English label in it – we shall have to give you a new identity.'

So . . . it was becoming clear now; there'd been no risk at all of this chance-met stranger turning him in. Whatever the danger to himself and his wife, he was involved in some local Resistance network.

'It seems that I was fortunate last night,' Robert said quietly. 'But it isn't fair to endanger you by staying here.'

'What is fair any more? We can only do what we think is right.' The man's face relaxed into a smile that suddenly turned him into a friend. 'France is a large country, thank God. Not even the Boche can be everywhere at once; in any case they feel safer in the towns.'

Clean and dressed again in shabby corduroys and a thick, homemade sweater, he was invited to take a place at the table. The farmer's wife reappeared, and breakfast began. The coffee was ersatz and the bread was hard, but when he followed his host's example and dipped his bread in the bowl of coffee it became enjoyable enough to eat with relish.

'Do you mind telling me where we are?' he asked suddenly.

'The *département* of Champagne,' his host explained. 'Reims is our nearest city.'

'Further south than I expected.' Robert relapsed into silence again, mentally surveying a map of France. Reims, to the east of Paris, was still an appallingly long way from the Spanish frontier.

'You won't do it on foot,' the farmer said suddenly, reading his thoughts. 'But despite the attentions of the RAF we have a sort of railway system left!'

Not sure whether it was a joke he was expected to smile at, Robert waited for what might come next. Madeleine Godard, watching their uninvited guest, saw his uncertainty and spoke directly to him for the first time.

'My husband means what he says – you'll have to travel by train. The railwaymen are always helpful – usually Communists of course, but good Resistance members as well.' She stared at Robert's fair head. 'We shall have to do something about your hair – no one would take you for a Frenchman, I'm afraid.'

The farmer looked at his watch and then stood up. 'I must go and get work started on the documents you'll need. I think you'd better be a schoolteacher – of English, *naturellement*! Not fit for military service, and called home for family reasons to the south. If anyone should come while I'm out Madeleine knows where to hide you.'

He smiled briefly at them both and then went out, leaving silence behind. His wife still sat at the table and Robert's guess was that she did so because she was very tired. He was clearly not the first fugitive this valiant couple had helped; she wasn't against helping him now, but the strain on her was becoming hard to bear.

'I feel very ashamed,' he said suddenly. 'There have certainly been Frenchmen making their way to England to fight, but even so we've tended to think that most people here were only too glad to accept Pétain's Armistice deal with the Germans. We reckoned we could hear them thanking God they were out of the war. It was a stupid point of view, but our only excuse is that we didn't know about men and women like you and your husband.'

Colour tinged her tired face for a moment but she shook

her head. 'I'm afraid your opinion is true of a lot of people, but you mustn't blame them – they still remember the last war and they're haunted by the military cemeteries that stretch from here to the Belgian frontier. We couldn't have survived the loss again of a million and a half young men, and the old Marshal knew that.'

'So why do *you* put yourself at so much risk – hatred of the Germans, or love of France?'

She gave the little shrug that seemed to be an essential part of any French conversation. 'I don't hate the German people, only the men who lead them into such wickedness. I don't even pay much attention to General de Gaulle broadcasting from London about saving the honour of France! We help men like you because our son was taken prisoner in May 1940. We haven't seen him since.'

She was a plain woman but not, Robert thought, when her face was touched with such love and aching loss as now. He stretched out a hand and touched hers where it rested on the table.

'The war won't last for ever. You *will* see him again,' he promised gravely.

She nodded and tried to smile. 'He'll wonder, poor boy, where all his clothes have disappeared to! He's not quite as tall as you, but you'll have to make do.' Recovered from the moment's weakness, she began to clear the table, ticking him off as calmly as she would have done her own son when he tried to help instead of resting his damaged foot.

The Godards kept him safe and fed for a week while his injuries slowly improved and his *carte d'identité* was manufactured in the name of Robert Dassin, schoolteacher, on his way home to inherit some property from a dead grandmother. His first destination would be Troyes, where a '*passeur*', whose name and address he had to memorise, would send him on the next stage of his journey. Speaking French as he did, he could at least be trusted to travel alone, but he was warned not to imagine that the journey would be less dangerous once he'd crossed the demarcation line into Vichy France; the Milice, Vichy's secret police, had modelled themselves on the Gestapo, and were bastards enough to match the Nazis, according to Jules Godard.

The morning planned for his departure arrived. His new life-story learned by heart, and his foot healed enough to be limped on, he was thankful to be removing from the Godards the danger that he represented. After a battle of wills with his host, he was allowed to put in the small attaché-case he'd been given his little book of sonnets. It was Madeleine who, after a glance at Robert's expression, helped to persuade her husband.

'It's *raisonable*, Jules – a teacher of English *would* have kept something like that to travel with.'

Robert gave her a grateful, goodbye kiss and pretended not to notice that she was beginning to weep. Five minutes later he was hidden among the sacks of vegetables Jules was taking to the market in Reims. The long journey to Spain had begun.

The train for Troyes arrived punctually, and it was a relief, because he felt somehow recognisably different from the other people on the platform. But when it came to a stop he found himself facing a coach reserved for the occupying forces. Unnerved, he moved along to a different coach, aware that his first close sight of German troops had been unexpectedly shocking. Those had been real, inimical men staring at him, a fact that attacking the enemy in purely aerial combat had somehow disguised until now.

He had to remind himself of whom he'd become – just another shabby, demoralised Frenchman ruled by Hitler's master race. After years in the north he was going home to claim a small inheritance. He was Robert Dassin. His identity-card said so, and his friends had promised that it would survive all but the most expert scrutiny.

A motherly woman in the seat opposite began a conversation, and he was earnestly embroidering a story about his mythical dead grandmother when the ticket inspector appeared. With him was a German NCO demanding to see identity-cards. There was a moment when he had to force himself to look at the man and command his hand not to tremble as he handed over the card. But it was returned to him unchallenged, and only when both men had left the coach did the woman opposite him enquire softly whether he felt all right – his face, she said, looked so very white. He managed to smile at her and explain that ever since he was a child sitting with his back to the engine had made him feel squeamish.

Twenty-four hours later he'd crossed the demarcation line into Vichy France. At Clermont-Ferrand he'd been recognised by another '*passeur*' and safely lodged for the night. The organisation of the network seemed to be superb and the men and women involved in it, just like the Godards, immeasurably brave. But at Agen, where he'd been told to leave the train, a shock awaited him. There were German soldiers in evidence again, carefully checking travellers through the station gates. The man beside him explained bitterly the reason why they were there. Because of Allied landings in North Africa, the Germans had decided to abandon the terms of the Armistice; the whole of France was now being occupied.

Robert agreed calmly that broken promises were all they could have expected from the Boche but, with his heart beating too fast, waited his turn to be interrogated, knowing that to try to avoid the inspection would be the most suicidal thing he could do. His card was examined, he explained his journey once again, and was let through. He could feel little runnels of sweat trickling down his back as he walked away, but knew he must keep walking – to the cousin he'd just invented as his host for the night.

The address he'd been given was hard to find – an arcaded street near the cathedral had sounded helpful enough as a direction, but Agen turned out to have numerous arcaded streets. The train had been very delayed and curfew hour was approaching, when it would be dangerous to be out of doors.

At last he found the address he'd memorised and knocked on the door with a sigh of relief. There was no reply and he had to risk the neighbours' curiosity by knocking again. Footsteps sounded inside on the tiled floor and a woman opened the door just wide enough to stare out at him.

'*Bonsoir, Madame – le Maître m'attend . . . je viens du Nord.*'

The identifying phrase he'd been instructed to use brought no invitation to step inside. The opposite, in fact; she made to close the door, and he repeated the words again more anxiously. '*Je viens du Nord, Madame. Ici c'est la maison du Maître Couvreur, n'est-ce-pas?*'

Her haggard face warned him of what was coming next. 'I don't know you,' she said fiercely. 'You must go away.'

He held the door ajar, hating himself for doing it and pitying her. 'Your husband knows *about* me. *Please* tell him I'm here – before a policeman notices me.'

Her eyes suddenly blazed in the dead pallor of her face. 'My husband was arrested this afternoon. I can't help you . . . I know nothing. Now go away before they come for me as well.'

It was impossible, in the face of that, to go on insisting. He murmured what he felt to be futile sympathy for her husband and turned away as the door closed behind him. The network had finally failed, but in the present circumstances what else could have been expected? He walked as if he knew where he was going, but his mind had become terrifyingly blank. He lacked shelter for the night and, probably worse, the precious thread that should have led him to his next contact had now been broken. It had begun to rain as night fell, and his suspicion was growing that he was being followed. The Milice, after arresting the lawyer, would almost certainly have watched his house to see who came calling on him.

A faint neon light illuminated a name ahead of him – the

Hotel Caprais – and without conscious thought he climbed the steps and went inside. A night's lodging there might use up most of the small supply of French money he'd been given, but he couldn't risk wandering aimlessly about the streets any longer.

The concierge was surly but didn't turn him away. His *carte* was taken, to be returned to him only when he left, but Robert wasn't alarmed by this – it was intended to prevent him absconding without paying. In exchange for food coupons he was given watery soup and an unidentifiable meat dish in the dining-room, but it was the atmosphere in the silent room that oppressed him. His fellow-diners looked sullen and without hope. If asked, he felt sure they'd have said that the Allied landings in North Africa had only made their own state worse.

In the morning the same concierge was behind the desk. When the bill had been paid, the moment came that he seemed to have been waiting for.

'I haven't your *carte d'identité*, Monsieur – the Milice took it away last night in one of their surprise visits. You must claim it from the Gendarmerie.'

It felt like a blow to the heart, but after a moment spent in folding his receipted bill very carefully, Robert was able to ask the obvious question.

'I'm a stranger here – where is the Gendarmerie?'

'On the far side of the Place de la Cathédrale. Even a stranger can't miss it.'

The faint emphasis on the word was deliberate, he felt sure; the man in front of him almost certainly guessed the bind he was caught in: was he to go to the Gendarmerie and have a false identity expertly demolished, or simply disappear and see how long he could survive without it? There wasn't any choice. He was certain now that he'd been followed from the lawyer's house, and the Milice's intention would be to try to beat out of him the names of the other people who had helped him.

He began to walk in the direction of the Cathedral Square, saw an alleyway whose entrance was briefly screened by a waiting van, and dived into it. While he loitered in a doorway, no one else followed him, and it seemed safe to assume that he wasn't being watched. The Milice felt certain, of course, that he couldn't leave without his *carte*. The alley led him to a shabbier district of the city – a neighbourhood of small workshops and poor houses. The people here looked no more prosperous than himself and he felt less visible.

In a cheap café he ordered coffee, in order to give himself time to stop and think. For the first time since meeting Jules Godard, his situation now looked hopeless: he had very little money, and nothing to show if challenged. It was time for Robert Dassin to die and Robert Ashton to reappear. With the aid of the compass he still had, he would walk south until he was caught. Then he'd admit to being who he was – an escapee who'd broken into an empty house and stolen money and the clothes he was wearing. If God was merciful he'd at least get far enough away from Agen for his captors not to know that he'd ever called at the lawyer's house, and the poor man's wife might then be safe. He felt curiously calm, as if this moment of being on his own had been awaiting him since he'd dropped into Jules Godard's woods. There was even a relief in knowing at last that no one else's life was now being risked for his own.

Four

He thought he'd counted three dawns since walking out of Agen, but he might have missed one now that the days and nights were becoming so jumbled in his mind. To avoid being stopped and questioned he'd only travelled after dark, mostly through relentless rain that had reminded him of pre-war walking holidays in Scotland. Holed up during the day in whatever abandoned shed or outhouse he could find, he'd slept fitfully in his sodden clothes. There'd been wizened apples and vegetables lying around, but his stomach had sickened of them. Hunger scarcely troubled him now – his unhealed foot was a greater problem, and the new pain in his side that was making it difficult to breathe.

The signposts were now pointing to Auch – a city, obviously, and something he would have tried to skirt at the beginning of his walk. Now, lightheaded with fever, Auch struck him as a place he ought to see, rather than avoid. He'd go there in daylight, spend his last francs on some hot food, then lie down somewhere and sleep the rest of his life away.

It seemed such a sensible programme that he felt resentful when Auch confronted him with endless flights of steps that needed to be climbed. Crawling up them on all fours would have been easier but he retained just enough grip on reality to know that crawling wasn't what grown men did. He was still upright at the top of them, and conscious of a building looming in front of him so huge that it must be a church. Jesus had welcomed sinners and outcasts – he remembered that. He'd go to the church, where at least no one could be blamed for letting him stay. But the locked doors stared blankly at him and, beaten at last, he sank to his knees in front of them.

'You can't stay here,' a voice murmured in his ear. 'If I help you, can you manage to walk a little way?'

He couldn't focus on the face leaning over him, but the soft voice belonged to a woman. He tried to whisper that she must leave him and go away, but her arm beneath his urged him up.

'*Try*, please – it isn't far to my home.'

Beyond thinking for himself, it seemed necessary to do what he was told. Together, arms linked like old friends, they shuffled back the way he'd come, but not as far as those terrible steps. The woman propped him against a door while she fumbled for a key and he fixed his eyes on the plate beside it. He knew what it was, could even read the name engraved on it – Dr Alain Mayer. His last conscious thought was that he'd come to the right place at last because there seemed no doubt that what he was most in need of was a doctor.

Memory fragmented after that; he could remember a man's voice speaking to someone called Marguerite. A nice name . . . he liked the sound of it; the voice was pleasant too, deep and gentle, and the hands touching him were full of kindness. Later, the scene changed. There was a night-time journey by car, because he could recall that dim lights had picked out a nameboard as the car swung from the road into a narrow lane. His vague idea of having died and gone to Heaven was obviously wrong, and something of a disappointment; he'd been rather looking forward to discovering what came next.

'So you've woken up at last.'

It wasn't the voice of his Auch saviour – younger, sharper altogether, and he didn't like it.

'You aren't Marguerite – I want to see *her*.'

He supposed the faint, querulous whine was his own. It didn't seem to impress the girl who now walked into his line of vision. She *was* young – eighteen perhaps, or not quite as much. Cropped dark hair framed a thin face noticeable only for strongly marked eyebrows, now drawn together in a frown.

'My parents had to leave you and go back to Auch,' she said briefly. 'You'll have to make do with me and my uncle.'

She was dressed in old trousers and a sweater several sizes too large for her, but she wore them with the air that French women seemed to be born with. He felt at a disadvantage, lying there weakened by illness, unkempt, and probably smelling objectionably.

'How long have I been here?' he asked next.

The girl gave a little shrug. 'Three days . . . four, maybe. You made a lot of noise to begin with – shouting in English. We nearly had to shoot you to make you quiet.'

It was some sort of joke, he then supposed, but when he got to know her better he realised that it probably hadn't been a joke at all.

'Should we introduce ourselves, do you think?' he suggested, to help a conversation that seemed to have ground to a halt.

'*No*, we shouldn't. The less we know about each other the better.'

She eased a knapsack off her shoulders and began to lay out its contents on a makeshift table. It made him realise that everything about him was makeshift – a square of carpeting covering the bare floor, the straw-mattressed truckle-bed on which he lay, and no ceiling above his head except the great timbered roof of what was obviously a barn. But his hiding place was very clean, and the sheets on his bed smelled of lavender.

'You're in the hayloft of my grandfather's barn,' she announced, seeing him glance around. 'Now, it's time to change the dressing on your leg. You'll make it worse if you fidget because I'm not a very skilful nurse.'

He was glad to find that he was wearing an antiquated nightshirt – something else belonging to her grandfather no doubt, but it was better than having this hostile girl gaze at his nakedness. She managed the messy dressing very well, and he felt obliged to explain.

'It healed up once, but I fell on it again.'

Her dark eyes glared at him. 'You also walked about with several bones in your foot out of place, and caught chronic pneumonia. You seem to have been remarkably careless all round. Now, swallow these pills.'

If he was expected to apologise, he was damned if he would; nor could he explain to this bossy, disapproving creature the acute discomfort he felt – he'd rather burst first. But suddenly she spoke again in the same gruff voice.

'My uncle will come up soon to see you. After that you can have some breakfast.'

Thank God, at least it wasn't left to her to carry away his slops – it would have been more shame than he could bear. He had cause to be deeply grateful to her but he found her tiring and unfriendly, and he wished she would go away. She walked to a gap in the wall, then turned round to deliver a parting shot.

'It won't stop him looking after you, but my uncle doesn't like the English.'

Robert closed his eyes to shut out the gleam of malice in her face. 'I can hardly wait to meet him,' he murmured politely.

There was a little silence before she spoke again. 'I think you won that round!'

It surprised him into looking at her, and he saw how greatly a glimmer of amusement changed her severe young face. But without saying anything else she dropped suddenly out of sight. Her place on the ladder she must have used was taken almost immediately by a man in whom he detected a strong family likeness – same dark hair and brows and sharply cut features. But instead of being small and slight, this was a mountain of a man who heaved himself through the gap in the wall.

'Good morning – my niece says you're making sense at last. I expect you need *this*.' He deposited a small bucket by the bed. 'You aren't up to managing the ladder yet. Breakfast arrives after my next visit.'

Ten minutes later bucket and contents had been removed; washing water was brought instead, and then a bowl filled with bread soaked in hot, sweet milk.

'The best we can manage in the way of invalid food,' he said, with his niece's abrupt way of talking. 'My mother says it will do you good. My father put some Armagnac in when she wasn't looking.'

Robert spooned it up, suddenly aware of feeling ravenously hungry. 'It's delicious – please thank them both for me.' He emptied the bowl and gave it to his host. 'I have to thank you all, of course, more than I can possibly say. But the Mayers shouldn't have brought me here – now you're all involved, if the Germans decide to search this place.'

The man watching him shrugged. 'They've already been – to see what food they could steal. We showed them the empty loft at the other end of the barn. This one's invisible from down below. My ancestors used it to hide from murdering *English* troops five hundred years ago.'

Robert apologised gravely. 'Sorry, we *were* a rough, marauding lot, but it was Eleanor of Aquitaine's fault – she shouldn't have given us an excuse by marrying an English king.'

He hoped to see a flicker of amusement in the man's impassive face, but it didn't change. Strength and the sort of self-control that would cope with any emergency he certainly possessed, but it seemed that he'd decided to yield nothing in the way of warmth or friendliness.

'I'll leave as soon as I can,' Robert said abruptly.

'You'll leave when there's a reasonable chance that you can make it back to England. Until then I'm afraid you'll have to stay here, mostly by yourself. My niece is too busy to keep you company and in any case she . . .'

'. . . doesn't like the English either,' Robert finished for him. 'She's already made that plain.'

A hand was lifted as if to acknowledge a fencer's hit, and then this visitor also stepped on to the ladder and disappeared.

The rest of the long day was marked only by the arrival of food – lunchtime soup and bread brought by the girl, evening meal of some delicious stew brought by her uncle. But he brought as well a lamp, and a book he suggested the patient might start reading when daylight came – a history of Gascony.

'Filled with references to the murdering English, I expect,' Robert suggested calmly.

'They crop up,' his host admitted with the faintest glimmer of a smile. 'You needn't worry about this small lamp – it can't be seen from outside. There's a deep overhang of the roof – an *auvent*, we call it – at this end of the barn. I'll see you in the morning.'

By the third day of this regimen of rest and food he was strong enough to walk about the hayloft, and become restive about staying there. But his relationship with the uncle and niece who tended him hadn't changed at all. He still didn't know their names, nor even where the farm was. All he could see through cunningly wrought slits in the walls of the loft that let in light and fresh air were glimpses of a valley flowing up to rolling hills. Cresting the one nearest him was the silhouette of a village, and at one end of it, like a stone exclamation mark, a tall, battlemented tower.

That morning he asked his nurse if she would bring his clothes.

'So that you can wander about and give yourself away

to the first neighbour who clatters past? *Not* a good idea, Monsieur.'

For want of anything else to call her he'd taken to addressing her as Mam'selle, and she responded in kind. It gave their conversations a formal, punctilious air, beneath which, as now, they seemed always to be fencing with each other.

'I have no intention of "wandering about" like a lunatic,' he pointed out. 'Let's just say I'd feel less vulnerable in something other than your grandfather's nightshirt.'

'Well you can stay as you are for the moment – my mother's coming this morning to see Granny who hasn't been well: I expect she'll want to check *you* over while she's here.'

Robert inspected the face of the girl holding out his daily dose of pills. 'I shall confirm what she can see for herself – the fact that I've been most carefully nursed. She probably *won't* see, and I shan't say, how much the nurse seems to resent her duties.' The pleasantness of his voice was misleading, and it took a moment for what he had just said to sink in. Before she could find an angry reply, he went calmly on. 'Why do you live here and not in Auch with your parents? Is it just because you're happier working on the farm, or are you going to point out that it's no business of mine either way?'

'Well, that's true enough,' she answered fiercely. 'The rest of the truth is that I'm more useful here. *Me voilà*, as we say!'

She had had to struggle, he thought, to finish up so carelessly, and it wasn't yet the whole truth that he'd been given. He would have sworn that for a brief moment of time he'd seen on her face some shadow of grief that she hadn't been able to hide. Amid his usual irritation at the belligerence she chose to wear like armour, he felt a sudden tug of pity. Her hostility might even not have much to do with him, but come instead from some desolation deep within herself.

'I shall be glad to see your mother again,' he said quietly. 'I have a great deal to thank her for.'

The girl in front of him had recovered and was looking maliciously amused again. 'You're looking much better but she still won't notice *your* manly charms at all, I'm afraid – she adores my father.'

'Rightly so, I'm sure,' he made himself answer evenly. 'I wasn't exactly in my right mind at the time we met, but my impression was of a man exceptionally clever and kind.'

As he'd seen once before, her mood suddenly changed. 'Put in my place again – you do rather make a habit of it! No wonder I seem to resent my duties. *Au revoir*, Monsieur.'

He examined that conversation again when she'd gone, trying to find in it a key that might make her complicated and difficult personality more easy to fathom. The clues were there, but she was adept at concealment and determined that he shouldn't understand her.

Marguerite Mayer was his next visitor, and she smiled with pleasure when, nightshirt notwithstanding, he got up and bowed over her hand.

'You're better – obviously *much* better than when we left you here. I'm very glad, and my husband will be too.'

'I've been most carefully looked after, but my first gratitude belongs to you. Without your help I'd have been imprisoned days ago – in fact probably dead by now.'

She nodded, not denying what he said, but simply putting it aside while she examined the healing wound in his leg, and then removed the strapping on his foot.

'Good, it's on the mend now that everything's in place again.'

She checked his temperature and pulse, put a stethoscope to his chest, and smiled at the question in his face. 'You're nearly well, but *please* don't go walking about the countryside in the rain again for days on end!'

'I'll try not to undo what's been done for me,' he promised gravely, 'but I mustn't stay here a moment longer than I have to – it's too unfair to your family.'

He saw Marguerite Mayer nod, and thought she understood

what he'd been careful not to put into words – the extent to which her brother and daughter would be glad to see the back of him.

'You aren't familiar with this part of France,' she pointed out. 'Very few English people come here as a rule. Men like my brother take time to accept someone from north of the Loire, so you mustn't expect them to make a friend of *you* without a struggle!'

Robert thought better of pointing out that her daughter was even less inclined to accept him on any terms at all. There was no reason why these people should regard him as anything but a dangerous burden foisted on them by the Mayers, but he couldn't add to this beautiful, kind woman's anxieties by saying so. Instead, he found something else to say.

'I'm not allowed to know names, so I have to call your daughter Mam'selle! I gather she likes living here, but you must miss her in Auch.'

Marguerite's expression grew sad. 'We miss her very much, but it's better for her to be here . . . safer, we hope.'

There was a moment when he thought she was tempted to say why that was so; but caution and wariness had become second nature to all these people now, and in the end she waved the subject aside.

'It's time I left – we have a clinic in Auch this afternoon. If I don't see you again, we wish you and your country well. My brother likes to . . . to denigrate perfidious Albion, but it's a pose, I think! At heart he knows that we must hold together if we are to win.'

She held out her hand and this time Robert kissed it, despite the ridiculous nightshirt that scarcely matched the gallant gesture.

'To the manner born!' she murmured with a glint of amusement that for a moment reminded him of her daughter. Then she turned and descended the ladder, leaving him with the sharp regret that what she'd said was probably true – it seemed unlikely that he would ever see her again. In less perilous times they might have become true friends. But he would always remember her as the essence of goodness and loving-kindness and wonder at the strange quirks of inherited genes that had produced a child so markedly different from herself. He sensed in her none of the sharp-edged impatience with fools that seemed to characterise her daughter. In fact, apart from a shared gift for suddenly switching moods, the two of them appeared to have nothing in common except their devotion to the fortunate Dr Mayer.

Five

That day, for the first time it wasn't an unfriendly girl who brought his lunch. There was a moment of sharp fear as an unknown face appeared at the top of his ladder, but the face was vaguely familiar after all.

'*N'inquiétez-vous pas, Monsieur l'Anglais – je suis le patron!*' It was Marguerite's father introducing himself.

Robert went to collect the soup bowl and shake hands with the newcomer. The patron wasn't quite as large as his son, but – probably in his middle sixties – still thickset and vigorous-looking. Beneath a thatch of silver hair his bright, dark eyes had the direct questioning glance that seemed to be a family trait, but there was something altogether less stern about him than his son, and more well disposed towards the *anglais* than his granddaughter allowed herself to be.

'The others are busy,' he explained cheerfully. 'The rain has held us up badly, you understand. But it's fine at last and they have to catch up with the ploughing.'

'All the more reason for *me* not to be a nuisance,' Robert pointed out. 'You know I can manage very well now – there's no need for me to be waited on, and I hate behaving like an invalid when the rest of you are slaving away. With my clothes on, I could at least empty my own slop-bucket when the coast is clear.'

The patron considered him for a moment. 'Well, if you *can* tackle the ladder now there's no reason why you shouldn't use the lavatory and wash-basin in the *chai*. You wouldn't need to go outside – there's a door into it at the other end of the barn. It's the wine-store really, but the men use it instead of coming to wash in the house.'

'The *chai* it shall be,' Robert said with huge relief, 'as long as you can find my clothes. Your granddaughter seemed to think I couldn't be trusted to stay well hidden, but I shan't be stupid, I promise.'

He was given a little smile that said even much-loved young women must occasionally be ignored.

'My wife will know where your clothes are. It was good for her to see our daughter this morning. We don't like Marguerite living in Auch – she ought to be here with us.'

'But at least you have your granddaughter.'

The patron's face broke into a smile. 'Yes, we have Jeanne,' he agreed.

He nodded and returned to ground level, unaware of having broken the rule of giving nothing away. Robert thought about the name he now knew. It had resonances in French history – Jeanne d'Arc, of course, and Jeanne d'Albrecht, a Gascon heroine. Now there was Jeanne Mayer as well, and the name sounded very like the girl herself – spare, unornamented, and definite. He was glad her grandfather had let the information fall, but he'd continue to call her Mam'selle; it had become a habit now.

When his clothes, cleaned and neatly darned, were returned a little later on, he ventured down from his loft and found the *chai*, a small, one-storey building tacked on to the far end of the barn. At last he could wash properly and rinse the remains of Madeleine Godard's gravy colouring out of his matted hair. Dressed and clean, he was himself again, capable of thinking about the future.

It was later than usual when supper arrived, brought by Jeanne instead of her uncle. The expression on her face at the sight of him warned him not to smile.

'You got round grandpère to bring your clothes,' she said furiously. 'He's a dear, foolish, old man.'

'He's nothing of the kind if you're implying that his

judgement isn't to be trusted.' Robert's own voice for once was suddenly very sharp. 'Don't you understand how much I've hated being a burden to you all, as well as a danger? I shan't be stupid – I'll only go downstairs when the coast is clear – but I *have* to start making my own decisions again.'

She regarded him in silence for a moment, aware of a change that she both resented and couldn't help approving of. He was still thin, and pale from being indoors; but no longer a wreck she could despise. She moved into the circle of lamplight and he could see *her* more clearly. A livid bruise was developing across her cheekbone.

'What happened to you?' he asked.

Her little shrug pushed the question aside. 'I was late home . . . from my music lesson. It was dark, cycling back. I didn't see a low branch hanging down.'

'From your *what*?' Anger crisped his voice again, mixed with disbelief. 'My dear girl, are you mad, cycling about an occupied country in the pitch dark, after curfew, just to have a music lesson?'

Instead of flying at him as he expected, she suddenly smiled, and for once the smile had no edge to it but was full of pure amusement instead. 'My teacher is very good, and I like playing the violin! I'll give you a recital one day.'

He didn't believe her, thinking it more likely that she'd gone to visit a lover who let *her* take all the risks. The man wasn't worthy of her. To say so would probably embroil them in a flaming row, but he was about to take the risk when a faint, distant noise diverted his attention. He listened more intently, aware that Jeanne was also listening. However unlikely it seemed, he recognised the sound now coming closer – an aircraft wasn't far from being overhead. But they were in '*la France profonde*', with not a factory or even a railway-line for many miles that the RAF might reckon worth trying to bomb.

'The wind's getting up – that's what you can hear,' Jeanne said, talking more loudly than usual.

Robert stood by the barn wall, trying to see out. 'The night is still, the moon is nearly full, and I know an aircraft engine when I hear one. Now tell me that one of our planes isn't up there, dropping supplies to your uncle and his friends.'

'Perhaps,' she mumbled. 'They're overdue; we need much more than they ever send. What are we supposed to resist the Germans *with* – our bare hands?'

He turned round to face her again. '"*We* need", you say. Does that mean that you're involved as well? If so, your people must be insane to allow it. Your mother thinks you're safer here than in Auch. I'll swear *she* doesn't know what you're up to.'

'Of course she doesn't know,' Jeanne said impatiently. 'But she and my father help to pass refugees from Alsace safely into Spain – they can't expect me not to be useful as well.'

'What does "being useful" mean exactly?'

She gave her usual little shrug. 'I carry the messages, that's all – between the network and the wireless-operator who talks to London. *His* is the dangerous bit.'

'Christ Almighty!' Robert said it as a prayer, not an oath. 'You're a child still. How dare your uncle embroil you in it.' He discovered that he wanted to shout at her, to rage all the more because she was smiling with the same amused smile of a moment ago; the truth was that she was young in years, but in every other respect nothing like the child he'd just called her.

'What happens if you're stopped?' he tried to ask calmly.

'I don't get stopped – I know the little lanes and byways, which the Germans avoid . . . They're afraid of being ambushed.'

There was a little silence before he spoke again. 'The only thing that gives away your youth is your determined intolerance of *me*. Your uncle claims to hate the English because of what we did here centuries ago. Is that your excuse as well?'

He recognised the mulish expression on her face and thought she wasn't going to answer; then she suddenly did.

'We had a dear friend nearby. I'd made up my mind he was the man I was going to marry as soon as I grew old enough, but he was called up first to serve in the army. In the retreat to the coast he got nearly to Dunkirk, but your ships left him there to be killed. A friend of his who got away wrote to tell us afterwards what had happened. Isn't that reason enough for me to hate the English?'

The dim lamp-glow fell on her downbent face, making it a tragic mask of light and shadow. She knew too much of grief already, and he'd been aware of it even before he knew the cause.

'I could offer you a case for our defence,' he answered slowly, 'but there'd be very little point. You'll believe what you want to believe. I'll say something else instead. This awful, bloody war *will* end, and when it does you'll still be young enough to start looking for happiness again.'

She stared at him across the space between them. 'Happiness doesn't last long enough to matter,' she said with certainty. 'It's living every minute that counts.'

'Well, for God's sake at least remember *that* when you next feel like playing hide and seek with a German patrol.'

She smiled again, thinking he'd misunderstood, but he knew very well what she meant. For Jeanne Mayer being alive was a matter of intensity, time experienced fully, nothing wasted. She turned to leave but he called after her.

'May I come down to breakfast tomorrow?'

'Certainly not – wait till you're invited!' and with that she disappeared.

The next morning breakfast was brought by her uncle. Obviously warned of what to expect, he didn't comment on the sight of the loft guest up and dressed. Robert felt sure he disapproved of the new state of affairs and had decided to surprise him again before he could say so.

'I hope you collected a good haul last night?' He shook

his head at the angry question in the face opposite. 'No one told me – I heard the plane, and I do know about aircraft engines.'

'For once it *was* a good haul,' the Gascon admitted reluctantly. 'Too often we're disappointed. The weather changes suddenly here, or it's bad over England and the plane can't take off. We've had many a wasted, anxious night waiting for a delivery that doesn't arrive.'

He put the subject aside with an abrupt gesture, and glared across the loft. 'I suppose *you* want to run before you can walk. I'll remind you that only a week ago we thought you were about to die.'

Robert dipped bread in his coffee-bowl in the way that had now become habitual. 'I'm not a fool – I don't claim to be in quite good enough shape yet to cross the Pyrenees in mid-winter.'

'I doubt if you'll cross them this side of the spring,' the brusque answer came back. 'The winter's set in early, and soon the passes will be blocked. There have been heavy falls of snow already.'

'Then I'll have to try a different route – go south to the coast and find a boat. What's *not* for arguing about is that I shall leave as soon as I can – I refuse to spend the next three months skulking in your father's hayloft.'

His host surveyed him without surprise. 'I knew you'd be difficult as soon as you started to recover. The English make a habit of being a nuisance – it's a fact that we French people have to live with.' He rubbed a hand across his eyes as he spoke, a small reminder that he'd probably been up half the night hiding his delivery of supplies.

'I don't mean to add to your problems,' Robert insisted. 'I want to lessen them as soon as I can, that's all, and I must try to get fit again. I can march up and down on the spot here, but it's a tedious way of taking exercise!'

'You can go outside at night. Not in daylight, I'm afraid.

People pass by, and they know who they expect to see here. I'm not saying they'd rush to the Milice, but it's better if they don't know anything at all. The ladder has to be hidden and the wall-shutter in place if you come down. The Germans mostly avoid us here, but they'll come if they want food.' A faint twitch lifted the corner of his mouth. 'You'll find my niece's bicycle downstairs – with a puncture in the rear wheel!'

'And you never know when she may need another violin lesson?' Robert enquired in a level voice.

'You don't approve, I gather. I don't know why not – there are a number of English women agents working in France.'

'They're professionals, specially trained; can't you see the difference?'

'Yes, since I'm not blind. But you don't know Marguerite's daughter if you think she'd be left out of anything that's going on. Now I must leave you. Have a care on the ladder!' About to add something else, he changed his mind and went away. The Englishman was showing more patient self-control than he could have produced himself in similar circumstances, but he didn't feel like saying so.

After he'd gone Robert descended the ladder and found the damaged bicycle. With the puncture easily mended, he examined the battered machine and then set to work again to overhaul and clean it. In the basket on the handlebars he found something to support Jeanne Mayer's violin-lesson story – a set of unaccompanied Bach chaconnes. The lines were annotated here and there with fingering instructions. This was music that someone actually played, and it seemed possible that she hadn't been joking about a recital after all.

With the bicycle roadworthy and shining again, he turned his attention to the tools hanging above the workbench. He was sharpening chisels on a whetstone when Jeanne walked in with his lunch.

'My uncle said you weren't to come down during the day,' she snapped. 'Suppose I'd been the police, or German military?'

He went on with his work, measuring a chisel's sharpness against his thumb. 'I assume they'd arrive like any other visitors from the road. With exceptionally long sight and very acute hearing, I *think* I could make it to the top of the ladder before they were half-way along the drive.'

Because he was now looking at her, she put up a hand to conceal the bruise on her face, now turning from purple to an unbecoming green. It was the first feminine gesture he'd seen her make, but, aware of it herself, she pointed instead at the bicycle propped up against the wall.

'You've mended the puncture, I see; thanks for that. It was a stupid waste of time to clean it, though.'

'I know, but time is something I have plenty of at the moment; besides, it pleased me to do it for you.'

At a loss for words for a moment, she stared uncertainly at him, and his own face broke into a charming smile. 'I'll give you a quotation from our English Bible for that: it was "the soft answer that turneth away wrath"!'

There was no doubt about it now; for once she had nothing to say, aware that he was older, more experienced, and probably more subtle altogether than she was herself. The thought led to another one which, without meaning to, she put into words.

'Who do you have waiting for you at home – a wife, a lover?'

He shook his head. 'Neither, at the moment I'm remarkably unattached.'

'Which explains why you're so careless about what happens to you, I suppose.'

'I shan't be careless now and endanger you or your family, if that's what is worrying you,' he pointed out quietly. 'Will it do if I promise you that?'

Again it seemed that their relative positions had changed;

he was in control of the conversation, not she, and disconcerted by the fact, she could only sound cross again.

'You might at least drink your soup while it's hot, *not* forgetting to keep an eye on the road, of course.'

She stalked away and, smiling faintly, he did as he was told. For as long as the light lasted he worked downstairs; then, when the late November dusk closed in, it was time to climb the ladder and hoist it up after him. The glow of his little lamp was hard to read by, and he set about remembering instead the rag-bag collection of poetry that he'd learned over the years. He was stuck at the fifth stanza of *The Rubáiyát* of Omar Khayyám:

> 'Iram indeed is gone with all his Rose,
> and Jamshýd's Sev'n-ringed Cup where no one knows;
> but . . .'

But *what* for Heaven's sake? He was still racking his memory for the next line when a voice shouted to him from below. He moved the shutter aside and looked down.

'My son said you'd be joining us this evening,' the patron called up.

'Your granddaughter told me to wait for an invitation!'

A chuckle – enriched by years of sipping Armagnac, Robert suspected – floated up to him. 'Then *I* invite you, *mon ami*! Hurry, the soup is waiting.'

Once more Robert descended the ladder, hid it in the straw, and followed his host out of the barn. There was time for a deep breath or two of cold night air before he was led into the kitchen of the farmhouse. The room was warm and full of the smell of good food being prepared. Jeanne was at the table, slicing bread. An older woman, her grandmother, of course, was stirring a saucepan on the stove.

'*L'Anglais, ma chère*,' the patron told his wife. '*Il s'appelle Robert.*'

She turned to smile at him, and he could see in her

lined face remnants of the beauty she'd passed on to her daughter.

'We're glad you've come – it must be so cold and lonely in the barn,' she said.

For a moment he found it unexpectedly hard to answer her. The lack of comfort in the hayloft didn't worry him, and his own company was something he was used to. But the suddenness – that was what it was, he told himself – the suddenness of being plunged into this warm family life made his voice unsteady.

'You weren't well, your daughter said. I hope you're feeling better, Madame.'

'She *isn't* well yet, and she ought to be lying down, but she's a difficult, obstinate woman,' Jeanne answered for her grandmother. The words were harsh but the smile that went with them was full of love, and it dramatically changed a face that had missed inherited beauty and too often spoiled its own charm by registering only disapproval or scorn.

When they were seated at the table, with the soup tureen in front of the patron, grace was said by Jeanne – another facet of her character that took Robert by surprise. She was unexpected in almost everything she did, apart from her refusal to see him as anything but a cross they had been asked to bear. The soup was followed by a dish that Madame *la patronne* explained was 'of the region'; a civet of hare cooked long and slowly with prunes.

'It's only peasant cooking, Monsieur Robert; that's all we can offer now,' she said with her gentle smile when he'd tasted it and pronounced it delicious.

No mention was made of the absent member of the family but Robert was content to be without him. It was enough to know that Jeanne's sharp glance was on him too often across the table. He supposed that she resented him there, and hoped to make him feel uncomfortable. Then there came an awkward moment when the conversation with his hostess faltered because she was looking instead at the silent girl sitting opposite him. He smiled at the older woman and shook his head.

'Take no notice of your granddaughter, Madame. Being English and therefore a barbarian, she suspects me of not knowing how to use a knife and fork – she's waiting to catch me out!'

'My son has filled her head with nonsense,' the patron said, 'historical nonsense about the English; nothing to do with the age we live in.'

It would have been easy to let the matter rest there, but Robert suddenly decided that he was damned if he would. Just once this valiant but tiresomely opinionated girl should hear *his* point of view.

'The age we live in also counts,' he said quietly. 'I've listened to conversations in trains, and it's been made clear here as well, that though many of you hate the Germans, you're anything but keen on *us*. By declaring war first (which we certainly did) we are blamed for pushing France into a war she didn't want to fight. By salvaging as much of our army as we could at Dunkirk, we are blamed for "running away". Forgive me if I insist – even though I have so much to thank you for – that both claims are unfair.'

He was embarrassed by the silence that followed his little speech. It would do no good, and probably cause still more ill-feeling. Then his hostess stood up, smiling at him very kindly. 'I'm not an expert like my son, Robert, but *I* think you were right to say what you did. And now, before my granddaughter bullies me again, I shall leave you and go to bed!'

He got to the door before she did and opened it. Then Jeanne marched out as well, announcing that she was going to help her grandmother.

'It's not like my small girl to quit the field of battle,' the patron remarked when Robert returned to his seat at the table. 'The truth is that she doesn't quite know what to make of you, and that annoys her!' He poured more wine and raised his glass. 'I drink to Angleterre, my friend. Is *that* fair enough?'

'It's generous,' Robert agreed, smiling at him.

After a moment the older man went on, speaking more quietly than usual. 'You were right about this country not wanting to fight. Our politicians were either useless or corrupt, and our generals thought they were still fighting the Franco-Prussian war. Clever men like my son and son-in-law knew that the Germans would fall on us through Belgium. To the Boche, the Maginot Line was laughable – something just to go round, not through.'

Robert thought it had been a hard admission for his host to make. 'Now, I'll drink to France,' he said, 'and assure you that our peacetime politicians and generals weren't much better than yours!' He drank his toast, then went on. 'I know about the young man your granddaughter hoped to marry.'

The patron gave a little shrug. 'He lived nearby, and she was often with us. It's true that she enjoys being here, but she's too like her father – clever, sensitive, *raffinée* as we say; not the perfect material for life with a struggling farmer!'

Robert remembered the violin music in the bicycle basket and wondered what the farmer would have made of it. 'Still, she chooses *not* to stay with her parents, it seems.'

His host's heavy face settled into lines of thoughtful sadness. 'I don't understand women's affairs, but my wife does. Marguerite and Alain love their daughter but they're wrapped up in each other and in their work. Jeanne adores them, her father especially, and she wants to be right inside their magic circle. Because she isn't, she chooses to stay as far outside as possible – that's what my clever Marie says.'

It seemed so true an insight into the girl's complex personality that Robert merely nodded. 'Your wife is lovely and kind,' he said instead. 'I'm sorry that she looks frail as well.'

'She wasn't when I married her. She was young and strong and ready to laugh at the hard times we knew then. But our elder son, Philippe, was killed at Verdun – he was just nineteen. She hasn't laughed much since then, and the name of Pétain is not valued in this house.' The patron cleared his throat and tried again. 'We don't tell her what is going on here now. You understand, Robert?'

'I understand.'

It seemed to bring the conversation to an end, and with a friendly handshake exchanged, they said goodnight. Robert crossed the courtyard, and fumbled his way back through the barn. It was later than his usual bedtime and he'd been given several glasses of the patron's strong wine, but there was a lot to think about before he finally fell asleep. His last conscious thought registered the strangeness of his present situation: he didn't know where he was, or even the name of the family whose life he shared. It didn't matter, he decided; he knew more important things about these people with whom he'd become so deeply involved.

Six

That day had changed things. From then on it was taken for granted that he'd cross the yard when darkness fell, and share in the family's evening meal. But he now used the hours of daylight to go through every physical exercise he could think of in an effort to get strong again. His foot, thanks to Alain Mayer's expert manipulation, was nearly normal; his leg had healed, and his lungs were clear of infection. It was only inaction that still ailed him, and the growing certainty that it was time to leave. He chose a moment to say so one evening when the women were out of the room.

'I've tried day and night-time travelling,' he finished up, 'and I know which I prefer. But without an identity-card I shall have to stick to walking in the dark.'

The patron looked at his son. 'Well . . . do we allow him to go?'

Their guest answered first. '"Allowing" doesn't come into it, I'm afraid. I refuse to stay here endangering you any longer. If I get caught there's nothing I can be made to say – I don't *know* anything.'

He was startled by his host's large fist descending on the table. 'I was thinking of *you*, boy, not us.'

Robert smiled apologetically but shook his head. 'You *should* be thinking of yourselves.'

Then the patron's son spoke. 'We could provide a *carte d'identité*, but there are problems. The first is that you look nothing like a Frenchman. The second is your age. Claiming to be one of us, you're likely to be rounded up anyway. Men below the age of forty, which you obviously are, are being sent to work in German factories to make good their labour shortage.'

'Forget the *carte*, then,' Robert amended. 'I'll go at night – make for the coast somewhere near Perpignan.'

A measuring glance met his across the table. 'There are others waiting to make the same journey, and it would be sensible for you all to reach the coast together. Will you at least be patient until I say that the necessary arrangements have been made? It won't be long – a week at the most.'

'I'll wait that long,' Robert agreed, and the conversation ended as Jeanne came back into the room.

Two evenings later, with a nearly full moon rising and the night sky cloudless, he had no need of a torch to guide him across the barn to the farmhouse. He was nearly at the door when it suddenly swung open. Heart thudding, he stepped behind a stack of hay as two men came in. Silhouetted against the sky outside, one of them was immediately recognisable, the other was a stranger. It was *he* who spoke in a low, urgent voice.

'There's only me, Cheval – le chien is out of action, and le chat was stupid this afternoon . . . got picked up. We shan't be able to keep the rendezvous tonight.'

'We *must*,' said the patron's son. 'God Almighty, what a night for things to go wrong. It isn't just a drop. They're landing a wireless operator we desperately need, and two sick agents have to be lifted back to London. We've *got* to be there.'

'But two of us can't manage the signals by ourselves . . . the pilot won't recognise them. So who are you going to ask – Jeanne, or your father?'

There was a tiny pause. 'I don't know yet . . . I'll have to think which it's to be.'

It was time for Robert to abandon his hiding place and step towards them.

'Why not think of *me*?' he suggested quietly.

The stranger made a leap at him, but he was grabbed in turn by his companion.

'Let go, you fool – it's only our Anglais. I should have remembered he'd be coming down.' A gleam of moonlight fell on their strained faces, but the patron's son spoke to Robert with his usual calmness. 'Sorry about that. Go on indoors, please. My friend and I still have some business to discuss.'

'Which you can't complete, it seems. I'm here; why not tell *me* what to do?' He saw the Gascon about to refuse and spoke more sharply. 'You *can't* send an elderly man or a girl out instead of me. Dammit all, it's an English plane, I take it? I have a *right* to be there.'

'Perhaps you have at that,' came the reluctant answer. 'All right: ETA is midnight; *we* meet at 2300, the others will arrive at 2330. *Ça va, mon ami*?'

The stranger nodded, suddenly extended a friendly hand to Robert, and disappeared without a sound into the night. The two men left behind fell into step together and crossed the yard.

'We leave at 2230,' Robert was told. 'Try not to look as if something is about to happen!'

It was more easily said than done. One of them talked too little and, to disguise the fact, Robert himself thought he talked too much. He was conscious, too, of Jeanne's bright glance on them, like an eagle observing its prey. She pounced first on her uncle.

'It's a beautiful night, just the sort you like, *n'est-ce-pas*?'

'So it is,' he agreed. 'But all farmers like fine weather – you should know that.'

She turned her attention to their guest. 'I promised you a recital. We'll have one tonight when Pappi and Mami have gone to bed – they don't enjoy my music!'

Before her grandparents could protest Robert answered with a sweet smile. '*Not* tonight . . . I don't quite feel up to it! I've walked the length of the barn forty times today, and tomorrow's target is fifty.'

She regarded him from beneath frowning brows, remembering a time when weakness had obliged him to do what she said.

'As you like, but I shan't offer again.'

'Then I shall never know what I've missed,' he said gently.

To sustain the fiction of an early night, he soon got up to leave, with only the faintest nod in the direction of the man on the other side of the table, now calmly cracking walnuts. An hour later he was outside again, waiting by the van that was used to carry vegetable deliveries to the neighbouring markets. He listened intently, but heard and saw nothing until a shadow appeared beside him.

'We push for a little while, otherwise my father will be down to see what's happening. Thank God the drive is only slightly uphill.'

A hundred yards further along they climbed in and drove in silence through the deserted countryside. It looked beautiful but unreal, Robert thought – every day-time colour lost in a silver-green wash of moonlight. Something else seemed unreal, too – the knowledge that the plane he was going to meet would return to England without him, its small passenger capacity absorbed by men who needed to escape even more than he did.

After twenty minutes or so they stopped in the shadow of a small wood. As well as being fine, the night was bitterly cold, and already frost was beginning to sparkle on the grass verge where they'd parked.

'We use the field across the road,' his companion murmured. 'It's flat, reasonably smooth, and its owner lives in Paris.'

'What more could we ask?' Robert turned up the collar of his borrowed coat against the piercing air coming through the opened window, and turned to the man beside him. 'Hadn't you better tell me what to do?'

'It isn't complicated. There's an agreed signal the pilot can recognise; unless we show it he won't even try to land. Three powerful torch beams point upwards, marking out the shape of the letter L. I'll be at one end, my friend at the other; your torch will be the one in the middle of the angle.' He looked at his watch by the glow of a tiny pencil torch and sounded anxious. 'Our third man's running it fine – the outward freight will be here soon. If you hear the word "Cheval" mentioned, by the way, it's my name in the circuit; forget it please.'

Ten minutes later they heard the sound of a car-engine. It stopped behind them, its lights blinked twice and then were switched off. 'Cheval', as Robert now tried to think of his companion, got out and walked back to the other car. Five minutes later he returned to the van, and his face looked lividly white and drawn in the moonlight.

'The plane's passengers have arrived, but not my friend. Something's gone wrong, because he's never unreliable.'

'The driver of that car can be our third torch-bearer, can't he?' Robert asked.

'He's got two sick people to get on board, and every minute the plane stays on the ground, the better the Germans' chances of tracking us down. If we have to we'll prop the bloody torch up with some empty boxes from the van.'

'You *won't* have to,' said a small, clear voice suddenly behind them. 'I can hold the torch as well as you can.'

While waiting for the explosion that would come, Robert had time to realise that the note of defiance sounding in Jeanne's voice was entirely typical of her. She could guess her uncle's furious reaction and would meet it head-on. He waited for her to emerge from a pile of boxes before he answered her. He couldn't risk a shout, but he made his anger felt well enough.

'We had an agreement, you and I. Now I shan't be able to trust you again.'

She tried to sound as if she didn't mind. 'Well, I guessed something was happening tonight, and I had a feeling you might need me. I was quite right, wasn't I?'

'We'll argue about it later. Now take this, and do *exactly* as you're told for once.'

She followed the other two out of the van, not saying a word to Robert; but her unrepentant glance at him was eloquent enough. If a mere Anglais was included in her uncle's doings, then all the more reason for a share in them herself.

They took up their positions in the field, marking out the small area in which the pilot would need to land. Robert didn't envy him his job – high skill would be needed even if the rendezvous went according to plan and they weren't at this moment being surrounded by a posse of German troops. The penalty for being caught would, more likely than not, be execution out of hand. He looked at the small, distant figure of Jeanne Mayer, and found that he'd begun to pray. Please God, at least let *her* be killed at once if they were caught – not abused, tormented, tortured until she told them what they wanted to know. He'd supposed that he felt afraid for himself, but what really consumed him, heart and mind, was fear for her. He wanted to run to where she stood, and shake her into promising never to accompany her uncle again. He needed her to admit that hostility between them was absurd, a silly, meaningless game they played. It wasn't possible to move, of course; he had to stay where he was, and what he wanted so badly to say would never be said. But suddenly he saw her hand lift in a gay little salute, and it seemed for a moment as if she'd heard after all and answered him.

The cold numbed their feet and fingers, and ominous swathes of cloud began to drift across the moon. The patron's son came to stand beside Robert for long enough to murmur that it looked as if the rendezvous had been aborted. But even as he spoke the low thrum of an engine sent him headlong back to his position again. Five minutes later the Lysander was touching down; then it taxied back to the down-wind end of the makeshift landing strip and turned into the wind again ready to take off; already the door was being opened.

The arriving operator and his precious equipment were unloaded while the first agent was being helped across the field. Behind them, 'Cheval' now carried the other passenger – a woman, Robert saw with a faint shiver, too weak to manage on her own. There was the usual brief exchange of handclasps and good wishes, and then the plane was moving again, lifting its nose into the wind. He watched it soar and bank round to the north, overwhelmed by the knowledge that it was going home.

'Don't stand dreaming,' said a sharp voice in his ear. 'It's time we got out of here as well.'

Back on the road again, they were given fresh instructions. 'Cheval' himself must see the wireless-operator installed in a safe house. Directed by Jeanne who knew the way, Robert was to drive the van back to the farm. They set off with nothing said, and Robert had no idea what the silent girl beside him was thinking until she suddenly muttered, 'I suppose you wanted to climb aboard that plane . . . Shake the dust of la belle France off your so English feet.'

'Would it be unreasonable if I did?' he asked after a moment or two.

'Probably not,' she agreed briefly.

He glanced at her face in the dim glow of the dashboard light. 'The truth is that I was praying something else: to deliver you home safely without running into trouble that I couldn't protect you from.'

She didn't answer beyond saying, 'You'd do better to be concentrating on the road, it climbs and twists all over the place.'

'And we mustn't, of course, behave like human beings and admit that we might feel anxious for one another.'

'The sentimental English,' she jeered. 'That's not the way to keep the empire you fought and schemed for.'

He brought the van to a halt that thumped her head against

the windscreen. 'One more dig at the English and you can get out and walk. Which is it to be?'

She rubbed her forehead, then pulled off the woollen cap she wore and ran her fingers through her hair. 'I'm too tired to walk. From now on I shan't say a word except tell you which way to go.'

It was exactly what she did, and he couldn't fairly complain if the silence of the dark, enclosed space they shared seemed more troubling than any conversation. With the moon now hidden, the world outside was mysterious as well as dangerous, and this strange journey was outside normal time and reality. The girl beside him, tiresome and intractable though she was, shouldn't be out here, but somewhere safe and warm and sleeping sweetly.

Suddenly he broke the silence himself, abruptly. 'I shall be leaving the farm soon. It's bad enough knowing that you'll go on pedalling messages about the countryside in your music-case; but you must promise me not to repeat tonight's piece of madness.'

She chose not to answer directly. 'I suppose you're afraid we might run into a German patrol. What would you do, I wonder?'

'The only thing left open to me: pretend to be German since I'm clearly not French. I'd be Ober-Lt Franz Von Hubner, and in my best Oxford High-Deutsch I'd swear at them for inconveniencing a superior officer when they were supposed to be hunting English spies.'

A small chuckle escaped the girl beside him. 'They're such fools, most of them, they might even believe you.'

'I doubt it,' he said briefly. 'Could you please try to remember that this isn't some lunatic game we're playing?'

Again she answered with another question. 'What would you be now if the war hadn't begun?'

'A schoolmaster!' He found it hard to believe himself, and it seemed to silence *her* altogether.

'Turn here,' she said at last. 'The track's bumpy, but

it brings us to the back of the yard. No one will hear us arrive.'

A few minutes later they climbed out of the van and Robert put out his hand to guide her through the darkness to the house. Her own hand was as cold as ice, and he was aware of a change in her. Reaction from the strain of the past hours was setting in, and she couldn't control the tremors beginning to shake her thin body.

Inside the kitchen he examined her sheet-white face. 'You need sleep, but you must get warm first. Your grandmother would probably prescribe a calming tisane, but I'm afraid that's beyond me. I could brew some coffee, though.'

A faint smile brought her face alive again. 'Pappi would probably prescribe coffee *and* Armagnac, I think!'

'Then that's what we'll have. I'll own up in the morning to pinching the brandy.'

He stoked up the fire, and she crouched down beside him on the rug, holding out her frozen hands to the warmth. Her face looked sad in the flickering light and beautiful in a way he hadn't noticed before. Then, in a small, sudden gesture of apology, her cold fingers touched his cheek. 'I'm sorry I poke fun at the English. It's only because I'm ashamed. They've done so much better than we have.'

'We haven't been overrun,' he said gently. 'And *no one* could do better than you and your family.' He wanted to offer her the comfort of his arms and the warmth of his own body, but it was suddenly necessary to remember why he was there – he was supposed to be making coffee. He forgot the Armagnac, she noticed, but she didn't remind him of it.

Nursing his coffee-mug between long, thin hands, he seemed content to stare at the fire. She watched him for a moment, thinking how different he was from the men she now lived among. His ways were gentle, and she'd chosen to underrate him because of that. It had been all the more stupid of her because her father was very much like this quiet Englishman; they would have got on well together.

'I don't know anything about you,' she said suddenly, '. . . don't even know how old you are.'

He smiled at a question he hadn't been expecting. 'Years older than you, twenty-three to be exact. It's reckoned to be a very advanced age for fighter-pilots!' She didn't smile back, and he cast around for something safer to talk about. 'I suppose your uncle will be back soon?'

'Not tonight. He must stay with the new man and teach him what to do.'

Robert glanced round the warm, shadowy room; it was time, more than time, to return to his cold hayloft in the barn. The hostility between himself and this small, complex creature had melted under the mixed tensions of the night into an unexpectedly sweet ending; but it *was* an ending, not the beginning of a different story. He was still telling himself that when she spoke again.

'Where is your home?'

'London – a house not far from the river at Greenwich. Maggie's still there, looking after it for me.'

'Maggie? I thought you said you were unattached?'

'She was my mother's nurse, then mine. I can't quite claim her as family, but she's the next best thing.'

'Why don't you count your parents?' Jeanne asked.

'Because my father died when I was five and I scarcely remember him. It didn't seem to matter, though. I had a gem of a mother – kind and clever and beautiful.' He steadied his voice and went on. 'She was killed in one of the first London air-raids of the war.'

The girl beside him said nothing and her silence pleased him; he hadn't wanted sympathy. But when he glanced at her, he saw tears trickling down her face, and her response both pleased and destroyed him.

'Don't cry . . . my dear girl, *please* don't cry. I shouldn't have told you; it was stupid of me.'

She shook her head, unable to speak, and his hands suddenly lifted her against him.

'A gentleman's supposed to have a nice clean hankie ready for these occasions, but my wardrobe isn't what it was,' he explained unevenly. 'I'll have to kiss the tears away if you'll let me.'

He intended a brief, gentle touch – merely the comfort she was due, no more. But she turned her head and it was her trembling lips that his mouth found instead, and then clung to.

The sweetness of the kiss, tentative at first and then not tentative at all, was hard to drag himself away from, but at last he managed it.

'This won't do,' he said unsteadily. 'After the past few hours you're overwrought, and God knows what I am – certainly not my sober, schoolmasterish self! It would be the easiest thing in the world to ask you to let me stay, and you might even be kind enough to agree. But in the morning you'd blame yourself and be back to hating me. I don't want that to happen, so I'll leave now.'

A faint smile touched her mouth at what he'd said, but she shook her head. 'I'm *not* overwrought, and you're the man you always are – the odd Anglais that my mother and my grandmother like so much!'

'Because they're sorry for me, that's all. You've never been that, I'm glad to say.' He made to get up but her hands kept him there.

'You said something about going away – when?'

'As soon as your uncle gives me the word – any day, I think.' His fingers gently traced the outline of her mouth. 'But I shall go knowing you at last, Mam'selle!'

She closed her eyes for a moment, as if caught by a stab of pain, then opened them and smiled at him. 'You *don't* know me, so stay, please.' She saw the sadness and refusal in his face, and spoke again with quiet insistence. 'My father is a good, wise man and I know what he would say. There has to be something more to life than violence and hatred if we're not to become simply hateful ourselves. So I'm asking you to stay and love me . . . just this once.'

Her hands pulled him down towards her and it was too late to remember the hayloft he should be returning to, or the terror-laden darkness outside the warm, firelit room. For the little time they had it seemed that they *must* love each other, must have a memory of joy and sweet delight to take with them into the cold morning world.

She slept at last cradled in his arms on the floor, but he lay awake watching for the moment when he must leave. The room grew cold but when he tried to make up the fire without disturbing her she woke and lay looking up at him, eyes dark and unreadable in the dimness of the room. He gently kissed her mouth, and then smoothed her tousled hair.

'I have to go, before your uncle comes back. Soon he'll tell me it's time to set out for the coast. Whatever happens, I refuse to believe I shall never see you again.'

She gave a little nod, and then her lovely, surprising grin. 'I might have got used to liking the English by the time you get back!'

The chiming of an antique clock on the wall insisted that the night was over. He got up, gathering his discarded coat and sweater, smiled at her for the last time, and then went to the door. She followed him there and stood waiting until the darkness outside swallowed him up. Then she quietly closed the door, but stood leaning against it for a long time, unaware of the tears that trickled down her face.

Seven

Washed and dressed again, he lay on his hayloft bed thinking about the night just past – the most memorable of his life. His behaviour had been shameful; there wasn't any doubt about that. He couldn't regret it, though; even now his body remembered the sweet contentment of the hours with Jeanne. It was a memory he wouldn't forget. Then, breaking into his thoughts, the patron's voice called from the gap in the wall.

'Sleeping late this morning, my friend?'

The question seemed pointed enough to make his heart turn over, but the Gascon's grin as he clambered into the loft was friendly and unconcerned.

'I was thinking,' Robert managed to answer truthfully, 'not sleeping.'

Coffee and bread were set down and it seemed as if his host had come intending to share it. When a chunk of the loaf had been broken off and handed over, the patron lowered his voice to what he was pleased to imagine was a confidential level.

'A busy night, I gather!'

It summed things up rather well, Robert reflected, but while he chewed a piece of bread and decided how to answer, his companion spoke again.

'Jeanne isn't forgiven yet, for disobeying my son's orders, but the pair of you seem to have been useful all the same.'

It seemed safe, now, to join in the conversation. 'I hope the "horse" got home safely.'

'Half an hour ago, and he knows what went wrong last

night. His friend's car tyres were spiked with nails.' The patron's large hands tightened into fists for a moment, then with an effort at self-control he loosened them again. 'Shall I tell you the worst thing about this terrible war? The bitterness it will leave behind. "Love thy neighbour as thyself," says one of the Commandments. How can we when we don't know who to trust, can never be sure who our enemies are?'

Then, with the sudden change of mood that was noticeable in his granddaughter, he began to smile instead. '*You* were supposed to be the enemy, according to my son. No wonder he doesn't know what to think about you!'

Robert brushed the comment aside. 'Let him forget about me and concentrate on Jeanne. She shouldn't have been anywhere near that field last night. He *must* keep her away from midnight rendezvous in future; God knows, what she does already is dangerous enough.'

'True . . . but I don't think she'll break the rules again. She's unlike herself this morning – very quiet, with her mind not on what she's doing at all.'

Robert reached absent-mindedly for another piece of bread while he thought about that and found something to say. 'You all work too hard, I think,' he finally murmured.

'Well, that's true. We've got good land but it's heavy clay – better ploughed with oxen than machines, though young men will tell you I'm a fool for saying so. We're underpopulated too; need more people.'

'Only you won't accept them unless they've been Gascons born and bred for the past five hundred years!'

'That may also be true,' the patron agreed cautiously. He finished his coffee and stood up. 'You're wanted in the barn soon, by the way, when my son's finished seeing to the animals. I think he's got news for you.'

Ten minutes later Robert waited down below in a dim corner screened from anyone crossing the yard. The tired-faced man who came to find him offered a small salute, acknowledging that the previous night's adventure had gone well after all. But he didn't waste words.

'Can you be ready to leave in fifteen minutes? A safe house in Tarbes will take you in, and we've found a guide ready to lead half a dozen of you down to the coast. Going on foot, you'd miss them; but I've got an excuse to make a call in that direction and I can drive you most of the way.'

It was the last stage of his bid for freedom – something he'd hankered after for weeks, managed to survive for. Fate was merely playing one of its usual malicious tricks in providing his chance to leave *now*, but there was nothing he could do but accept it. 'I can be ready – I've nothing to do except say my thanks and goodbyes,' he murmured after a moment's hesitation.

'You must leave your goodbyes to me, I'm afraid. I want you hidden in here until I've got the van at the door of the barn. The Germans know a plane landed last night, and they're going through the district with a fine-tooth comb. Jeanne's out at market, and the sooner *we're* away the better.'

Hearts didn't actually throb with pain, Robert told himself; it was an extravagant phrase coined by lady novelists. He was merely disorientated by the suddenness with which his life was being turned upside down again. It was a shock to leave quite so abruptly – *that* was why he felt sick and heart-sore. 'You won't thank your parents and . . . and Jeanne . . . nearly enough,' he said slowly.

'Probably not; you know far more words than I do. My mother's putting some food together. Be ready and watch for the van to drive up.'

It scarcely seemed possible, ten minutes later, that he should be leaving, hidden under a pile of evil-smelling sacks. One moment he'd still been a part of their lives, the next he was a part of their past, merely a dangerous nuisance wished on them by Marguerite and her husband. They wouldn't be human if they weren't glad to see the back of him. Would

Jeanne be glad, too? That question, to which he might never know the answer, would haunt him through the years to come. He wouldn't think of it now, though, or visualise her face when she returned home to find him gone.

His dream had always ended there, with his departure from the farm. The remainder of the journey down to the coast and his return to England seemed scarcely worth remembering. It took a conscious effort to recall the sequence of events, but it was something to think about while William Harcourt still slumbered peacefully in the opposite berth and the night-sleeper hurtled them towards Calais. Safely back in England with his own squadron, he'd upset his CO by asking for a transfer out of Fighter Command. His request to join F Section of the SOE instead had been even less well received, but he'd managed it in the end by sheer persistence, and at F. Section he'd had the good fortune to meet William. They'd worked together for the rest of the war, Robert flying out the Resistance supplies and money that William's effrontery wheedled from the Ministries concerned. Then, at the end of the war, his friend had offered him a very different future from the one he'd originally planned.

Now, five years on, Robert still had things to learn about vineyards and the making and selling of fine wines, but his mentor and guide was very content with his progress. William reckoned that the world could do without another indifferent schoolmaster; but a judge of wine nearly as expert as himself *would* do the human race some good.

That afternoon, standing together on the deck of the ferry approaching Dover, William gestured at the cliffs ahead of them.

'Just here I always forget how much I love France, and wish I need never leave England. I suppose the truth is that I want to belong to both.' Then he blew out a little sigh. 'That wouldn't do for Christine, I'm afraid. Like a lot of English people, she has a sad disability – no ear at all for anyone else's language;

which, of course, largely spoils the fun of being in a different country. It's something she got from her mother, I think. My brother was musical enough.'

To William it was perfectly clear: languages and music went together; the ear that heard one could always hear the other, and in this one respect his much-loved niece was deaf.

'I failed Christine,' he said sadly. 'After all, I brought her up more than her parents did, but I still can't get her to sit through an opera without fidgeting.'

'Give her time,' Robert suggested cheerfully. 'No – tell her that Grand Opera is something she's not quite ready for. If I know Christine, that should do the trick!'

William shot a glance at his companion's face, pleasantly inscrutable as usual. Robert Ashton had been little more than a fair-haired, handsome youth when they first met – trained and disciplined in one direction, of course, but otherwise still unshaped. Now he was an experienced man – clever, assured, with a charm of manner that concealed his unusual self-containment. It was time he took a wife, and who better than bright, vital Christine to persuade him to let down the guard he'd always kept around himself.

'I don't think you enjoyed your Gascony trip,' William suggested gently. 'Revisiting the past rarely turns out a success; expectation is set too high, I think.'

'I tried not to set it at any level at all, and that was just as well.' Robert pushed aside the memory of his abortive reunion with Pierre Darroze and did his best to sound no more than impersonally involved in the subject. 'France is almost unmatchably lovely, but it's not a country at ease with itself.'

'Dear boy, are *we* . . . a mere five years after a disastrous war? Like the French, we're still rationed, still poor, and still in the devil of a mess, with less excuse for that than they have.'

'I know, but at least we have a government, not a procession of discredited politicians walking in and out of office.'

He could see William waiting to interrupt but went firmly on. 'We *don't* try to vilify our neighbours because they did too little in the war or too much. And, as far as I know, we aren't trying to rewrite history, to make it look less discreditable than it actually was.'

'You're thinking of some of de Gaulle's high-flown words, I expect,' William admitted miserably. 'It's rhetoric, I grant you, much of what he says; but so were many of Churchill's wartime speeches. The point is that they worked.' Then a more cheerful thought occurred to him. 'Well, at least you care what happens to France. I agree with you that it hasn't come to terms yet with its recent past; but remember what it's suffered in the first half of this blood-strewn century. Despite the horrors of two hideous wars, it's still France, still functioning, still able to heal its wounds. Just give it time.'

Robert watched the port of Dover emerge in front of them from the afternoon mist. 'You could also have reminded me of its men and women who kept me alive. I can scarcely complain that *they* weren't more like us!'

'There's that as well,' William agreed. He was silent for a moment, then spoke in a different tone of voice. 'I've remembered the instructions I was given: you aren't allowed to go straight home to dinner this evening. Christine is expecting us both.'

'And we always do what she expects, of course!'

There was no sting in the words, only an amused acceptance of the pleasure it gave her to order their lives. But William wondered how often in the past his niece *had* made assumptions that Robert Ashton would have preferred not to accept. She'd returned from wartime evacuation in America a beautiful, wilful girl of sixteen. Robert, still in uniform, had been laid claim to at once. Lonely and war-sick, he hadn't seemed to mind then, and the Harcourts' home had become almost his as well. It was still, but there'd always been some obstacle to the prize Christine had set her heart on. At last, though, perhaps it was going to be all right. With time and patience things usually did turn out as they should, in William's opinion; but, being a bachelor not very well versed in affairs of the heart, he hadn't been able to feel sure.

At Victoria Station there was a queue for taxis, and dusk was falling over the city by the time they trundled through the evening traffic to Wapping. William peered out of the window at the familiar landmarks.

'I hope we never take anything for granted again,' he said suddenly, pointing to the lamps that made a garland of light across the river. 'But, human nature being what it is, I expect we *shall* soon have forgotten the long nights of stumbling about in the dark.'

Robert turned to smile at the small, rotund figure beside him. 'I'll remember the black-out if you like, but *not* the smell of a gas-mask, or the taste of reconstituted egg! Some things are better forgotten.' Then, as the taxi slowed down, he stared out at what they'd come to – the beautiful eighteenth-century Customs House that was William's home. 'I don't take *this* for granted. It's a miracle that it was ever built here at all, and still more of a miracle that it survived when everything else for miles around was knocked flat.'

'The ever-present ghost of my grandfather watched over it, I expect,' William suggested. 'He was a very formidable old party by all accounts!' He chuckled at the thought and then looked at his companion. 'I'm glad you love this odd bit of London as much as I do.'

'"Liquid 'istory",' Robert quoted. 'I love the whiff of something exotic in the air – the last trace of the spice warehouses that once upon a time lined the river. I'm rather sorry we missed the great days when just about every commodity on earth came and went on London's waterway.'

'Well, great indeed; but we also missed some of their violence and vice as well. I doubt if Grandmama dared go out of doors except to step into a carriage.'

He waited while Robert paid off the cabbie, and then the two of them climbed the elegant flight of steps together.

'Shall you mention your visit to Gascony?' he enquired tentatively.

The question was answered with more sharpness than Robert intended. 'No . . . what would be the point? Pierre Darroze was right; the past is over and done with.'

He was convinced of it now and could smile easily at the sight of Christine opening the door. If she had been lovely at sixteen, she was more beautiful still now – blue eyes combined unusually with Titian hair, near-flawless features, and the glow of health and vitality that most Londoners had lacked since the war. She kissed them both, then surveyed first one and then the other.

'Uncle Will, *you're* looking very pleased with life, you must have found some treasure you weren't expecting! Robert's less easy to read, of course, but I do believe there's *something* to notice about him as well.'

'Hunger, probably,' he suggested helpfully. 'We had a miserable sandwich on the boat, and I *was* lured here with the promise of dinner!'

His smile was warm, more openly affectionate than usual. She was adept at noticing such things, but all the same she'd keep hope on a tight rein; there'd been too long a wait to fling caution to the winds now, just because he seemed happy to be back and was looking at her as if seeing her for the first time.

'Dinner's only shepherd's pie,' she said with a wry grimace, '. . . nothing to get excited about when you've probably been eating like lords in France.'

'Not quite, but in any case I *like* shepherd's pie – it's your dear uncle who's a snob about food, not me.'

The sparkle of amusement in his eyes allowed her stranglehold on hope to be released another notch or two. He *was* different – no longer the charmingly unknowable friend who'd gone away refusing to insist that she must be there when he got back. She offered him a radiant grin, but managed to sound unconcerned.

'Well, you're lucky to get anything at all. I've landed a part in a new play, and I've been at the theatre most of the day.'

'Well done, dear girl! Something jolly for a change,' William ventured hopefully, 'or are you one of King Lear's beastly daughters again, or grim and godly Mother Courage herself?'

Christine tried to look solemn and failed. 'It's a translation from the French, Anouilh's *Ring Round the Moon*. My part's not huge, but the production is *very* prestigious.' She linked an arm in each of theirs to lead them to the dining-room. 'You'd better hear the rest over the pie – it's probably getting a bit dried up by now.'

Helped by William's wine, it seemed to taste all right, and by the time it was consumed Christine had exhausted the subject of the play for the time being and wanted to hear how the visit to France had gone.

'Robert can fill you in,' her uncle suggested neatly. 'I'm going to abandon you and catch up on some mail.'

He left a silence behind that her companion seemed in no hurry to break, but she had the exciting feeling of something about to happen. There was an electric tingle in the air, and she was perfectly aware of him watching every move she made. Chin resting on her hands, she tried to sound unconcerned.

'You're supposed to be filling me in.'

'So I am. Well, your uncle found an undiscovered vineyard, which is rather like pointing a truffle-hound in the very best direction of all. He's come back a happy man.'

'I can see that. What about you?'

'I was taken to meet all his old friends – useful for the future and very enjoyable.'

She examined his face for a moment. 'Something *wasn't* enjoyable, though. Did you find it painful, going back to France?'

He'd forgotten how quick she was, how perceptive about

others when she wasn't concentrating fully on herself. 'I tried not very successfully to find some people I once knew. It scarcely matters now, so let's talk about you. Have you told your parents about the new play?'

She accepted the change of subject, no longer interested in people from the past when he could say so casually that they hadn't mattered.

'Of course I've told them – to stop them nagging me to go and stay in Washington. Aside from my career, I must be here to keep an eye on Uncle Will – some designing widow might sink her talons in him without me to look after him!'

'He wouldn't notice if she did, and even the most determined widow needs a little encouragement, I fancy.' Robert took another sip of wine. 'You might give your career more of a push in America – have you thought of that?'

'Yes, but I like living here, even if it isn't as comfortable as life in Washington. I got off scot-free during the war – I'm due for a little hardship now!'

He smiled at the idea, thinking how little she knew about hardship even now, but there was something touching about her all the same; she was a beguiling mixture of a girl. It seemed hard to remember now why he'd ever doubted that, if he wanted a wife at all, it should be this lovely, self-confident creature. He *did* want a wife, and he owed William a great deal. Marrying the girl *he* looked on as a daughter would simply and surely mean happiness for them all. He stretched out his hands suddenly across the table and Christine put hers into them.

'In between the career and Uncle Will, would there be a little room for me? Sweetheart, I don't know what sort of a husband I'd be, I'm not much in the habit of normal family life, but I'd do my best to take care of you and make you happy.'

The words, fading into the room's quietness, struck him as pompous, bordering on the insanely inadequate. Why couldn't he, like any normal man, have spoken of love and longing and desire? She wasn't laughing at him but she wasn't looking in the least entranced, and he certainly couldn't blame her. His hands tightened suddenly on hers. 'Was that just about the worst offer of marriage a girl ever received?'

She gave a small, considering nod. 'There *was* a touch about it of a middle-aged Victorian suitor contemplating a child bride! But I liked the bit about making me happy.'

'I meant it,' he said gravely. 'I'd love and honour you, and remain faithful all the days of my life, if that sounds any better.' She didn't reply, and he answered himself. 'No, I don't think it did. The truth is that I've taken too long to sort out the muddle I was in. The dashing wartime flyer has become a rather boring, respectable wine-shipper hopeless at putting his feelings into words or actions. *You*, on the other hand, are about to set Shaftesbury Avenue alight! This poor fish has missed the bus, and serve him bloody well right, I'm afraid.'

She shook her head, half-laughing, half on the point of tears. 'The bus has been waiting very patiently!' She pulled her hands free so that she could go and twine her arms around his neck. 'Darling Robert, I like the idea of being a famous actress, but all that really matters is to be your wife. That's why I wouldn't go to Washington after RADA – you *had* to notice in the end that I'd grown up still not seeing any man but you! I shall *teach* you the right words and actions.'

'You put me to shame,' he said unsteadily. 'But I promise to get the hang of being a doting husband. Sweetheart, I do promise you that.'

Looking at her radiant face it seemed the easiest promise he'd ever made. He confirmed it by kissing her mouth, then kissed her again because her lips invited him and because he'd wasted too much time already. Breathless and trembling she was at last allowed to speak.

'Actions shaping up quite well already, I'd say! Let's go and tell Uncle Will. He'll think it's even better news than a new vineyard!'

Eight

Maggie received his news at Greenwich the following morning with no surprise at all. In fact she seemed to suggest that it was long overdue, given the years of closeness with the Harcourts. She knew Christine only by hearsay, of course, but no doubt his young lady would now be brought across the river and properly introduced.

Obedient to the hint, he conducted Christine to his home, confident that the two women in his life would get on happily together. The first hint of trouble came when Christine corrected his handmaiden's expectation of a wedding in church. Seeing Maggie frown, Robert hurried into the conversation.

'We'd all prefer it, I expect, but what would be the point when we haven't belonged to a congregation since every church in the district was damaged or blown to smithereens?'

Maggie sniffed but held her tongue. She registered instead the fact that the house she'd cleaned and polished until every corner of it shone evoked no comment at all from this beautiful, carelessly friendly girl she'd laboured to please.

Nothing apropos the visit or the wedding was said for several days. Then, seeing Maggie's expression as she brushed the dust out of an awe-inspiring hat of pre-war vintage, Robert decided to grasp the nettle.

'You don't like the idea of a registry-office wedding. What else don't you like? The fact that Christine isn't going to give up being an actress? Maggie, love, girls don't only want to be housewives nowadays.'

'What I like doesn't matter. Your future life's nothing to

do with me. I'm planning to retire.' She delivered the salvo calmly, still brushing away at her hat.

'Don't be silly,' he managed to say after a stunned silence. 'You're much too young to retire. In any case this house is your home, and there's more than room enough in it for the three of us.'

'I'm sixty-nine, and I've been looking after you for too long. Besides, your young lady doesn't like this side of the river. She'd rather stay where she is.'

'Stop calling her my "young lady", for Heaven's sake. You know her name.'

But he couldn't complain about the rest of what she'd said. As usual, Maggie had put her finger on the truth. He liked his comfortable Edwardian-villa home, but he knew it hadn't measured up to the Georgian elegance Christine was used to. More sadly still, he realised that his dear, blunt Cockney hadn't appealed to a girl who couldn't know her for the staunch-hearted treasure that she was.

'I'm going to move in with my widowed sister-in-law,' Maggie announced next. 'The poor thing's lost without a husband. It's all fixed.'

He could tell that it was. With her mind made up, he could as easily deflect a London bus as get her to go in a different direction. But she saw the trouble in his face and put out her hand in a rare gesture of affection.

'No need to fret, dearie. I'll be all right and tight, and your Ma wouldn't have expected you to stay here for ever. It's Christine you have to think of now.'

With that settled between them, it didn't seem to matter when William broached his great idea. Rather than have two houses half-empty, why didn't they make their home on the unused top floor of the Customs House? Why not indeed, except that it felt as if his entire life was being wedded to the Harcourts. But he told himself that he was the gainer, not they; and in any case he must do what would make Christine happy.

* * *

Their wedding was on a fine day in June. The bridegroom's guest-list was small, but the beautiful reception rooms of William's home were filled with his legion of friends, Christine's theatricals, and her parents' acquaintance with most of diplomatic London. Maggie, straw hat firmly skewered with long pins, was stiff to begin with, but if William's champagne hadn't mellowed her in the end, his way of treating her like a duchess certainly would have done. She was even ready to concede that she'd been wrong; the marriage was going to turn out well after all.

With the Anouilh play about to open, they couldn't have a honeymoon, but Christine assured her husband that night that life was perfect as it was. He kissed her for the compliment and felt convinced that she was right. So beautiful and responsive a wife was more good fortune than he deserved. It seemed the most natural thing in the world to take possession of her body, and to have her gladly accept pleasure in return. Only when she was lying asleep beside him did the memory of a different night surface in his mind, unbidden and certainly unwanted. He'd kept that remembered sweetness hidden away like a secret store of treasure, but it was time to let it go now. Jeanne Mayer had been another man's wife for years, and to remember her at all seemed disloyal when he had a wife of his own.

The play's opening night put the final gloss on Christine's happiness. The critics were kind, the public enchanted; the production was set for a long run. It was easy for Robert to share her pleasure in its success, less easy for him to enjoy what went with it – the tinselled theatre world that fascinated her so much. Behind the illusion of glamour was a reality she didn't seem to mind, of backstage gossip and intrigue. He fetched his wife home from the theatre at night cheerfully enough, but it was harder to pretend to feel at ease among her close-knit coterie of friends.

Late in the summer came an interruption to the usual

routine their life had settled into. William was unwell, but the champagne vineyards in eastern France had to be visited. Robert spent a busy fortnight there, but found time to call on the Godards, traced in the Reims telephone directory. He was given a welcome that touched him to the point of tears.

'You got back to England,' Jules Godard said more than once. 'That's all we wanted – for you to get safely home. But we heard that the line had broken down, and it seemed certain that you'd been caught.'

Over the meal they insisted that he stay and share, Robert told them the rest of the story, and saw Madeleine Godard weep for the death of a woman she hadn't known. To cheer her again, he offered the gifts he'd brought – a delicately engraved rose-bowl for her, tobacco for her husband. He hesitated about handing over his third package, but she understood his uncertainty.

'It's all right, Robert; our son came safely home . . . Half-starved of course, but he's well again now.'

'Then perhaps he can make use of my flying-jacket – not new, but guaranteed never to wear out! Do you remember that I walked away with most of his wardrobe?'

Her fingers stroked the sheepskin-lined leather. 'He'll be proud to use it, won't he, Jules?'

All in all it was a wonderful reunion and, still thinking of it on the journey home, Robert realised that it was time to share his memories with Christine. He hadn't told her about his French adventure but now he would – not quite all of it, but most of it.

He half-expected her to meet him at Victoria, but she wasn't there, and he found her at home instead. It seemed that she was both glad to have him back and deeply irritated about something as well.

'You look beautiful but cross, my dearest,' he said, smiling at her. 'Did I stay away too long? I tried not to.'

'I'm not *feeling* beautiful,' she answered sharply. 'Uncle Will's doctor tells me I'm pregnant.'

It took a moment to realise that she was serious in being upset. His own immediate reaction was delight, but he could see that it wasn't being shared by his wife. He framed her face in his hands so that she had to look at him.

'My love, it's too soon – is that the trouble? But by the time you have to leave the cast the run might be finishing. Even if it isn't, you'll probably be tired by then of doing the same thing six nights out of seven.'

Her blue eyes stared coldly at him. 'It *won't* be finishing, and of course I shan't be bored. That's the sort of stupid thing a non-actor always says.'

'Then forgive me for being stupid, but *please* be glad about the baby. It's such lovely news.'

The pleading in his face at least persuaded her, not very enthusiastically, to say that she supposed she would get used to the idea of motherhood. He was gentle and tender, but found that he no longer wanted to tell her about his visit to Jules and Madeleine Godard. She hadn't known the war, so how could she be expected to value the private heroisms of such people? Even so, he knew that if she failed to understand he would find it hard to forgive her.

Their daily routine was re-established, he working hard during the day, Christine leaving for the theatre just as he was arriving home. It didn't strike him as an ideal way to live, but it was what made her happy. Then one afternoon at the Customs House, conducting an important client to the door, he found Christine coming in, white-faced and tense. He disposed hurriedly of his guest, but she brushed past him and posed dramatically at the foot of the stairs.

'My dear, what's wrong?' he asked quickly. 'Aren't you feeling well?'

'I'm as well as can be expected, given my condition, and a very tiring understudy rehearsal.'

He struggled not to be sharp with her, nor to say something that would only serve to irritate her again. 'Then why not give it up? There'll be other plays when you're ready for them.'

The flash of anger he expected didn't come; instead, her eyes filled with tears. '*This* one's going to Broadway, and the American producer offered *me* the lead this afternoon. You can't possibly imagine what it felt like to have to turn it down.'

He went to stand beside her, his hand covering hers where it clutched the banister. 'Perhaps I can't properly understand, but I can at least say that I'm truly sorry for your disappointment.'

She lifted her shoulders in a sad, fatalistic shrug and turned to climb the stairs. He watched her go, aware of having been inadequate; but there was something more serious as well – he had just realised for the first time the extent to which they might always be going to fail each other in the things they considered important. The coming baby could make a difference, of course; child-birth altered a woman. He clung to this, and explained to William, who noticed her frequent spurts of ill-temper from then on, that she was simply tired and regretting having to leave the cast. Domesticity wasn't something she enjoyed, he admitted, and she was getting bored at home.

Two months later their daughter was born and Robert adored her from the first moment of seeing her. Christine, after a long and difficult labour, sounded disappointed.

'She looks ugly, poor little thing. I suppose they've brought us the right child?'

He forgave her because she looked so tired, and promised that Miss Daisy Ashton would soon be nearly as beautiful as her mother.

'Daisy?' Christine queried at once.

'Only if you'd like it, too. It's our version of a French name – Marguerite.'

'And I suppose you fell in love with a French Daisy during the war,' Christine suggested wearily.

'Hardly – I'm only aware of meeting her twice. But she deserves to be remembered. She saved the lives of other people like me but couldn't save herself. She died in a concentration camp.'

Christine gave a faint shrug. 'All right – we'll call our daughter Daisy, but it's rather a sad history to saddle the poor child with, assuming that she ever understands it.'

Robert smiled at his sleeping daughter. 'She will when she's old enough to be told. I think she looks the sort of girl who'll understand all sorts of things.'

Christine stretched out a hand to the flowers by her bed. 'I expect Uncle Will's disappointed, he'll have wanted a boy to carry on Harcourt's.' She glanced briefly at Robert, then looked away again. 'Don't promise him we'll try to manage a son next time. This will have to be the extent of our family – I don't want any more babies.'

He didn't answer immediately. Expecting an explosion or at least a reproach, Christine was almost resentful when he went instead to stand beside the cot and stroke his daughter's cheek.

'In that case,' he said quietly, 'I shall have to make the most of Daisy.'

She couldn't reasonably complain that he didn't make a fuss, and yet she had the feeling that a complaint was justified – gentle though he always was, he *ought* to have been angry or upset. It wasn't until visiting-time ended and he went away that she finally worked it out – the dead French girl, Marguerite, had been remembered; that was the important thing. His living wife didn't matter nearly as much.

In the years that followed he supposed they were taken for a very fortunate couple: she an ornament of the London stage, he not famous, but at least known to be a highly successful businessman. Obviously blessed by the gods, they were the envy of less favoured mortals who, in order to secure an invitation to the beautiful house at Wapping, had to pretend they didn't mind this unfair share-out of advantages.

Robert would have agreed with them about his own good fortune. He had a wise, compassionate friend and business-partner whom he revered; he had an elegant home and a celebrated wife. Above all, he had Daisy. Watching her grow from babyhood into a lovable and vividly attractive schoolgirl had become the joy of his life. She made up for what he didn't have – a marriage that was real. The façade of domestic happiness remained intact but it seemed to him that what he and Christine played together was one of the drawing-room comedies that she appeared in so successfully onstage. The façade suited *her* very well, and for as long as it did he would pretend to be content with it.

Then, when he'd given up expecting their life to change, an alteration there suddenly was. She returned to London from an absence in New York – but only to ask for a divorce.

'It won't hurt Daisy now,' she added, anticipating what he would say. 'She's almost grown-up. I know what she'll choose – to stay here with you.'

Robert stared at his wife, registering again after a gap of several months how lovely she was. Now in her mid-thirties she was probably at the peak of her beauty. Success had added self-assurance, and wealth had merely helped to gild the lily. He observed the fact without the slightest excitement or desire and, knowing it, thought he couldn't blame her for wanting not to stay with him. Even so, vanity was piqued; that at least, he hoped, was one natural reaction to have to the news that his wife was about to walk out for good.

'The divorce is so that you can marry someone else?'

'Yes,' she answered calmly, 'Arnold Goldman. He's the man who wanted me to go to New York long ago – before Daisy was born.'

'Then he's been very patient!'

The irony stung a little but she managed to smile. 'Not as

patient as all that – we're already living together. That makes me an adulterous woman, I'm afraid.'

She watched his face, its features as finely etched now as they had been twenty years ago, and still as unrevealing. He'd been a maddeningly reticent man altogether, difficult to bait, and nearly impossible to quarrel with. She knew that other people, always happy to make assessments of blame, would heap it all on her. But it would be unfair, and just once she wanted to say so.

'I expect you're wondering why I've suddenly decided to go now. It's because I've finally woken up to what I'm missing. Instead of a polite companion, I've got a lover – a man who actually sees *me*. I could have fought a living, breathing woman, but not that ghost from the past who still haunts your imagination. Do you remember her every time you speak Daisy's name?'

He wanted to shout that she was wrong. Whatever memory he still kept of Marguerite Mayer had done nothing to destroy their marriage; but he wouldn't have it dragged into this bitter discussion.

'Blame me if you like,' he said instead, 'but I'll just remind you that you were the one who insisted on going on with your career! Has Arnold Goldman been warned not to interrupt it, in case *he* should want to give you a child?'

Her face whitened but she answered calmly. 'He understands what the theatre means to me . . . Well, of course; he's part of it himself. But what you *never* understood was that I knew the truth almost from the beginning. I wasn't the woman you really wanted. I *am* the woman Arnold wants; it's why we're happy together.'

There was the ring of truth in that and it suddenly defeated his anger. 'Then of course you must be free to marry him,' he said quietly. 'We'll get the lawyers to fix it as soon as they can.' He wanted to ask her if she loved Arnold Goldman, wondered if the question would mean anything, and then decided that he hadn't the right to ask it anyway. In any case it was more important to ask something else. 'Shall I tell Daisy and William, or will you?'

A ghost of her lovely smile glimmered for a moment. 'I'd better, I think. You might heap coals of fire on my head by pretending that I've been the perfect wife. But I'll give you the job of telling Maggie – at least *she*'ll be pleased!'

He didn't argue with that, or want to know afterwards in what terms she'd broken her news. Having taken refuge in his office, he was tracked there by William who, looking very upset, merely said how sorry he was. Then, a little later, Daisy also appeared.

'You've got to come and say goodbye to Mummy, please – she's getting ready to go.' His daughter's face was pale, but her voice didn't tremble. 'I've been helping her pack.'

He thought he might have guessed that it was exactly what she *would* have done. She was adult beyond her years, but already blessed with more loving-kindness than most adults could lay claim to. He went with her upstairs, feeling ashamed of his own behaviour. Christine was standing in the hall, with suitcases heaped up around her. She tried to smile at him.

'I haven't grabbed the family silver! These are just clothes, books, personal things.'

'You're free to grab anything you want. I'll help you take it wherever you have to go.'

She accepted the peace offering but shook her head. 'All I need is a taxi. Arnold's waiting for me at the Connaught. He was kind enough to refuse to let me come over here alone.'

She sounded calm but he recognised the effort an accomplished actress was having to make. Her eyes were full of sadness, and this departure *wasn't* the easy choice she was trying to make it seem. Nothing, in fact, was ever simple or without regret, and she'd learned enough about life to know it very well.

She put out a hand to touch her daughter's cheek. 'Will you come and see me when you get a little older? New York's an exciting place to visit. In the meantime I'd look forward to a letter . . . just now and then.'

Daisy nodded gravely. 'I'll write, and one day I'll come.'

Christine's self-control wavered, but she was a disciplined professional and had promised herself she wouldn't allow this farewell scene to become unbearable. She even managed to smile at Robert. 'I hate saying goodbyes, so I'm going to hurry away. Take care of Daisy and Uncle Will for me.'

Five minutes later, with a taxi at the door, they stowed her luggage inside. A final, unsteady smile and then she climbed in herself and was driven away. The cab turned the corner and disappeared but Robert still stood there, engulfed by something that seemed less straightforward than simple pain. Shocked awareness of his own blindness had begun to figure in it rather strongly.

'Don't look sad,' a voice said beside him, and he turned to find Daisy watching him anxiously. 'We couldn't keep her if she didn't want to stay. It isn't *your* fault. Shall we blame Mr Goldman instead?'

He resisted the shameful temptation to agree. 'Your mother blamed me. I didn't have the grace to agree with her then but she was right. I couldn't make her happy; I only looked after her and expected *that* to make her feel grateful. It's what Mr Pickwick, and probably Arnold Goldman as well, would call humbug, I'm afraid!'

He smiled at his troubled daughter. She hadn't grown conventionally beautiful after all, despite his promise to Christine, but her face was intelligent and sensitive, and she had a smile to lift a watcher's heart. 'I'm sorry I've spoiled things for *you*, Daisy love – that's the worst of it.'

She gave a firm little shake of the head, a gesture he was familiar with. 'I'll manage nicely with you and Great-Uncle Will. I might even be better friends with Mummy if we have the ocean in between. I used to think she didn't like me very much, but I got the feeling just now that she really wanted me to write.'

She hesitated for a moment and he thought he could guess the question in her mind. How did it come about that two people who began by loving each other ended as strangers, or worse? But she didn't put the question into words, fearing that it would hurt him. Instead, she tucked her arm in his and led him back into the house. One day, he thought, he'd explain how their failure had come about. She wasn't old enough yet to understand, but when the right time came he'd tell her the story from the moment it had started – with his unpremeditated descent on to Jules Goddard's land.

Nine

Christine's departure from the Customs House saddened Robert most for the failure that it seemed to represent; but his anxiety was for its effect on Daisy. He made sure the divorce that followed had as little bitterness attached to it as possible but even so, a schoolgirl of fifteen had been left in the company of a father approaching middle-age and an elderly great-uncle.

He had to guess at the grief Daisy felt, because she seemed determined to give no sign of being an unhappy, disturbed, or angry adolescent. As time went by, Robert saw her commandeer instead the role of loving autocrat whose self-appointed mission was to rule their muddled, male lives. Her student friends filled the house with noise and laughter but whenever she saw William begin to tire of them, they were bundled out at once; there was no doubt that Daisy was in charge. The miracle was, her father thought, that she didn't get spoiled, but remained the girl she'd always been – funny and sharp and sweet.

Her choice of career remained constant too. She was going to write for a living. To everyone else's astonishment but hers, success came early, and her very first novel, no sooner submitted than snapped up by a publisher, set her on the road to what might eventually be fame.

Robert supposed that one day she would leave him and William alone in the rather echoing spaces of the Customs House, but for the moment, now aged twenty-four, she was still there. He should have remembered, though, that she liked to spring surprises. One evening, sitting with some sewing by the fire, she suddenly suggested that it was time they left London and went to live in France. She made the proposal casually enough – it might have been a Chinese take-away she was offering him, or a visit to a cinema – but he suspected her of a plot more deeply-laid and hatched. It took him a moment or two to decide how to answer, but in the end he pretended that she hadn't been serious.

'You're tired of this filthy winter, you're yearning for a blue Provençal sky and a whiff of mimosa blossom! Cheer up, my love – spring will even come to Wapping one of these days.'

She wasn't looking at him, being engrossed in the patchwork quilt she was constructing. 'Not Provence – it's getting spoiled along the coast, and inland it's too harsh and arid. I was thinking of somewhere further west – Gascony, say.'

There was another silence while he registered the power that the name still had to touch him. 'I was thinking you weren't serious,' he said at last, 'but in fact perhaps you were.'

She nodded, confirming it. 'Will you at least consider the idea?'

'I already have, to some extent!' The admission, calmly made, took some of the wind out of her sails, but he only smiled at her astonished face and went on. 'William's had a miserable winter and he needs a warmer climate. But he loves this house and he's lived here all his life; it's hard enough to suggest a different home – I hadn't thought of recommending a different country as well.'

This time, frowning at the effect of a crimson square alongside fuschia-pink, Daisy shook her head. 'France *isn't* a different country to Uncle Will. It's where he almost seems to belong. I'm not so sure about you.' She put down the piece of material she was holding and stared at her father instead. 'It's more of a love-hate thing with you, but at least that might make for an interesting life!'

'You don't think I should be allowed to sink into a peaceful if unexciting dotage here?'

The smiling question was briskly waved aside. 'Dotage is a long way off; you're a mere youthful fifty-five. There's no one to keep you here now that dear Maggie is dead, and you need a new challenge. It might be too late in ten years' time.'

Robert thought that it was probably true. 'All right, we're agreed that William must have warmth and I'm in need of a fresh start. We would have to sell this house – where would that leave you? Does New York beckon?'

'Not as a place to live, though I enjoy visiting Mum and Arnold there. I'd find a flat in London eventually, but you and Uncle Will would have to be settled in first. You'd get in an awful muddle by yourselves.' She folded up her sewing and got to her feet. 'Now for a delightful evening with the music of Arnold Schoenberg, whose centenary I'm told it is! My new admirer is hoping to convert me to the 12-tone scale, but I've warned him that I shall probably nod off before the interval.'

'I doubt it – you'll find it much too noisy,' her father pointed out. 'Before you go, tell me why you thought of Gascony; it's not a part of France that people usually pick on.'

Daisy pondered the question for a moment. 'Because you've both been to the Bordeaux region so often, I expect; you've got friends there. The climate's better than Provence – no Mistral, for one thing! And aren't the people supposed to be rather jolly?'

'That's the legend,' he agreed, 'not altogether supported by my own experience.'

She was about to delve into this, but the ringing of the doorbell downstairs reprieved him.

'There's your admirer. Better not keep him waiting – I believe it creates a bad impression on a new man.'

She grinned and went away, leaving the argument to continue in his mind. William should be got out of the dank, Thames-side atmosphere before another winter set in; there was no doubt about that. It was also true that he was ready for a change himself. He was tired of travelling, tired of being so deeply involved in the trading life of the City. Men had been carefully trained to follow him at Harcourt's, and he'd like for their sake as well as his own to hand over the reins soon. But France hadn't figured in his vague imaginings of where he and William might go. Trust Daisy to confront him with the very thing he'd been dodging.

He'd told her briefly long ago of his wartime journey through France, but only to explain how she came to have been given Marguerite's name. The man called 'Cheval' had been described but Jeanne Mayer was scarcely mentioned, and Daisy must certainly suppose by now that all the people involved in the adventure had long since faded from his mind. Her love-hate comment was shrewd, but only arose because, in moments of irritation with the French, he'd been heard to say that France was too good for them; she couldn't really know how little *any* of his memories had faded. At last he put the problem aside as one that only concerned himself and went to sound out his old friend downstairs.

William was huddled over the fire in his study, looking pale and woebegone, but he cheered up immediately at the sight of his visitor. 'I thought you were out, Robert. I only puff up the stairs nowadays if I'm sure you're there. Pour yourself a glass of port, and half a glass for me – it's all that killjoy leech allows me.'

With the wine poured, Robert settled himself on the other side of the fireplace. Unable to think of any tactful way of approaching what he'd come to talk about, his only option seemed to be to plunge straight in.

'Daisy reckons it's time we left the Customs House. She says *you* need sunshine and warmth, which is true; I apparently need something else to do, which may also be true but is less urgent. How does it strike you, William?'

He didn't know quite what reaction he expected: shock, perhaps, or anger; at the least, a stubborn refusal to even consider the idea. But William merely sat looking at the ruby wine in his glass as if it absorbed his entire attention. Disconcerted, Robert felt obliged to spell out the suggestion a little more. 'Daisy also reckons we need to go abroad – you know what a bossy piece she is!'

At last William looked across at his friend with a faint grin. 'Just "abroad"? You mean she hadn't decided on the exact spot? Well, not Spain, I think, although its sunshine is probably assured! With Franco dead at last – thank God! – there's no telling what's going to happen there. Not Tuscany, either – it's getting very full of English tax-exiles, I hear.'

Robert shook his head, puzzled but relieved. 'This isn't at all how I imagined the conversation would go. I expected you to say you'd only be taken out of here feet first, not calmly discuss where we might pitch our tent next!'

William's pale face was suddenly tinged with pink. 'Daisy's right. I've loved this house, and so have you, but it's time to leave it now. I think *she* only stays because she's afraid we need looking after here, but she ought to feel free to do whatever she wants. What say we find a lovely, peaceful spot and plant a little vineyard? I've always wanted to do that – watch the vines grow, and make some wine ourselves. Château Ashton-Harcourt we'd call it!'

Robert grinned affectionately at his friend. 'I was thinking in terms of a farmhouse, not a castle! But we shan't get rid of Daisy immediately – she intends to see us safely installed. She did have a suggestion to make, by the way. Perhaps she even anticipated the vineyard, because she picked on Gascony!'

'Of course she did, dear boy. What Daisy doesn't know by instinct isn't worth knowing.' He smiled happily at the thought, and half an hour later Robert went back to his own part of the house astonished at the change in William: restored to gaiety, he'd also suddenly recovered his old drive. As he'd pointed out, a man of seventy-five who wanted to enjoy his own grape harvest couldn't afford to dilly-dally; they had to press on fast.

Determined not to procrastinate, William set off a month later for France, shepherded by Daisy. Their plan was to settle into an hotel in Auch, and to explore the district from there: northward into the lovely valleys of the River Lot, southward into Gascony proper. Somewhere in all that delectable countryside, William said contentedly, would be the house they were looking for. It was just a matter of tracking it down.

Robert's own task was to find a buyer for the Customs House, and to arrange for the shipment of the bulk of its contents to France. He had insisted on this division of labour knowing that William would find it easier to drive away from his home one day and not look back. Disposing of it would be less painful if the actual job was left to someone else.

At the beginning of May he was finally ready to set off himself, the house sold and Harcourt's safely handed over to its new management. Walking along the riverbank for the last time, he discovered that what he would miss most of all was this odd neighbourhood itself, so rich in London's history. If he came back again it would be as a visitor, not as someone who belonged. He wouldn't be there as a matter of course to see the gulls squabbling over some find on the glistening flats left by the outgoing tide; he'd never hear the mournful toot of a tug on a misty evening, or sniff the composite smell of mud, tar, and sea-water that was the river's distinctive and unforgettable aroma. But enough of regret! He was going to live in France; he would be grateful for the fact and look forward now, not back.

Two days later he drove into the courtyard of the Relais de Gascogne and found William and Daisy waiting for him inside. They both looked fit after several weeks of fine spring weather, but also remarkably pleased with themselves. The farmhouse Robert had requested had been found – needing a little renovation here and there, William admitted gaily, but structurally sound and weatherproof. There was some land with it, but not too much. They would allow him time to recover from the journey over a brief déjeuner, and then he must inspect the property before the deal was signed in front of the notaire.

After a hasty meal of soup and jambon de Bayonne he was in William's car with Daisy at the wheel. They drove southwards out of the city, but Robert told himself it was only in his imagination that the route seemed familiar. He hadn't come this way for twenty-five years; how could he remember it as the same road he'd taken when he was looking for the Cheval's farm? But when Daisy turned off the main road, bumped along a rutted lane, and stopped in front of an old, weathered house, he knew there was no mistake. He could even see the donjon on the neighbouring hilltop; this *was* where a disagreeable farmer and his ill-tempered dog had hustled him off the premises all those years ago.

Forgetting to look at the house in front of him, he frowned at the only thought that filled his mind: the Darroze farm could be only a few kilometres away. Daisy, watching him, saw his withdrawn expression and grabbed hold of his hand.

'You're not *looking* properly. Don't make up your mind yet – it gets better inside, I promise.'

He managed to smile at her anxious face. 'All right, lead on, my love, even though I shall be hard to convince that this is where we ought to live.'

But at the end of half an hour he had to agree that the house would suit them very well; it was the right size, its roof and ancient colombarded walls were sound, and on the surrounding slopes were even the remnants of what had once been a vineyard. The land had been neglected, and the house obviously not lived in for some time, but there was nothing wrong with it that they couldn't put right. Outside again, Daisy looked at her father, still sensing in him some deep resistance that she couldn't understand. For once she didn't attempt to argue or persuade, and it was left to William to try to talk him round.

'You don't like it as much as we do, I'm afraid, and if you couldn't feel happy here there's no point in going on.

But the truth is that we've covered a lot of ground and had a fair number of disappointments. There isn't much to choose between our estate-agents at home and the ones we've dealt with here – they've sent us off hot-foot after the most unsuitable houses you ever clapped eyes on. Even Daisy, in whom hope springs nearly eternal, was close to giving up, and we couldn't believe our luck when this suddenly came on the market. It seemed well-nigh perfect to us. Is there something awful about it that we've missed?'

Robert turned to look again at the old house in front of him. No, there was nothing awful about it at all; in fact it looked very pleasing. Its walls, half-timbered and plastered in the Gascon fashion, glowed warmly in the May sunlight, in nice contrast to the window shutters that had weathered to a soft silver-grey; it belonged in the landscape.

'I think it's a nice house,' Daisy said, unable to keep quiet, 'it just needs a bit of affection, that's all, to make it beautiful again.'

Her father finally nodded his head. 'You're probably right, both of you. It will do very well. I was put off because by the most odd of chances, this neighbourhood is where I happened to be years ago. When I came back again the then owner didn't take kindly to stray visitors and for two pins would have set his dog on me. It doesn't look as if he prospered much after that.'

Daisy looked happy to have matters explained so simply. 'It doesn't sound as if he deserved to prosper, but it wasn't the house's fault. I think it's been waiting for you to come back and give the story a happier ending.'

Her father's face looked pained. 'Whimsy, my dear Watson; this is simply an old, neglected building for heaven's sake, not a sentient human being!'

She smiled at him, taking no offence, but when she'd gone out of earshot to relock the front door, William had something more to say.

'You must have called here when you were looking for your friends. Does that mean they're living close by?'

'Pierre Darroze probably still is. I imagine that his parents are dead by now.'

'Does it matter?' William asked gently. 'Is that what made you hesitate?'

Robert nodded, then put his anxiety into words. 'Daisy takes a romantic view of life. She'd imagine nothing nicer than a wartime comrade on our doorstep, but I can't help feeling that Pierre Darroze *wouldn't* want us here. He has a lifetime's prejudice against the English, and if ever a man born of woman was incapable of changing his views, I'd say that man was him. The name of "Cheval" wasn't given to him in the Resistance because he was easily led.'

William's cherubic smile appeared. 'I'm about to offer you more whimsy, I'm afraid. You have to admit that the strangest coincidence brought Daisy and me *here*, instead of to a dozen other places; it seems to confirm my theory that our lives are required to make completed patterns. Your own connections with this country *aren't* complete – you still haven't decided whether you like it or even understand it. Suppose the unfinished pattern required you to come back here and meet Pierre Darroze again?'

Robert didn't answer for a moment. 'You may be right,' he said at last, 'but I bet you all I possess that Pierre himself would never agree that the pattern of *his* life needs me to complete it!'

He watched Daisy walk back towards them, sunlight glinting on her hair, and a little smile tilting up the corners of her mouth. 'Still, my daughter looks happy, so we'd better go and clinch the deal with the notaire. Another bidder might step in ahead of us and then where would all your high-flown speculations about patterns be?'

It was Annette Darroze, Pierre's wife, who took back to the farm a report of the morning's conversation at the boulangerie. An English girl had come in to buy bread, and two cars with GB plates had been seen in the locality. Tourists were scarce in Foutances, and no one in the shop admitted to having guests, so it had made a nice little mystery to discuss over the purchase of the day's baguettes.

At the lunch-table, Pierre brushed the gossip aside. 'They'll just have been passing through, you know what the English are: they don't want to be a part of Europe, but they like coming here well enough.'

'It's their climate,' his step-daughter explained. 'The poor things need to find the sun.' Jacqueline was accepted as being an expert on the subject of the English, having, unlike the rest of them, once been taken across the Channel on a school trip.

The only other person present – Pierre's great-nephew, Daniel Lescaut – had no view to offer, and the conversation reverted as usual to farm matters.

But it was Daniel who found an English car the following morning, blocking the track that led to the rear of the farm. A girl was in the driver's seat, with a map spread out beside her. She wound down her window at the sight of him.

'Good morning – I'm lost, I'm afraid! A signpost or two would help newcomers like me.'

Her friendly smile brought no response from the stern-faced man looking at her.

'This is Darroze land. My great-uncle isn't obliged to signpost it for people who trespass on private property.'

'Then I apologise,' she said quickly, aware of being at fault but irritated by his manner. 'Direct me to a house called the Petit Manoir if you can and I'll get out of your way.'

Her French, though fluent, was strewn with errors, and she supposed for a moment that it was the cause of his deepening frown; the French were so very touchy on the subject of their precious *langue*. But it seemed that he had something else to criticise.

'You must have the name wrong – the Petit Manoir has been empty for years.'

Daisy smiled again, very sweetly. 'No longer. My father

and great-uncle live there now, and I'm staying with them for the time being.'

She would have sworn that it was shock his expression now registered; certainly something more than her small trespass on his great-uncle's land was upsetting him. In fact, she was inclined to think he'd forgotten she was there at all.

'We moved in a week ago,' she added helpfully. 'That's why I'm not quite *au fait* with the district yet. I was looking for a short-cut home.'

It seemed at least to remind him of how the conversation had begun. 'Turn round – if you can, that is, without knocking down our fence posts. You branched left too soon, your turning is five kilometres further on.'

'Thank you. M. Lambert, the notaire, should have warned us that our neighbours wouldn't be very welcoming. We'll try not to trouble you in future.'

She gave him a little nod, decided that discretion was the better part of valour in the matter of a difficult turn while the damned man stood watching, and reversed along the track to the road. Then, with an impudent toot on the horn, she drove away. A sparring-match with a personable male was usually enjoyable – and memory confirmed that he *had* indeed been personable – but she found herself depressed by the encounter. There'd been so little cause for the man's hostility, and it reminded her too vividly of what her father had said about his reception there years ago. However much they grew to like their new home, some of its pleasure would certainly be spoiled if they couldn't get on terms with their neighbours. She drove away wondering whether to mention the incident or not, and decided in the end to make light of it – her well-known charm had fallen flat on its face for once. She would leave it to her father and Uncle Will to do a little public relations work among these not-so-jolly Gascons.

Ten

Daniel Lescaut watched Daisy's car out of sight before he turned to walk back to the barn. The loss of Gaston's property was a blow, but something else nagged at his mind as well. The girl's comment about unfriendly neighbours still felt like a barb stuck in his skin. She shouldn't have been there of course, but he'd behaved like an ill-mannered lout. The trouble was that she'd looked the kind of sophisticated, self-assured female he particularly disliked. The confident smile had given her away, saying too clearly, 'Look at me; I'm worth it.' Added to that had been the fact that she was English, and his great-uncle had taught him to believe that they were slippery people – hard to fathom, because what they said was so often the opposite of what they actually meant you to understand.

He shrugged the memory of the girl aside and went straight to the office in the barn. Pierre Darroze was there, frowning over farm accounts. He leaned back in his chair and smiled at Daniel, then stared at him.

'Something wrong?'

'Something extraordinary, at least. It seems that the English people Annette heard about yesterday are our new neighbours – they've bought the Petit Manoir.'

'Nonsense,' Pierre said sharply. 'The lawyers are still wrangling about who owns it. Old Gaston's relatives are scattered far and wide and the inheritance can't be settled till they're all agreed about what happens to it.'

Daniel shook his head. 'That's what we were supposed to

think, but the English people have been there for a week; I've just bumped into one of them. I suppose they were ready to pay through the nose for it, and between them Deschamps and the notaire were willing to bend the rules a little.'

His great-uncle's lined face suddenly looked tired and grim. 'I expect so; it would certainly have suited Lambert to have a private sale engineered by his estate-agent crony. At a public auction they couldn't have stopped *me* bidding for it.'

There was a little silence that Daniel finally broke. '*Why?* Why are they so determined to spite you?'

Pierre gave his usual shrug. 'Because, more than thirty years ago, I faced the people here with a hard choice. Some of them fought with me against the Germans, many did not. The Lambert family certainly suffered because of what we did: the elder son was taken and shot – a reprisal to teach us a lesson, and to make us hated by people who only wanted to keep their heads down and stay out of trouble. It was a long time ago but memories die slowly here.'

'If they ever die at all,' Daniel suggested quietly. Then he tried to smile at his companion. 'Look at *you* – still mistrusting the English because they burned some village down five hundred years ago!'

'True,' Pierre conceded, 'who am I to preach tolerance and forgiveness? Now come and sort out these damned accounts for me – you're better at them than I am. I'm going visiting.'

'Our new neighbours? They won't reckon you're dressed for a social call!'

'So much the better,' Pierre said, considering his faded shirt and much-patched jeans. 'I'm a working farmer, not a city gentleman pretending to enjoy the rustic life.'

He picked up a saddle on his way out of the barn and threw it over the back of a chestnut mare grazing in the paddock. Daniel watched him go, thinking how typical it was of his great-uncle to make no effort at all to impress his new neighbours. He hadn't asked which one had been met, and Daniel was thankful for that – he didn't wanted to admit that a smiling foreign girl had made him feel like a country bumpkin.

Trotting through what had been Gaston's fields, Pierre was freshly irritated by the signs of neglect; the land could have been made productive again, and the house itself would have been useful when he and Annette were ready to retire. Now all those possibilities were lost and he'd been cheated out of them. Anger burned in him no less strongly because he was a man who held his tongue and hid his feelings, but there was a kind of sick despair as well, nothing changed as the slow years went by; the old vendettas remained even now to poison goodwill, and Daniel was right, perhaps they always would.

The surroundings of the Petit Manoir looked as he remembered them, unkempt and rankly overgrown. But there were clear signs of work in progress around the house itself. A builder's van was parked there, and materials were neatly heaped under the shelter of the barn's overhang. Mindful that he wasn't making a social call, Pierre walked round to the rear of the house. The door leading to the kitchen quarters was wide open. Inside, he could see a girl standing at a table, stirring paint. Like himself she wore working garb – jeans and a shirt – but the resemblance stopped there, he had to admit. She was young and slender; her sandy-red hair was tied back in a businesslike way, and the sun had sprinkled freckles across her nose and cheekbones.

She said 'good morning' at once, but called to someone he couldn't see. 'Uncle Will, come please, we've got a visitor, and I can't leave the paint.' Then she smiled at the large, thickset man standing in the doorway. 'Excuse me for not staying, but my wall is drying upstairs! My father's out, but my great-uncle will come and welcome you.'

She walked away with her can of paint, leaving him to realise that Daniel hadn't told him which of them he'd met. Then a small, elderly round man came bustling into the room.

He had soft white hair fringing a bald pate, a pleasant smile, and, when he spoke, an accent that suggested he was perfectly at home in the French language.

'How kind of you to call on us, Monsieur. My name's William Harcourt. That was my great-niece, Daisy, you saw just now; perhaps she explained that her father is out shopping for all the things we seem to need to get the house in order.'

He waited for the visitor to introduce himself and, briefly as usual, Pierre did. 'Pierre Darroze,' he admitted, 'your nearest neighbour.' The name had been recognised, he realised, but that wasn't surprising – Lambert would have mentioned it. 'I came to make sure the news I've just heard is correct. My own information was that this house wasn't on the market yet.'

William decided to ignore the belligerent manner but not the sense of injury that seemed to underlie it. 'I believe we were lucky to approach the estate-agent at just the right moment; but I'm sorry if we snapped up something you might have wanted yourself.'

Robert could have explained that it was his friend's usual way of tackling opponents – the cunning mixture of candour and courtesy that left them flummoxed and disarmed. In the present case William had the added advantage of knowing who this hostile neighbour was. There was no question of resenting his manner, the man reckoned he had reason to feel misused, but much more than that, it was he who'd sheltered Robert long ago at hideous risk to himself and his family.

After a moment or two Pierre decided to meet frankness with frankness. 'Most of Gaston's land went bit by bit over the years – he was a bad farmer. What remains runs alongside the river. It would have been very useful to me in our long, hot summers.'

'The house goes with the land,' William pointed out gently. 'Would you have wanted that as well?'

'Not immediately – later on, when my wife and I retire and Daniel takes over the farm.'

'Your son, Daniel?'

'My niece's son; I have step-children, none of my own. Daniel still lives with his mother, Jeanne Lescaut, for the moment.'

It was more than he meant to give away, but the small man in front of him had a knack, it seemed, of extracting information. For the moment, though, William wasn't thinking of Pierre Darroze. Instead, an echo had chimed faint but clear in his memory; Jeanne had been the name of the girl Robert had gone back to find, only to discover her already married to someone else. William was reminded, too, of his own glib suggestion that unfinished patterns needed completing. Robert's own resistance to living at the Petit Manoir had been due to the probability of having to dig up the past, but it seemed likely that this angry man would refuse to acknowledge it at all.

'We'll try not to be bad neighbours, Monsieur Darroze,' he said at last, with a small, quiet note of authority not lost on his visitor. 'We shall look after the property, not neglect it, because we love France, cherish its past, and know the wounds it's suffered in this century.' He hesitated briefly, then leapt the hurdle in front of him. 'By the way, Daisy's other name is Ashton. I think you knew her father, Robert Ashton, a long time ago. He arrived a week or two after us to find that the house we'd set our hearts on was on *your* doorstep. It took some effort to persuade him that this ought to be our new home.'

The silence grew heavy in the room while William waited for the visitor to finally dredge up a reference to Robert, or at least some conventional words of welcome. But the man merely lifted his hand at last in a gesture William couldn't interpret and then marched out of the room. The odd, uneasy interview was over.

Daniel was left to wonder about his great-uncle's sudden impulse to go visiting. It was unusual behaviour for a man who didn't normally obey the whim of the moment. However much he might regret losing Gaston's property, there was nothing he could do about it now, and a visit to the intruders at the Petit Manoir could only be a waste of valuable time.

It wasn't until lunch-time came round that an enquiry could be made as to how the visit had gone. Even then Daniel had to ask – his great-uncle seemed disinclined to talk at all, or to listen to the conversation round the table.

'Who did you see at the Petit Manoir?' Daniel finally asked point-blank. 'It was a girl I met, parked along the track.' He shook his head at Pierre's step-daughter who had pricked up her ears. '*Not* a blonde English beauty – she had odd red hair and a self-confident smile; I didn't like the look of her at all.'

'She's called . . . Daisy.' Pierre brought out the unfamiliar name after a struggle to recall it from the morning's conversation. 'I talked to an old man – well, older than me – who said he was her great-uncle. They're putting the house in order; going to live there, by the look of it, not just come when it suits them.'

'Does it matter?' Annette asked. 'They might call here for milk and eggs, but that's as much as we shall see of them.' She noticed her husband's grim expression and spoke more sharply to him. 'It's stupid to let them upset you. What's done is done, and we're no worse off now than when Gaston was alive.'

He took a moment or two to answer her question. 'No, it doesn't matter. But in the strange way that coincidences happen, the girl's father – the man I *didn't* see this morning – turns out to be someone I knew a long time ago. His plane had been shot down and he was trying to get back to England. My sister brought him here because he was sick. Jeanne nursed him, rather against her will – she didn't like him. Eventually he did get home: one of our success stories!'

It was a long speech for Pierre Darroze to have made, and Daniel detected beneath its staccato sentences a seam of emotion that was also unusual. 'How did you know he escaped, did he get in touch with you afterwards?'

'He called here some years after the war – to thank us, I suppose. But that was a long time ago as well.' Pierre's hand waved the subject aside, but Daniel hadn't finished with it.

'My mother didn't like him, you said. What about you?'

'Annette's right, it doesn't matter,' the answer came back curtly. 'What happened thirty years ago is ancient history, and we and the Anglais next door won't be living in each other's pockets.'

It put an end to the conversation, but Jacqueline reverted to it when her mother and step-father had left the room.

'I've a feeling that we didn't hear the whole story. Perhaps you could get the rest of it from your mother?'

'I shan't ask her,' he said firmly. 'Let's forget the damned war; it's haunted us long enough.'

Jacqueline didn't argue; instead she leaned over and kissed his cheek. It wasn't the most she could do when given the chance, but at least it reminded him of the softness of her body against his. Growing up had been a race against serious odds, because Daniel was years older than she was and he might easily have fixed on some other girl by now. But she'd been lucky; he wouldn't leave home all the time his father was slowly dying. Now that Jacques Lescaut was dead, and Jeanne could manage well enough on her own, things were different. Jacqueline, at nineteen, was more than ready for marriage, and she was doing her best to make sure that Daniel couldn't hold out much longer. There was no blood tie between them, and he was her step-father's heir to the farm. It was perfectly clear to all of them that he and she would end up man and wife. She wasn't troubled by the thought of the English girl that Daniel hadn't liked; he never said one thing and thought another.

All the same, it was he who met Daisy again. One morning, with farm business to attend to in Foutances, he saw a van being reversed so carelessly that it backed into a bicycle parked at the kerb. The driver roared off out of the square a moment before the owner of the bicycle reappeared.

Daisy was confronting the wreckage – a hopelessly buckled front wheel, and the contents of her basket scattered over the pavement – when a tall man she recognised came and stood beside her.

'If you're about to tell me that I'm where I shouldn't be yet again, please don't bother,' she said hotly.

Daniel thought it wouldn't be advisable to smile. 'I came to say that I took the number of the van. It may not do much good, but we should give it to the police.'

'I think it would do no good at all,' Daisy pointed out. 'I and my English bicycle are probably reckoned fair game around here. I wish I knew what we've done to upset you all so much.'

Daniel was squatting on the ground now, reassembling her shopping. He stood up, registering the distress as well as anger in her face. 'You need a cup of coffee, I think.'

Her arm was taken in a grip that couldn't be argued with, and she was piloted across the square to one of the pavement tables outside the café.

'Sit here and calm down,' he suggested quietly. 'I'll be back as soon as I've ordered the coffee and phoned that number through to the police.'

Aware that anger had now turned into a ridiculous desire to weep, Daisy did as she was told. Five minutes later Daniel returned and sat down opposite her.

'It was a stolen van – which explains why the driver didn't hang around to apologise.' He stopped to thank the waiter who put coffee in front of them, and then went on. 'Why do you think being English makes you some sort of target here?'

She'd recovered enough to answer him, but her eyes were still bright with anger. 'That's all you know about us, so what other reason can there be to dislike us?'

He stirred sugar into his cup, as if looking for an answer

there that she might accept. 'We're Gascons, you have to remember. I doubt if we'd make *any* foreigners welcome, at least not straight away.'

'My father and William Harcourt *aren't* "any foreigners",' she nearly shouted at him. 'I wasn't born at the time, but I know what happened during the war. Where would Pierre Darroze and his friends have been without the help that was flown to them night after night from England by pilots like my father? If General de Gaulle could decorate Uncle Will in person, how dare *any* of you think he hasn't the right to live here if he wants to?'

The man opposite her stilled her agitated fingers by suddenly covering them with his own warm ones. The gesture made her look at him, and now she could see in his brown face that unexpected amusement had chased hostility away.

'I think I'd like you on my side in a fight; you remind me of my mother – very formidable when roused!'

It wasn't altogether a compliment, Daisy suspected. If a fight *wasn't* in question he probably preferred women who were docile and tactful. She was tempted to say so, but he didn't give her the chance.

'If your family helped this country during the war you probably expect us to feel grateful. We should be, of course, but the truth is that it's not something we're good at.'

'Understatement *quite* worthy of an Englishman,' she said approvingly.

Daniel took no notice of an interruption intended to provoke. 'We're also tired of being reminded of the fact that *we* capitulated and you did not. But what you insist on calling the *English* Channel – there's hubris for you; why "English" may I ask? – is something we didn't have between us and the Germans. Why not admit that it's what saved *you*?'

She was silent for a moment, smarting under the attack, but aware that her father would probably accept what had just been said if he were there. 'We aren't going to agree, are we?' she suggested at last. 'You think we claim too much in the way of heroism; we think your leaders and generals, at least, didn't show enough. It ought not to affect how we see one another now, but I'm afraid it still does. It was my stupid idea that we should come here, my father and Uncle Will ought to have told me it wouldn't work.'

Daniel remembered telling Jacqueline that he didn't like the look of this English girl, but he hadn't seen her then as she was now – unhappy and ready to admit to having been wrong. She wasn't a beauty, didn't try to remind him of her femininity as Jacqueline frequently did, and clearly didn't care whether she made an impression on him or not. She was different from the women he knew; that was what it amounted to. But he could recognise some elusive quality in her that appealed to him. Abruptly, he signalled for the bill and brought the little episode to a close.

'I'll drive you home, but I'll keep your bicycle in the jeep, and see if it's worth mending.'

He was going out of his way to be kind, but with so little apparent pleasure that she was tempted to tell him not to bother. She remembered in time how stupid it would be to cut off her nose to spite her face, and followed him silently instead to the jeep parked across the square.

They made the short journey without speaking, Daisy polishing up a farewell sentence that would combine frigid gratitude with the strong hint that she hoped not to bump into him again. But the sentence wasn't delivered because her father was outside the house when they arrived, repairing a broken shutter. He laid down hammer and nails at once, and came over to help her out of the jeep.

'Something wrong, my love?'

She quickly explained, and then introduced him to the man who had jumped down from the driver's seat. 'I can't introduce *you* – I don't know your name,' she pointed out to Daniel.

'But I think I know from William who he is,' her father said with a smile – 'Jeanne Lescaut's son.' He held out a friendly hand. 'Thank you for bringing Daisy home. Will you come in and have a drink?'

The refusal came stiffly. 'I'm afraid not, there's work waiting for me.' His glance settled for a moment on Daisy, now standing with an arm linked through her father's. 'I'm told we haven't made you properly welcome.'

'By my daughter, no doubt,' Robert said calmly. 'Take no notice. She can't resist pointing out to people the error of their ways, but she means very well.'

Daniel watched the two of them exchange smiles, and realised once again the extent to which they were different from the people he was used to. 'We're in the habit of taking things slowly here,' he felt the need to explain. 'I'm barely reckoned a Gascon yet myself. The Lescauts originally came from Alsace, and so did my maternal grandfather's family.'

That strong element of northern ancestry accounted for eyes that were unexpectedly blue in his sunburned face. Otherwise, Robert thought, he was entirely Jeanne's son. If he ever smiled, which on present showing seemed unlikely, his smile would probably be hers, too.

'Your mother might remember me,' Daniel heard the Englishman say diffidently. 'Would she mind if I called on her one day? I must be sure about that because I have the impression that people here often don't want to be reminded of the war; given what they suffered it's understandable enough.'

'I'll tell her you're here,' Daniel answered. 'Why not let her call on *you* if she wants to?'

He gave them a brief nod, and drove away before Daisy could suggest that he and his mother must be sure not to go to too much trouble. Balked of this, she turned on her father instead. 'What *is* it with these people? Damn them, why *can't* they like us?'

Robert put a comforting arm around her shoulders because she sounded close to tears. 'Don't fret, Daisy, love. You're afraid we made a mistake in coming here. I don't think we have. The house suits us down to the ground, and we'll get on terms with our neighbours – slowly, as that dour young man suggested we should! William's our secret weapon; he's bound to charm them out of their bunker in the end, if only because he loves France so dearly.'

He saw her smile with the relief of thinking he might be right, but her next question took him by surprise.

'Do you suppose Madame Lescaut *will* call? She might prefer you to remember her as she was; she must have been young at the time, and I expect she was brave and beautiful.'

'Young and brave certainly,' he answered after a small pause, 'but only intermittently beautiful; rather in the way that you are in fact!'

Never making any claim to beauty, Daisy was rather pleased with this tribute. 'Well what about my namesake, Marguerite?'

'She was Jeanne's mother, and she *was* beautiful.'

The quiet answer confirmed what Daisy had long believed. Her parents' marriage might have foundered anyway on Christine Ashton's determination to have a stage career, but beautiful, lost Marguerite had had a good deal to do with their failure as well.

Daisy stopped suddenly to inspect her father's face. 'I know Uncle Will loves it here already, but are *you* sorry we came?'

He had to lean down a little to kiss her cheek. 'Don't be daft, child. How could I regret being in such a lovely place?'

It hadn't, she thought, quite answered her question, but she knew it would be all the answer she would get. On balance she hoped Jeanne didn't call, and she was prepared to do without her bicycle rather than have to meet the lady's awkward son again.

Eleven

Still thinking about his visit to the Petit Manoir, Daniel drove straight back to his own home on the outskirts of Foutances. He knew his mother would be there – she didn't teach on Saturdays. The day being fine, she was certain to be in the garden she'd made out of an unpromising bit of land at the back of the house. Its only virtue to begin with had been that it ran down to the river that skirted their small town. Now it was a secluded, tranquil oasis where his father had mostly spent the last months of his life, content to enjoy the beauty Jeanne Lescaut had created for him.

She was on her knees examining a rosebush when Daniel walked out to find her. 'Look, my favourite Boule de Neige is covered in these damned insects. Why can't they leave her alone?'

'Because she looks and smells beautiful, I expect,' he suggested reasonably. Then he smiled at his mother with the sweetness that he reserved only for her. 'Come and sit down. I'll fetch you a glass of wine and then I've got something to tell you.'

She thought she could guess what he was going to say – he'd finally made up his mind about marrying Jacqueline. Sooner or later, because there was an old-fashioned streak in her son, he would have got round to insisting on the sacrament of marriage. He quite often stayed overnight at the farm if work had gone on late into the evening and she didn't suppose he'd tried very hard to keep Jacqueline out of a bed the girl was only too eager to share. Jeanne knew she would miss him very much, but it was time he settled down.

She'd got on terms with Pierre's wife over the years, and accepted that Annette's daughter would make Daniel a good, if less than ideal, wife. There was also much to be said for arranging the future of the farm so neatly. Pierre's step-son, a successful lawyer in Toulouse, had no interest in it; all the more reason, therefore, for Daniel to share his inheritance with Jacqueline by marrying her.

He came back now and set down a tray of wine and glasses on the terrace table. Jeanne watched his quiet face, hoping suddenly that the unspoken pressures they'd all put on him hadn't been unfair.

'What took you so long this morning?' she asked. 'I thought you must have run into our dear mayor, and he'd implored you to help him run the Fête again.'

Daniel poured the golden Alsatian wine that Jacques Lescaut had taught them to drink as an aperitif, and handed his mother a glass. 'Not the mayor, but I did meet someone else. First, though, I must tell you the beginning of the story.' He described briefly what he hadn't mentioned before – the English trespasser on the farm track, and Pierre Darroze's visit afterwards to the Petit Manoir.

'You can guess his reaction to the news of its sale,' Daniel interrupted himself, 'imagining Lambert and friends laughing behind his back.'

'I *can*,' Jeanne agreed. 'Still, English owners can't be any worse than the thieves who tricked Gaston out of the rest of his land.'

'True, and at least they aren't going to plant acres of maize and sunflowers, just to claim fat subsidies from Brussels.' Daniel frowned over that, but went on with his story. 'This morning I happened to meet the English girl again – her bicycle had just been wrecked in the square by a lout in a stolen van. I bought her a cup of coffee while she calmed down and then drove her home. Unlike Uncle Pierre, who only saw an elderly relative when he called, I met her father.'

Jeanne's face suddenly sparkled with amusement. 'Shall I guess the rest? The girl is very pretty and her father, who has nice English manners, thanked you in atrocious French for taking care of his daughter!'

'Well, not quite. The girl is what *you*'d call interesting, I think; not pretty. What's more, they all seem to speak French like natives.'

'Not their usual habit,' his mother pointed out. 'I wonder what brought them *here*?'

'The past, perhaps,' Daniel suggested. 'It turns out that the girl's father has been before. Uncle Pierre wasn't eager to talk about it for some reason, but it seems that you both knew the Englishman as an escaping RAF officer. His name is Robert Ashton.'

He had to wait a long time for a response, and when it came Jeanne's voice wasn't quite as level as usual. 'We never told him where he was, or even who we were, and he left us as suddenly as he arrived. I got home one day to find him gone. If he made it back to England at all it seemed unlikely that he'd survive the war; not many fighter-pilots did.' Her voice faded altogether, and she made an unnecessary business of taking a sip of wine.

'Ashton asked if he could call on you.' Daniel went on with his story. 'I remembered what Uncle Pierre rather insisted, that you hadn't liked him all those years ago, and said he'd better leave it to you to visit *him* if you wanted to.' Daniel hesitated a moment. 'I rather liked him, as a matter of fact. He had a nice, laughing way of apologising for his daughter's habit of telling other people what to do! She and I *didn't* take to one another – she was sharp and I was rude.' He remembered a moment when the girl had seemed sad, but brushed it aside in registering the strange fact that his mother's thin, brown face looked full of pain. Suddenly it seemed likely that Jacqueline had been right about a story they didn't know. He might have risked asking whether his mother would visit the Ashtons or not, but she abruptly switched the conversation to himself.

'Whenever I see Annette she drops little hints about possessive mothers. I think I'm required to push you out of here by force if need be. I shan't do any pushing, but I *would* like to be sure you aren't still here because you think I can't manage on my own.'

He smiled at her with deep affection and a glimmer of amusement. 'You could manage in the Gobi Desert, I dare say! I know that Annette is anxious for the marriage, but it seemed only fair to give Jacqueline a chance to look around. What seems the perfect arrangement to everyone else might not have been so to her.'

Jeanne stared at him rather sadly. 'Or to you, if you can make it sound so very little like a romance! *Don't* marry, please, just because Annette is manoeuvring you into it, or because you think you're obliged to take care of Jacqueline. She'll want to be loved as well as provided for. If you can't manage that, leave her to someone who can.'

He patted her hand, and then stood up. 'You worry too much. We shall manage very well together.'

It hadn't quite answered what she'd said, but she allowed the subject to drop and he picked up the tray and took it back to the house. She stayed where she was, pretending to enjoy the fragrance of a cascade of Madame Albertine above her head. But she wasn't thinking of the rose or even considering the matter of her son's marriage; instead, she thought about the family at the Petit Manoir. At last she made up her mind. Courtesy seemed to insist that she must call on them, but the truth was, of course, that she must also see what the years had done to Robert Ashton. Honesty even pushed her into another admission as well; she had to meet the woman he'd chosen as his wife.

The house was slowly but surely becoming their home.

Even Daisy, whose standards were exacting, admitted to being pleased with the team of workmen found for them by the ever-helpful Monsieur Lambert. Masons, plumbers and electricians between them had transformed Gaston's nightmare kitchen, constructed two bathrooms upstairs, and converted the *chai* attached to the back of the house into a working utility room. Daisy had insisted on the old tiled floors throughout the ground floor being simply scrubbed and repolished, and she'd been equally insistent that the vast stone fireplaces should be repointed but otherwise left intact and unspoiled. To the pleasure of them all, the lovely antique furniture that had grown old as the Customs House grew old now looked just as much at home in their Gascon farmhouse; the Petit Manoir, neglected nearly to the point of ruin, was beautifully recovering health and life.

Indoors, it was she and William who planned, decided and oversaw. Outside, Robert took charge; first of all, in the redemption of the land around the house. His most immediate project was to make a garden; William's vineyard and his own dream of replanting the orchards as well must wait until later.

By the end of June the thermometer was climbing steadily, and one cloudless, early summer day followed another so inevitably that it was hard to remember the times when they'd waited hopefully for the sun to gild the river at Wapping. It was becoming too hot to work out of doors after midday, and Robert's routine was to rise soon after dawn, and knock off when Daisy called him back to the shade of the terrace for their pre-lunch glass of beer or *citron-pressé*.

She watched him walking towards her one morning, pulling on his discarded shirt, and thought how fit he looked. The move had been a huge upheaval in their lives, and the difficulties with their neighbours hadn't yet been overcome, but she was no longer afraid their decision had been the wrong one. Uncle Will was a thoroughly happy man, and her father daily seemed to be putting age into reverse and becoming young again.

'Uncle Will's in earnest consultation with Alphonse,' she now explained. 'They're supposed to be deciding when to repair the loose tiles on the roof; but what I think I actually overheard was a spirited argument on the rival merits of Vieux Cahors and Châteauneuf du Pape!'

'That's what you get for living in France – intelligent conversation with the builder about important things.'

Daisy grinned and poured the lemonade. 'It's all right, isn't it?' she said suddenly. 'I know I keep asking, but things aren't quite perfect; I want to be sure we didn't make a mistake in coming here.'

'No mistake at all,' her father said firmly. He glanced at her down-bent face, now so freckled by the sun that her pale skin gave the appearance of being tanned. 'We'd love you to stay for ever of course, but it isn't necessary. You must live your own life, Daisy, not spend all your precious youth on us. Just come in future when you feel inclined.'

She smiled at him, thinking that she loved him very much; no man she'd ever met so far had had a hope of dislodging him from the core of her affections.

'I promised myself the summer here,' she said at last. 'But this place has begun to put a story in my head, so I won't go back to London with nothing to show for an extended vacation.' Then, about to say something else, she suddenly stopped. An unknown woman had rounded the corner of the house and was walking towards them.

'I banged on the door but nothing happened,' said the visitor. 'At home I'd be out in the garden; I thought you might be too.' She stared at the tall man who'd risen to his feet, and offered him a faint smile. 'It's a long time ago that you lived in the hayloft in my grandfather's barn.'

The remark identified her for Daisy – fortunately, she thought, since her father seemed unable to find anything to say. Then the woman spoke again herself. 'I mention that in case you're trying desperately to remember who I am!'

He freed himself at last from whatever paralysis had gripped him, and pulled out a chair. 'There's no effort involved in recognising you. Daisy, let me introduce Daniel's mother, Madame Jeanne Lescaut. She was "Mam'selle" when I knew her, but I did eventually discover her name.'

The two women shook hands, and Daisy smiled with her usual friendliness, trying to disregard the strange tension in the air. 'Excuse me while I fetch Uncle Will,' she suggested, 'he hates to miss a visitor.' Without waiting for an answer, she walked back towards the house, hoping that the awkwardness of bridging a long gap of years might be managed more easily when she wasn't there.

Jeanne's quick glance skimmed over the quiet man, now seated again, opposite her. Aware of the changes in herself, she almost resented that *he* seemed to have changed not at all, except for the scattering of silver in his fair hair. The sort of male beauty that he'd possessed was unfairly resistant to age. But at least she'd taken him unawares deliberately, wanting the advantage of surprise.

'Daisy resembles her mother, I take it – she doesn't look much like you,' she said quite calmly.

Robert pulled himself together sufficiently to smile. 'She'd be the first to tell you that she isn't nearly as beautiful as her mother, but it's true that she's inherited Christine's colouring.'

'I hope your wife is happy here,' Jeanne said politely.

'She wouldn't be happy *here* at all,' he pointed out. 'She's a rather well-known actress who lives in New York with her second husband. Rural France would have no appeal, I'm afraid.'

This time it was Jeanne who fell silent and Robert who suddenly knew what he wanted to say. 'Even after all these years I don't know how to talk about what happened to your parents. I saw their window in Auch Cathedral when I came back after the war, looking for you. I managed to find the farm and Pierre told me you'd married, had a son. He decided it would be pointless to tell me where you were, and by then I knew better than he did that he was perfectly right. I went back to England and married William's niece.'

'He didn't tell me about your visit,' Jeanne answered after a small pause. 'Perhaps he was right about that too.'

She was looking back into the past, but her thin face was more schooled than it had been thirty years ago. He couldn't even make a guess at what she was feeling. But maturity suited her, he thought; she'd acquired, no doubt under the pressure of experience, an attractive air of serenity that the young Jeanne hadn't had.

'My daughter and her great-uncle found this house while I was still in England,' Robert suddenly found himself explaining. 'It was too late when I arrived to say that this wasn't where I'd have chosen to live.'

Her dark eyes suddenly held his. 'Too many unpleasant memories, perhaps?'

'No,' he contradicted her gently. 'But I thought Pierre had been right – the past *was* better left undisturbed. I rather gather that *he* still thinks so.'

She suddenly rapped the table with her brown hands. 'Don't you see it's not just *you*? It's more complicated than that. He's angry, true, but not with you. There are people here who pretend the war is over and forgotten, but they *still* nurse old wounds and pay off old scores.'

It confirmed a view of his own that William refused to share: more time was needed yet for France to come to terms with what had happened in 1940 and afterwards. There were harrowing truths still to be admitted, and painful adjustments to be made to the official version of wartime events. The notaire who'd been so helpful to *them* was obviously one of the people ranged against Pierre Darroze. He was about to say so when Jeanne asked a question of her own that took him by surprise.

'What made you choose the name of Daisy for your daughter?'

'It's our English word for Marguerite,' he answered after a small pause.

'That's what I thought,' she agreed quietly.

That, it seemed, completed everything they had to say to each other. The rest wouldn't go into any words he could think of, and he was thankful to see William coming towards them, followed by Daisy carrying a tray of wine and fresh glasses. With them at the table, he could smile and instruct William to make his bow to their neighbour's niece, who had been a Resistance heroine.

For such a one William was prepared to do more than bow. He advanced on Jeanne to kiss the hand she held out with a grace to match any Frenchman's. All went smoothly after that until he suggested that she should bring her husband to dine with them one day.

There was a little pause before she answered. 'You don't know, Monsieur, but my dear Jacques died six months ago after a long illness. Our son still shares the house with me, though not for much longer because he's planning to marry Pierre's step-daughter.' A glimmer of amusement suddenly changed her sad face, making it look young again. 'It's a good French habit – keeping things in the family!' Then she turned to Daisy. 'You're only here to escape the English summer, I suppose. It must seem very quiet and dull after life in London.'

'Blessedly quiet,' Daisy amended, 'but far from being dull. To someone like me who aims to write for a living there's plenty of material here.' She smiled, wondering what had caused the woman watching her to pull dark brows together in a frown of disapproval.

'I hope you haven't got some highly coloured, touched-up wartime adventure in mind,' Jeanne Lescaut said bluntly. 'You're too young to know what really happened.'

Feeling rebuked, Daisy gave a little shrug borrowed from

the people she was living among. 'I don't have to "know", she pointed out. 'Fiction writers are allowed to invent!'

Jeanne's glance met hers across the table, acknowledging the small clash of personalities, and it was obvious to her now why Daniel hadn't liked Robert Ashton's daughter.

She got up, not pointedly ignoring the Ashtons, but explaining to William that it was time she left. All three of them walked with her to her car, parked at the front of the house, and waited while she drove away. Then Robert turned to his daughter.

'Tell me why you seemed to be crossing swords with Jeanne Lescaut just now. You aren't usually so belligerent. We're here to learn to live with these people, *not* to shove our own point of view down their throats.'

'She's like her son,' said Daisy, leaving her meaning obscure. 'I feel rather sorry for *him* as a matter of fact – being pushed into marrying for the convenience of the family. What do you bet that his bride-to-be is on the wrong side of thirty, has bad teeth and no dress-sense at all?'

'You'd lose your money,' her father said firmly. 'If she's the girl I saw him with the other day, she's years younger than he is and extremely seductive. Furthermore the Frenchwoman hasn't yet been born who has no dress-sense, as you well know.'

'I'm squashed – deservedly!' Daisy admitted with a disarming grin. Then her face grew serious again. 'I don't know why I got so prickly. Perhaps it's because I expect all these people to be *more* friendly towards us because of the past, not less; but that isn't how it seems to be working out. Even *you* weren't yourself when Madame Lescaut walked in.'

It was true enough to silence Robert for a moment or two. Then he tucked her arm in his. 'I know, love. We're still a bit hung up on the people we were thirty years ago. No doubt we'll sort ourselves out eventually and settle into some sedate and neighbourly relationship.'

Her great-uncle smilingly agreed that this was so, and

they walked back together to the house. But when lunch was over and Robert went outside again on the pretext of examining the flower border he'd laid out that morning, it was because he didn't want even Daisy's company. He had to confront by himself the sort of fool he'd been in imagining how his reunion with Jeanne Mayer would go. That was how he still thought of her, and it was his first mistake. He'd expected, God help him, some sign of warmth, or at least some friendly recognition of a relationship that hadn't been merely 'neighbourly'. Instead, her face had expressed nothing except impersonal curiosity about the man he now was, leaving him with the knowledge that his own memories of the past had become simply an embarrassment.

It left him with an overwhelming sense of sadness. He would have liked to tell her that he remembered, even now, every moment of his stay at the Ferme Darroze. He would have wanted to say that, whatever grief the years had brought, they'd left her serenely mistress of herself, an elegant and distinctive woman. But the moment for saying these things had come and gone, and now there wouldn't, he felt sure, be another opportunity. All he could look forward to was a reunion with Pierre Darroze – from whom at least he need expect nothing in the way of exuberant friendship.

Twelve

The garden was not so much taking shape as being rediscovered. Hidden among the accumulated jungle of creeper and bramble Robert was finding more desirable things, such as mimosas, tamarisks and oleanders; there was even a delicate lemon-tree that had somehow survived the winters under its blanket of greenery. He didn't intend to lose sight of the fact that their new home, an ancient Gascon farmhouse, almost grew out of the soil of southern France; but he'd explained to William and Daisy that its proper setting nevertheless must be not the raggedly mown field at present in front of it but a simple sweep of English lawn that would become the house and establish their credentials at the same time.

He was marking out its shape one morning when a Land Rover ambled along the drive, as if its occupant was taking stock of everything he saw. Robert waited for it to stop and watched the driver climb out – a youngish middle-aged man wearing the usual working uniform of shirt and jeans, but with an air about him of the city rather than the countryside.

Robert offered him a friendly 'bonjour', then waited for the stranger to introduce himself and say why he was there.

'Good morning, Mr Ashton – Lambert gave me your name. I'm Michel Bonnard; I farm the land from your boundary as far as Foutances.'

'So it was you who bought the rest of Gaston's property to add to your own. It's a big holding you have,' Robert commented.

'My syndicate's holding, in fact,' Bonnard corrected him. 'It's the only way to manage farms nowadays – in large plots, *arpentages* we call them, that allow machines to be used efficiently.'

'I can remember being told differently by an old patron from these parts,' Robert in turn suggested pleasantly. 'He used to say the land was too heavy for tractors, whereas oxen not only pulled the ploughs but manured the soil at the same time!'

Michel Bonnard smiled briefly. 'A patron from the Dark Ages, I should think. He's either dead or long since bankrupt.' Another measuring glance round brought the visitor's eyes back to Robert's face. 'You're making some much-needed improvements to Gaston's old house, I see. Are you going to be summer visitors, may I ask?'

'Ask by all means, but we intend to live here. My daughter had the idea that the Petit Manoir would respond to affection.'

The visitor smiled again, pityingly this time, as Robert had suspected he would. The Anglais were living up to their usual reputation – mad but harmless.

'It was the *house* you wanted, of course; you're not interested in the few miserable hectares of neglected land that went with it.' Bonnard paused a moment. 'My partners and I would consider taking them off your hands, Monsieur. When we bought the rest of Gaston's land he was still living here, and clinging to the pathetic idea of being a vigneron!'

Robert appeared to consider the matter, not pointing out that the Petit Manoir's remaining boundary across the river effectively cut off Bonnard's access to it. Old Gaston hadn't been entirely stupid when it came to selling things. At last he shook his head. 'It's too soon to make hasty decisions,' he said almost reluctantly. 'We shall play with our few hectares for a while – who knows, they might be made to yield some grapes again!'

'Not by an amateur, believe me,' said Bonnard, with the

reluctant air of a man who disliked sounding brutal. 'All you'll do is waste your time and money.'

'Then in that case we'll consider your kind offer again – if it still stands.'

Bonnard nodded, and fished a card out of his pocket. 'First refusal ours, I hope, Monsieur Ashton, when you decide to sell?'

'By all means,' Robert agreed affably. 'We'll shake hands on it, shall we?'

The visitor accepted the gesture, pleasantly sure of having spiked the guns of Pierre Darroze. He hadn't got what he wanted immediately, but it would fall into his lap when the Englishman got tired of wasting his money. The visit had been perfectly timed.

'You're hoping to make a lawn here, I see,' was Bonnard's parting shot as he opened the door of the Land Rover. 'I shouldn't bother if I were you – you're not in England's everlasting rainclouds now. The grass will die in no time at all.'

'I expect you're right,' Robert agreed cheerfully, 'but the trouble with us is that we never know when we're beaten! Au revoir, Monsieur.'

His neighbour roared off showily along the drive, and Daisy came out a moment later to find Robert still standing there, smiling to himself.

'I hope you're going to share the joke, whatever it is,' she told him. 'And if your visitor was so entertaining you might have brought him indoors.'

'He was informative rather than entertaining,' her father replied, 'and I repaid him rather unkindly by behaving like an amiable fool and leading him up the garden path a little. Now *there's* an English idiom to break a translator's heart – I must ask William what *he*'d make of it.'

'You're prevaricating,' Daisy said accusingly. 'Who *was* the poor misled visitor?'

'A neighbour of ours, except that from his card I see he lives in Foutances, instead of on his farm. That's probably why I didn't like him. Daisy, love, do something for me, please: ring Daniel to enquire about your bicycle, and say that I've also got a business matter to discuss. It might even be enough to get Pierre Darroze over the hurdle of coming to see me himself.'

'You're getting very Machiavellian,' she pointed out severely.

'I know – it's my new career. You said I ought to have one!' He smiled at her lovingly. 'I promise I'll share the joke with you as soon as William gets back!' Then he returned to measuring out his lawn.

He was cutting down some overgrown bamboos the following morning, carefully setting aside the long, straight stems for future use, when another visitor arrived. This one, more unusually, rode Daisy's bicycle but led a horse at the same time. Even from some distance away he was instantly recognisable. The Cheval *had* decided to come instead of Daniel.

Man and horse disappeared round the side of the house, but Robert didn't stop what he was doing, knowing that Daisy was there, planting up pots of herbs on the terrace. The stack of bamboo canes was neatly lashed together when a gruff voice spoke beside him. He should have remembered Pierre's trick of moving without making any sound.

'Your daughter told me where to find you. She's ruining my mare's teeth by feeding her sugar; apart from that she seems all right.'

'She *is* all right,' Robert agreed. 'It was good of you and Daniel to see to her bicycle.'

'She thanked me by planting a kiss on my cheek. Is that how you've brought her up to greet strange men?'

'At the age of twenty-four she decides for herself who to kiss. But I dare say she was also thanking you for looking after me a long time ago. Daisy's a firm believer in gratitude.'

There was something wrong with this conversation, Pierre decided. The faintly smiling, self-possessed man in front of him was altogether too much in charge of it, for one thing. He'd been successful, obviously; that was nothing to hold against him, but he shouldn't be so damned pleasant and sure of himself.

Robert's smile deepened as the inspection went on. '*You've* worn very well if I may say so! I know you don't want us in this house, but I'd offer you a cold beer if you'd agree to sit down and drink it.'

Pierre hesitated, then gave a little nod. 'Daniel said something about a business matter. I'll hear what it is, but I haven't got time to waste in pointless chat about events best forgotten.'

'We'll pretend if you like that we're meeting for the first time, though it seems rather silly to me!' Then, not waiting for the answer Pierre seemed unable to give, he led the way back to the terrace. Daisy, still there but now talking to the mare tied up to a post, smiled on both of them.

'I expect you'd like some nice chilled beer,' she said obligingly.

'Yes please, sweetheart,' her father agreed, 'and William is needed too if you can find him.'

She went indoors and tracked down her great-uncle from the tortured strains of 'I Pagliacci' coming from his bedroom. 'Uncle Will, you're wanted outside – the great Pierre Darroze has come to call.'

When he'd followed her down to the kitchen she glowered at him. 'I'm not invited to join in the conversation. How am I to write a story if I don't know what's going on?'

'You make it up, my love; as you suggested you would to Madame Lescaut.'

Setting out glasses on a tray, she now grinned at him instead. 'Quite right, of course. I think, don't you, that "le grand Pierre" is rather sweet?'

William blinked at her in astonishment. 'Well, yes, if you think a hungry, *grand* brown bear is also "rather sweet"!'

She shook her head, handing him the tray. 'It takes a

student of human nature like me to see beneath the surface.'

He was kind enough to agree that she might be right, and then walked outside into the sunlit morning to form his own opinion about their taciturn neighbour.

It was Robert who opened the conversation. 'What do you know of a man called Michel Bonnard who turned up here yesterday?'

'Nothing good,' Pierre growled. 'He pretends he's a farmer; he isn't – he's a businessman, screwing the last franc he can get out of the land and out of his crooked dealings in Brussels. I think he lent Gaston money and then called in the loan; that's how he got his hands on most of the farm. But the wily old devil clung to the house and what had been the original demesne – said it belonged to his heirs! That's what you now own.'

Robert's nod agreed, then he spoke again himself. 'Bonnard offered to buy us out yesterday, although I don't think he wants the house.'

'Of course not – the fool would rather live in town. What he wants is the river frontage so that he can draw out all the water he needs.' Pierre shot a glance at his host. 'Are you thinking of making a quick profit by selling and going somewhere else?'

'We happen to like it here,' Robert said calmly. 'But I promised him first refusal if we should ever decide to sell. The poor fellow went away more optimistic than he should have been, I'm afraid.'

A slow grin worked its way across Pierre's face. 'Perfidious Albion – you English never change. Still, it serves the sod right.'

'It also brings us back to the question of the river. William and I aren't farmers; we only want a garden, and in time a little vineyard. We'll replant the orchard, and grow our own fruit and vegetables as well. That's the limit of our ambition, and for that we have all the water we need; there seem to be half a dozen wells scattered about. So what William and I would like to suggest is that *you* make use of the water. We don't know how it can be done – that's for you and Daniel to work out – but you are welcome to run a pipe across our land.'

There was so long a silence that William supposed the grizzled, weatherbeaten man opposite him was framing a sentence that would demolish the idea. Robert, knowing him better, remembered that, unlike Daisy, Pierre Darroze wasn't good at handling gratitude.

But at last he cleared his throat and found something to say. 'I'll talk to Daniel – he's clever at mechanical things, much better than me. We're short of water every summer; it's spoiled crops more times than I can remember. We shall . . . well, we shall be much obliged to you both.' He swallowed the remainder of his beer, and then stood up. 'Best be getting back before that girl of yours lays claim to my mare!' Then he did what so far he'd refused to do – swallowed up William's small paw in his own huge one, and shook Robert's hand as well.

They walked with him to where a grateful horse was now being fed handfuls of clover. He swung himself on to the mare's back, lifted his whip in a little salute and trotted away down the drive. Daisy inspected the pair of them.

'You're looking very pleased with yourselves. Are you going to tell me why?'

William offered her his guileless smile. 'I think you were right about the bear after all.'

Pierre Darroze wasn't a man to be seen to give up fixed habits of thought overnight, but even he had to admit to his family that they could do worse than have the English as their neighbours. Daniel interpreted this correctly as a significant change of heart, but he was still surprised to be invited to accompany his great-uncle on a visit to the Petit Manoir. On the way there he was told about Robert's offer, and asked to think how it could be used to provide a source of good water for their own land.

'My first thought is that we must do it without Bonnard getting wind of it,' Daniel pointed out. 'I don't know that it's illegal, but he'd get some expensive lawyer to try to prove that it was.' Then he smiled at Pierre. 'It's a problem, but a nicer one than most!'

They found Robert outside, and the three of them walked as far as the river together. It was clear from then on that Daniel would be in charge; he had the sort of brain that revelled in finding ways round obstacles, and only Daisy's assertion one morning later that even he couldn't make water run uphill seemed likely to hold him up for long.

In the following days he became a frequent visitor, doing most of the building himself of the small reservoir that was eventually agreed upon. From there, the water could be pumped and piped where needed on their own adjacent land. More often than not it seemed silly not to accept Robert's invitation to share their lunch on the terrace – an al fresco, happy meal so different from what he was accustomed to at the farm that to begin with he seemed ill at ease. Unable to share the fun and cross-talk and discussion about anything under the sun, he said nothing at all. Feeling sorry for him, Daisy kindly explained one afternoon that the three of them had lived together a long time, and knew each other very well.

'I expect it's the same with you and your family,' she suggested, '. . . conversation's hardly necessary; though that doesn't stop *us* talking, I'm bound to say!'

She smiled as she admitted it, and he thought how strange it was that he'd begun by deciding not to like her. It seemed, now, to be the most futile decision of his life, because a man would have to be blind and daft not to like Daisy Ashton. He tried hard not to compare her with Jacqueline; it was far too unfair when this girl had had advantages, travelled, lived a cosmopolitan and sophisticated life. But the confusing truth was that despite it all she was *more* straightforward than Annette's daughter, not less; Daisy was as clear and refreshing as running water, and more inclined to make him laugh than imply that what they ought to do was make for the nearest bed. The effect of *that*, of course, was that he perversely found himself wanting to look at her far too much.

Aware of the muddle he was getting into, he sounded sharp one day when she asked to go with him to inspect the reservoir.

'You don't have to ask permission – it's your father's land.'

'So it is,' she agreed, disconcerted by his reaction. 'But I won't come if you don't want me to. I'll go to my room instead and toss off a best-seller or two.'

He answered her by holding out his hand and, after a moment's hesitation, she put her own into it.

It was a mistake, he realised; her hand felt so right in his that he wanted to go on holding it, but that wouldn't do. He released her and spoke in a level, indifferent-sounding voice.

'I suppose you'll be going back to London soon. You must be getting very bored here.'

'Your mother suggested that too, which is odd when you both clearly love the place to death. I'm *not* bored, but it's true that I haven't come to live here for ever. For one thing I always visit my own mother once a year in New York.'

'Of course, the globe-trotting Miss Ashton! We must be grateful to have detained you so long.'

The jibe brought a flush of colour to her skin, but she stopped in her tracks and stared at him. 'Go to the reservoir by yourself; I've lost interest in it. Are all French people the same, or is it just *you* with a monumental chip on your shoulder? We like to think we're making a little headway in the business of understanding one another, but it isn't so; all the old prejudice and distrust are still simmering away underneath. Thank God for the *English* Channel say I, that keeps us separate from France.'

Robert could have warned her to expect a change of mood that would topple her off her high horse, but she wasn't prepared for Jeanne's son to suddenly smile so irresistibly that anger was impossible. He caught hold of her hand again and carried it to his lips.

'*Mes compliments, Mademoiselle*; I deserved that ticking off! Now will you forgive me and walk to the reservoir after all?' His eyes, so brilliantly blue in the brownness of his face, held warmth as well as humour, and she told herself that he'd apologised so nicely that it would be unkind to reject an offer to make amends. But when it became clear that they were to walk hand in hand, she freed herself very firmly. There was the girl who *wasn't* middle-aged and dowdy to be thought of, and if Daniel wasn't disposed to remember her, *she* must.

But as if her own discomfort had communicated itself to him, he suddenly launched into a technical explanation of how water *could* be made to flow uphill. Jacqueline herself listening to the rest of the conversation wouldn't have felt the smallest twinge of anxiety about them.

That night as usual he described to his mother the progress they were making and it was she who enquired casually whether he lunched every day at the Petit Manoir.

'Not every day, of course not,' he answered, 'only when I happen to be there around midday.' He glanced at her across the supper-table, aware that her expression of polite interest concealed something else. 'They're nice people,' he felt obliged to explain. 'I can't describe how they're different from us, except that they like to be solemn about silly things and treat serious things lightly. It was confusing to begin with, but I'm getting the hang of them now; in a funny sort of way I even feel at home with them.' His mother's face expressed nothing at all as far as he could see, and he suddenly wanted *her* to give something away. 'I don't need to explain Robert Ashton to you –

you and Uncle Pierre must have got to know him well enough.'

Jeanne gave her usual little shrug. 'We were living through strange times, and we probably all behaved strangely. But my poor frail grandmother fell in love with a young man who treated her like Dresden china, and my mother was determined that he wasn't going to be allowed to die on our hands.' She hesitated a moment and then went on. 'His daughter's name is the English version of hers – Marguerite.'

'Robert Ashton's way of saying thank-you?' Daniel suggested gently.

Jeanne nodded, and then wondered whether she would regret that confession. Her strong impression was that her son found the people at the Petit Manoir all too appealing as it was.

Thirteen

It had been a strict rule made long ago that Robert wouldn't allow himself to interfere in his daughter's life. She was enjoying this summer in France, and a friendship with Daniel Lescaut that had seemed unlikely to begin with was merely adding to her pleasure in the long, sunlit days spent mostly out of doors. He was content if she was happy, and reluctant to remind her of Jeanne's warning that her son's marriage was all but arranged. They were adults, not adolescents, and didn't need an interfering parent to point out that in a triangular relationship someone usually ended up getting hurt.

He had, in any case, a sadness of his own to contend with, that gave the summer a peculiarly bittersweet flavour. They were now on terms of friendship with Daniel, and on something that occasionally felt like that with Pierre Darroze, although there'd been no invitation to the farm so far. Robert regretted that because he was curious to meet the woman Pierre had selected rather late in life as a wife. His private unhappiness concerned Jeanne Lescaut. She'd refused both of William's attempts to invite her to repeat her visit to the house and Robert had told him, too sharply, not to try again. Aware of Daisy's interest, he'd made an unconvincing joke of it. '*You* may reckon we're irresistible, but it's obvious that we're not Madame Lescaut's cup of tea. You'll have to be content with your undoubted success in charming Giselle Lambert instead!'

The subject wasn't discussed again and, knowing how much he would dislike it, Daisy had resisted the temptation to tackle Daniel about his mother's refusal to bury whatever hatchet she imagined existed. Then, one morning in Foutances, Robert found himself outside her front door. He wasn't there by any conscious intention; it had simply happened because it was time that it did.

The house was pleasantly set back from the wide pavement that ran round each side of the square, arcaded in the way of old bastide towns. But it offered little to see from the outside except a handsome front door. He heard footsteps on the tiled floor inside, and a moment later Jeanne looked at him while he was still trying to decide what to say. She was a small woman and had to tilt her chin to look up at him.

'Have I forgotten inviting you?'

He wanted to smile for the typical lack of welcome, and for the pleasure of seeing her nevertheless, but thought better of it. 'You didn't invite me at all, I'm afraid; I'm what's known as presuming to call! Daniel tells me you're an inspired gardener – I wanted to pinch some of your ideas.'

He didn't see how so tempting an offer could be refused, and after a moment's thought Jeanne reluctantly allowed him inside. Without speaking, she led him to a door at the far end of the passage, and then into the garden beyond. It lay below a short flight of wrought-iron steps, and his first sight of it made him exclaim with pleasure.

'It's a small, hidden paradise – I wonder you don't live out here all the time.'

'I almost do,' she admitted, suddenly ceasing to frown. 'Jacques hated it if the weather drove him indoors. Even when he was dying he was happy out here.' She glanced at Robert's entranced face and smiled in spite of herself. 'You can wander about by yourself while I make some coffee.'

He was content to do that, and had to be called away from inspecting the rich variety of plants along the river bank when she came back.

'It's a lovely place; I congratulate you,' he said quietly.

She made him a little bow, accepting a true compliment.

'Life was very difficult here even after the war ended. You can't imagine the bitterness. *Epuration*, it was called – the punishment of criminals and collaborators. But dreadful things were done in the name of justice. Jacques and I kept ourselves sane by making this garden.'

Now that she had begun to talk Robert was afraid of checking her by saying the wrong thing. 'You had Daniel as well,' he ventured.

'Yes,' she agreed, 'we had our dear Daniel.' She paused, also seeing a need to choose words carefully. 'He seems to spend quite a lot of time with you at the moment.'

'We don't see much of him – he's too busy laying pipes and building a reservoir. You have a very nice son, not to mention an extremely competent one. I can see why Pierre depends on him.'

Jeanne nodded, hesitated, then decided to go on. 'I think I mentioned that he's going to marry Annette's daughter. He's enjoying the . . . the English company at the Petit Manoir, but it's not where he belongs. Could you and your daughter remember that, please?'

Robert's glance met hers across the table. 'Are you asking me to warn Daisy off a friendship they both seem to enjoy?'

Jeanne gave a little shrug. 'What do I know about her? She may have a lover waiting for her in England; she may just see Daniel as a pleasant summer companion. But *his* life is here with Jacqueline. Daisy mustn't spoil it for them.'

'She's not in the habit of hurting people,' he said stiffly.

'If not, then she might find that she gets hurt herself. Daniel's too attractive not to make an impression.' Jeanne offered the man watching her a wry smile. 'Be honest – can you see your daughter as a farmer's wife deep in rural France?'

'Perhaps not,' he admitted. 'On the other hand love changes people – as if they weren't unpredictable enough in the first place.'

She pushed the subject aside with a gesture he remembered, then glanced at her watch. 'I can't talk plants with you now; I have to leave for work in ten minutes' time.'

'What sort of work?' he asked, obeying the hint by standing up to go.

'I'll show you on your way out!'

He was led back to the front door and out to where her car was parked under the arcade. On the back seat was a battered violin-case, so poignant a reminder of the past that his heart seemed to turn over.

'I can't part with it, even if it falls to pieces,' she said quietly. 'I teach at a school for disturbed children. In some strange way music helps them to become tractable, and even capable of learning other things. It's the most satisfying thing I've ever done.' She suddenly smiled at him, a smile wholehearted and sweet. 'You never did get your recital!'

He wanted to touch her, kiss her, promise to protect her with his life; he'd never ceased wanting those things, he realised. But he had no hope at all that she might want them too. 'Pierre says we should forget the past,' he said unevenly. 'I can't do that however hard I try, but I promise not to remind you of it. All I ask is that we recognise each other as friends. Could you manage that, do you think?'

She only nodded by way of an answer but it was enough. His hand touched her cheek in a fleeting gesture, and then he turned away, suddenly aware that he had no recollection at all of where he'd left his car. He got home at last to find William alone; Daisy, it seemed, had offered to keep Daniel company on a trip he had to make to Auch.

'Why can't Jacqueline keep him company?' Robert wanted to know, reminded uncomfortably of what Jeanne had said about his daughter.

'Because she works during the day. Don't you remember what Daniel said? She's a guide of some sort at the Armagnac Museum at Cassaigne. Which reminds me, I must include a mention of it – it's an interesting place.'

William paused to make a mental note for the memoir he was happily engaged in compiling, an anecdotal tour of all his favourite vineyards; it distracted him now from asking why Daisy shouldn't have driven off with Daniel for the day. Robert was glad to let the subject rest but he could see that something might have to be said, even though his forthright Daisy would probably point out that the role of heavy-handed father didn't suit him.

She returned in time for supper with them, and he couldn't for the life of him decide whether the day had been a tedious bore, time enjoyably spent, or an interlude in her life that she might always remember. Daisy could have told him, but she intended to keep the knowledge to herself.

They'd set off with little said, having reached that stage in their friendship where conversation wasn't always necessary. Daniel had attended to the business he had to do, and then turned to smile at her.

'The rest of the day's a holiday! What shall we do?'

She'd answered gravely that she wanted first of all to see the window in the cathedral that her father had described. They'd stood in front of it in silence, and she'd been very glad when Daniel took hold of her hand. Afterwards they'd bought bread and cheese and fruit and wine, and driven out into the beautiful green countryside again for what Daisy said would be a proper picnic, not the sort of nonsensically elaborate meal in the open air that the French preferred to settle down to.

'What's wrong with doing it in comfort?' Daniel had asked, happy to tease her, happy just to be with her. 'The trouble with the English is that they *will* always think their ways of doing things are better than anyone else's.'

'The trouble with the English from everyone else's point of view is that their ways usually *are* . . .' It was as far as she was allowed to get before Daniel made a grab at her and rolled her back on to the grass. She didn't protest, but lay smiling up at him.

'You talk too much, and there's only one way to stop you,' he murmured unsteadily. The kiss that followed was so long and sweet that when she was finally allowed to sit up it seemed clear to both of them that it had changed the world. They sat in silence for a moment, coming to terms with so strange an alteration, still holding hands but not looking at each other.

'I'm sorry,' Daniel said quietly after a while. 'No, I'm not sorry at all, but I shouldn't have done that yet. There are . . . things in the way; things that have to be sorted out first.'

She knew what he meant – Jacqueline, and the damnably convenient marriage arrangement that he'd had no reason not to accept until now. It was too late to remember that three into two was a sum no one could do. All she could manage, for him and for herself, was to leave him in peace to disentangle himself from the web of relationships that had been his entire life. She could see clearly enough that one of them, Jacqueline or herself, would have to go without him. It was a terrible truth, but it needn't be faced just yet.

'We've got the rest of the day still,' she suggested. 'Let's enjoy it, Daniel; every single minute of it if we can.'

From then on the day was dusted with the special magic of a happiness that might not last because it was so perfect. But on the drive back conversation deserted them; they were nearly home when Daniel suddenly asked a question.

'Tell me what you're thinking about.'

'It's *who*, not what,' Daisy replied. 'I was remembering my namesake, your grandmother – just in case I should think of feeling sorry for myself.' She turned and glanced at him very briefly. 'Hurry now, please. Our lovely day is over and I want to get home.'

A meeting with Jacqueline after that matchless day came as no surprise; in fact Daisy found herself half-expecting it, as part of the unpleasant game of tit-for-tat that Fate so often liked to play.

It was market-day in Foutances, and the square was crammed with stalls. She was turning away from a wonderful array of vegetables, having bought too much of everything as usual, when a dark-haired girl beside her suddenly spoke.

'I'm Pierre Darroze's step-daughter, and you're Daisy Ashton. I'd like to talk to you, please.'

'Over a cup of coffee?' Daisy suggested. 'We need to sit down, don't you think?' She began to walk to where the café had set out its pavement tables – her second meeting-place with Daniel, she remembered. 'We haven't met,' she said to the girl beside her. 'How did you know who I was?'

'I've heard a lot about you, and you don't exactly look like one of us.'

It was true, but Jacqueline's dark eyes flickered over her again, deciding why that was. The English girl had a slender, almost boyish body, pale skin, and fair to reddish hair tied back severely with a ribbon. No *femme fatale*, for sure, but she'd been intelligent enough to realise that. Her cream linen trousers and coral shirt were faultless, and she possessed something a Frenchwoman was obliged to recognise – a certain effortless style. Jacqueline was aware that Daniel would appreciate that.

'The coffee's on me,' Daisy said as they sat down; she spoke to the hovering waiter, and then turned to Jacqueline. 'I suppose it's Daniel you want to talk about.'

The calm statement should have made the conversation easier to start, but for Jacqueline it had the opposite effect. This enemy had the usual sang-froid of her maddening race; against another Latin she would have known better where she was. Still, the aces were in her own hand, not Daisy Ashton's; all she had to do was remember that.

'Daniel spends a lot of time at the Petit Manoir,' she pointed out as matter-of-factly as she could.

'He has a lot of work to do for your step-father,' Daisy countered.

'My mother expects him home for lunch – he stays with you instead.'

'If you're not there yourself perhaps he sees no reason to rush back to the farm and then have to return again.'

It was like a horrible fencing-match, Daisy reflected, thrust and parry to and fro. It was also dishonest, of course, and that knowledge troubled her.

'The work is taking too long, Pierre says – because you hold Daniel up.' It wasn't quite what her step-father had said, but never mind; it might still be the truth. 'You spent the whole day with him in Auch too. I asked him and he admitted it.'

Pale, now, beneath her freckles, Daisy admitted it too, waiting for what would obviously come next.

'Daniel and I are promised to each other. We could have been married by now, but he kept thinking I wasn't old enough. Even Frenchmen never really understand women, and I'm told your own men are much worse.' Confident of having scored a hit, Jacqueline's taut face relaxed into a slightly pitying smile. She felt in charge of the conversation now.

The waiter interrupted them by setting down their coffee, hoping to linger and enjoy a little chat, but he was dismissed with a pleasant word of thanks. Then Daisy looked instead at the girl watching her across the table. She *was* pretty – there was no question about that – and quite as seductive as a man could wish, with rounded breasts, neat waist, and small bottom encased in well-cut jeans. It was bitterly difficult to pretend that Daniel was being coerced by gratitude into partnership with an ageing slut. But did he know with Jacqueline the contentment and joy that had flowered so unexpectedly between him and herself?

'Do you love him?' Daisy asked abruptly. 'I know the other reasons why it seems right for you to marry him, but even with love it's hard enough to make marriage work.'

'Of course I love him; how could I not when I'm *his* already,' Jacqueline said dramatically. It *was* just true. Daniel had always refused to sleep with her at the farm – it wouldn't be *comme il faut*, he had said, when he was a guest in his great-uncle's house – but there'd been an evening when she'd provoked him enough to fall on top of her out in the barn and they'd made love there instead.

'I can see that temptation would have been hard to resist,' Daisy admitted, 'but have you "been his", as you so nicely put it, since I've been here?' She was most terribly tempted to claim that *she* had, but a congenital inability to lie held her back. The answer to her question was clear in Jacqueline's face in any case, and she suddenly found herself hating the conversation.

'I think this discussion isn't going to get us anywhere,' she said curtly. 'If we both love the same man, what can we do but let *him* choose? It's not what's supposed to happen nowadays in this brave new women's world, but I always reckoned feminists were leading us up the garden path!'

She prayed that on this lighter note they could agree to part company. But Jacqueline had heard only the beginning of the speech. Anger, now beginning to be laced with fear, drove her into playing the ace she had intended keeping in her hand.

'I doubt if Daniel could ever choose *you*, of all people!'

'Why not? Tell me *why* you feel so sure,' Daisy insisted. 'Because I'm English? Because I'm not a farmer's daughter?'

Jacqueline gave a shrill laugh. 'Because you're probably his half-sister, that's why!'

Suddenly white beneath her freckles, Daisy stared at the girl opposite her. 'I don't believe you,' she answered at last.

'Well, perhaps you should. Jeanne married Jacques Lescaut *very* suddenly, soon after your father left the farm during the war. He was years older than her, a friend of my step-father, and it came as a *great* surprise to everybody when he managed to give her a child. Of course no one knew about the English airman having been at the farm. Pierre always believed your father was responsible – he once told my mother so years ago.'

Jacqueline watched Daisy's stricken face, half-frightened and half-triumphant at what she'd done. 'Daniel doesn't know, of course; well, no one knows for certain, except Jeanne, and she'll *never* admit that Jacques Lescaut wasn't his father.'

Daisy lifted her hand stiffly, as an old woman might, and signalled to the waiter. 'My friend is just leaving, but I'd like some more coffee, please.' Then she spoke to Jacqueline. 'You've said all you had to say, I'm sure. Don't let me keep you any longer.' It seemed a pitifully small but necessary victory that it should be Annette's daughter who had to leave, but after a moment's uncertainty Jacqueline did get up and walk away.

The coffee came and Daisy sat holding the cup between her hands. She didn't believe it, she'd said, but that wasn't altogether true. Jacqueline's version of those long-ago events would explain so many things that had been puzzling – Pierre's determined hostility to her father, Jeanne Lescaut's refusal to have anything to do with them, Robert's obvious sadness about it, and Daniel's surprisingly blue eyes, so similar in colour to her own. But there was even something more – the feeling of recognition that had grown so beautifully out of their initial dislike of one another. She hadn't known it with any other man, but it was scarcely surprising to find it in her own father's son.

She got up at last, remembering to place some notes under the ashtray on the table. She forgot her basket, but a passer-by called out to her, and she thanked him and went back for it. She remembered to retrieve her bicycle and pedalled away from the small town, wondering whether she'd ever enter it again without feeling sick. Then, half-way home, she suddenly stopped, with relief flooding her in a blinding wave. Jacqueline was *wrong*, quite wrong; it wasn't Jeanne Lescaut her father had loved, but the woman called Marguerite, who hadn't been at the farm at all.

Fourteen

The spell of fine weather was suddenly broken that night by a tremendous thunderstorm and torrential rain. Each workman who'd come to the house had warned them that it happened every summer, but insisted that the sun always returned, and would stay probably until the end of October. They just had to remember that when it rained in Gascony, the good God knew it really rained!

Daisy was grateful for the storm; it conveniently explained the migraine that engulfed her in the early hours of the morning. After another bout of sickness she crawled downstairs to report that she could do nothing but return to bed. Only William was still at the breakfast-table, drinking coffee and reading a day-old copy of *Le Monde*.

'My poor girl – you look awful,' he said at once. 'Your father's out already, but what can I do for you?'

'Nothing, thanks, Uncle Will. I shall recover in an hour or two.'

But an air of desolation about her made him persist. 'You're sure it's nothing else – only the beastly migraine?'

'Quite sure. I'll see you later on.'

'No message for Daniel if he comes?'

She fought a wave of nausea and shook her head. 'No message at all.'

It wasn't until early evening that she came downstairs again to find the house empty. Her headache had gone, leaving behind the lassitude that followed a bout of pain; but inertia had to be fought because she must either do something herself to establish what was truth and what was lie, or have Daniel walk blindfold into a minefield he knew nothing about. At this hour of the evening William would be on the terrace, enjoying a pre-dinner glass of wine; if he was home now, her father would be there as well. She went outside to find William entertaining instead the last woman she felt ready to confront at the moment.

'Daisy, love, you're looking a little better,' William said happily. 'Here's Madame Lescaut come to talk gardens with your father, and he's not back from Toulouse.'

She shook hands with the visitor, chose mineral water instead of wine, and did her best to sound normal. 'Don't let me interrupt your conversation. I'm going to do what the Spaniards like to do – *tomar el fresco*. It smells lovely after last night's rain.'

'The famous reservoir must have some water in it already,' Jeanne remarked pleasantly. 'I hope you understand how grateful my uncle is – he's not a man who expresses thanks very easily!'

William began to insist that between friends thanks weren't necessary, but he was cut off by the ringing of the telephone inside the house. He went to answer it, leaving a silence behind that Jeanne was the first to break.

'You've been unwell – I'm sorry.'

Daisy managed a smile. 'Too much sun yesterday, too much thunder last night. I'm recovered now.'

'You've been to Auch, I believe.'

Did the whole damn world know she'd been there with Daniel? Roused by a jab of anger, she agreed that she had.

'My son mentioned your visit to the cathedral, that's how I know,' Jeanne explained quietly.

Anger stood no chance against that, and Daisy felt ashamed of it anyway. 'We went to see the window my father told me about a long time ago. It's too beautiful for what it commemorates, but perhaps that's the only salvation we have – to somehow transmute evil into beauty.'

Jeanne was silent for a moment, reminding herself that this girl was Robert's daughter and therefore easily capable of a remark like that. It was cruel that she could have made so perfect a companion for Daniel; but it was absolutely necessary that she should be driven away. Fate had played one of its merciless tricks on them by letting the Ashtons come back at all.

Daisy glanced at the visitor's withdrawn face, wondering for a moment why it looked so painfully sad. But a moment was all she could spare from the realisation of something else: the opportunity she needed was here, *now*; somehow she must force her tired mind to produce the opening that Daniel's mother must respond to.

'I expect you understand why I was given my name,' she began hesitantly. 'I feel very privileged, but my own mother saw it differently, of course. She was always aware that Marguerite had never been forgotten.'

Jeanne's faint smile shone for a moment. 'My mother *was* beautiful as well as brave and kind. I *wasn't* kind – I chose to laugh at a young man who . . . who fell a little in love with her, I think!'

'He said *you* didn't like him – for being a nuisance, and for being English into the bargain.' Daisy did her best to sound amused, unaware of the desperate pleading in her eyes. 'I bumped into Jacqueline the other day. We talked about the war and *she* had a much more romantic idea. She reckoned that my handsome father and a heroine like you, thrown together, were certain to have fallen for each other!'

Jeanne stared at the pale-faced girl opposite her, feeling slightly sick herself. It wasn't difficult to guess what else Jacqueline had said, but who could blame her when she was fighting an opponent who had advantages she didn't have? She hadn't even invented the idea she'd passed on – Annette had hinted at it long ago in the course of some now-forgotten row.

Jeanne examined the choices in front of her: she could tell

Robert Ashton's daughter the truth, she could lie, or she could tread a perilous path between the two. With her mind finally made up, and in a voice made hoarse with the stress of the moment, she began to explain.

'I doubt if I can make you understand what our life was like in those dreadful years. We were even unsure of staying alive from day to day; enemies suddenly became lovers, and so-called friends became traitors overnight. There was only the excitement, the grief, the happiness of the moment; the future didn't exist. But that was our mistake, of course. What we did then affected everything that happened afterwards. It still affects all our lives now, however much we wish it didn't.'

Daisy listened quietly, remembering what Jacqueline had said. Jeanne Lescaut would never admit in words that Jacques hadn't been the father of her son; but she didn't need to. What she *had* forced herself to say, and the aching regret in her face, made the truth clear enough. Daisy examined her own hands, pleased to find them not trembling. With a little more effort she could survive the rest of this conversation that had just destroyed her hope of happiness. But Jeanne was speaking again, and it was necessary to try to listen.

'When I came here once before I mentioned that Daniel and Jacqueline were going to marry. I'm afraid I made it sound a rather "French" arrangement based on common sense. The truth is that their relationship is based on affection, trust, and a life of shared interests. Does that sound too little to marry on for an Anglo-Saxon like you?'

White-lipped, Daisy merely shook her head, aware that there was still a little more to come.

'Annette's husband was a youth at the beginning of the war,' Jeanne went on. 'He saved my uncle's life but got seriously injured himself. He died afterwards still quite young, leaving her with two small children. Pierre eventually married her, and the farm became the only home Jacqueline can remember. Daniel would never forgive himself if . . . if she were made to leave it.'

Daisy looked up at the woman watching her, and forced her lips to smile. 'Of course he wouldn't, and no doubt every other marriageable female for miles around, understanding that, knows better than to waste a smile on him!'

Jeanne waited a moment before asking briefly, 'What will you do?'

'Go back to London soon. It's time I got back to work and I can't pretend that I'm still needed here.'

Jeanne nodded, but found that she couldn't bear to sit there any longer. 'I must go home. It would have been more sensible to make sure your father was here before I came.' She hesitated over holding out her hand; there was a good chance that it would be ignored. 'I'd like to say that I hope you find happiness, but perhaps you won't believe me.'

Daisy managed another smile. 'Oh, I usually do believe what people say. I'll tell my father you tried to see him.'

Feeling in some way that she deserved to be dismissed, Jeanne walked away. She told herself on the way home that her real object in going to the Petit Manoir had been achieved. *That* was what mattered; the grief she'd caused could be survived. It always was – the war had taught her that.

An unexpected telephone call from London provided Daisy with the excuse to leave that she needed so badly. Better still, Daniel had just arrived when she walked outside to tell her father the news. She pinned a bright smile to her mouth and sounded cheerful.

'An SOS from Nicola in London. She wants to marry before she changes her mind, and I'm needed to support her up the aisle, or whatever's the Registry Office equivalent!'

'But you'll come back afterwards.' It wasn't really a question; Daniel thought he knew the answer.

Daisy shook her head. 'I'm afraid not. My friend wants a tenant for her very nice flat. I must grab it before someone else does – we're desperate for living space in London.' She smiled carelessly at him. 'In any case it's time I got back to work. I've idled away almost the whole summer.'

Her glance moved hurriedly on from his stunned face and rested on her father. It begged him, he realised, not to leave, even if he took no part in the conversation. He realised something else as well. For a reason unknown to him she'd decided not to fight for Jeanne's son. Perhaps she didn't love him after all, but there'd been times in the past when she'd detached herself easily enough from admirers who didn't make the grade; she didn't need his help for that. This was different – a fight she reckoned she couldn't win. This time *she* was the one who was getting hurt.

'When *will* you come back?' Daniel's hoarse voice asked the question.

Daisy gave a little shrug. 'I'm not sure – probably not before the spring. I'm expected in New York for Christmas, and that's always rather fun.'

It sounded so unpleasantly bright and brittle that her glance at Robert asked him to forgive her for it. He still said nothing, and Daniel's voice again broke the silence.

'Of course, I was forgetting: the sophisticated Miss Ashton will have had enough of Gascony's simple pleasures by now.'

Then, as if she'd already disappeared from their lives, he spoke only to her father about some farm matter. Daisy watched them for a moment and then walked away. She'd just demolished Daniel's brief attachment to her with a single, brilliant stroke; there wasn't anything more to stay for now.

She didn't see him again before she left, and knew that he was avoiding the Petit Manoir deliberately. It was Pierre who took home the news that William Harcourt gave him in Foutances one morning.

'Robert Ashton and his daughter are on the way to Toulouse – she has a plane to catch for London.'

'Well, she couldn't stay for ever,' Annette Darroze pointed

out. 'There's nothing here for a girl who's used to a different kind of life.' No one argued with her and she went cheerfully on. 'I'm told Michel Bonnard's in the market for a wife again, but I can't see even Daisy Ashton looking at *him*.'

For once Pierre *had* listened to his wife's conversation. 'What do you mean, "even Daisy Ashton"?'

Annette's glance rested on her daughter complacently. 'Well, she can't have much choice, can she? Odd, thin creature that she is.'

Jacqueline was watching Daniel's expressionless face, but said nothing. It was left to Pierre to deliver a parting shot as he walked to the door. 'I liked the odd, thin creature, as a matter of fact – I liked her very much!' Then he offered his wife a brief smile and walked out.

After Daisy's departure the weather became unsettled again. The summer was ending earlier than usual and, as the evenings grew cool, it became a pleasure to light the log fire in the room they called William's study. There, companionably silent, the two of them were busy – William working on his memoir, and Robert pouring over seed catalogues and manuals of garden design.

With the wet weather had come the chance to sow his lawn. Pierre Darroze laughed at the ambition – a '*folie anglaise*', he called it – but Robert smiled and went on with it all the same. But he did accept advice about the sad remnants of Gaston's vineyard; nothing to be done about *them*, said Pierre, but grub them up and start again. This had now been done, and the ground turned and cleared of weeds. Robert was determined that when the spring came his old friend and Pierre as well should see the slopes behind the house veiled in the greenery of newly planted vines.

They acquired a housekeeper who came daily from Foutances and arranged life at home comfortably for them. In the town they were also pleasantly aware of having been accepted. It was only with the Darroze family that they seemed to make no lasting headway. Pierre freely gave advice and criticism when asked, but he never came purely as a friend. Annette regularly called with milk, eggs, and the fresh vegetables that Robert's own plot wasn't yet producing, but these were mere business transactions. Daniel came briefly if there were farm matters to discuss; and Jeanne came not at all.

Robert regretted their lost friendship with her son and felt deeply sorry for him; but his dear Daisy had been damaged as well. She'd have stayed for ever if Daniel had been free to ask her to; but presumably he'd seen no way out of the bind in which he was caught. As for Jeanne, Robert didn't even know what the difficulty was. She'd seemed to agree that they were friends, but now even William had given up hope of having her call in at the Petit Manoir.

Then, one morning, he walked into the church that dominated the town's central square and she was there as well, in front of the candle-stand.

'Jacques' anniversary,' she explained briefly, after a glance at him.

'My mother's also,' Robert agreed, lighting a candle of his own. 'It would be nice if you were to offer me a cup of coffee at home, but I doubt if you will. You seem as determined as your son not to have anything to do with us.' He spoke gently but she couldn't mistake the sense of hurt.

'Come if you want to,' she said without enthusiasm. 'But you *could* try to remember that Daniel's always busy, and so am I.'

He didn't answer, even to say that it wasn't much of an excuse, and they walked in silence the hundred yards to her house. This being November, he was led into the pleasant kitchen that overlooked the garden; Jeanne brewed coffee, and set it in front of him.

'Perhaps you haven't heard our news,' she said at last. 'Daniel and Jacqueline are to be married soon after Christmas. It's a slack time at the farm, so they can manage a visit to Morocco after the wedding.'

Robert sipped his coffee, watched her over the rim of the cup, and decided to be less than truthful. 'I got it all wrong, then – reckoned he avoided us because he was angry with Daisy for going away. Something else must have upset him, and I wish I knew what it was.'

Jeanne tried to speak as casually as he had done. 'Daisy unsettled him a little. What can you expect? She's different from the girls here, and a man would have to be blind not to see her attraction. Daniel enjoyed her company but he knew they had no future together. For the moment I expect he doesn't want to be reminded of the very pleasant way life is lived at the Petit Manoir.'

She was aware of having been less than truthful herself, and half-expected Robert to tell her so. Instead, he asked a more difficult question. 'You've explained Daniel to me. Now tell me why *you* avoid us?'

Flummoxed, she could only go on to the attack. 'I expect because I'm content *here*. I'd visit you if I wanted to.'

'But you *don't* want to, of course. Silly of me to have needed telling!' The wry comment was made lightly, but she knew she had hurt him and would have softened what she'd said if he'd allowed her the chance. Instead, he went on to speak of his daughter. 'In case you have the slightest interest in what Daisy's up to, I'll mention that she's going to spend Christmas with her mother in New York. We shan't have her back here until *after* Daniel's marriage.'

'A quiet Christmas for you, then,' Jeanne merely suggested.

'We shouldn't mind if it were, but William tells me we're invited to the Lamberts. They've been very kind to us all along.'

'They would be, of course, and so would anyone else who wasn't aware of what you and William Harcourt did during the war. They'll drop you soon enough if the truth gets out.'

Robert put down his cup, and covered her hand with his

own. 'My dear girl, the war ended thirty years ago. The bitterness *has* to end if this country is ever to live at peace with itself.'

She snatched her hand away and nursed it as if some pain had been felt because of his touch. 'The reasons for the bitterness have to be faced first, not run away from. Half the people who now run France were collaborators in one way or another. They only became brave Resisters when it was clear that Germany would be beaten.'

She was looking back into the past again, lost in the memory of all its pain and confusion. He couldn't follow her there, only thank God that somehow she'd survived it. To a month or two he could guess her age, and the bright winter sunlight showed him a face marked clearly enough by painful experience. But in every way that mattered she was the same Jeanne – still brave and honest, still infinitely precious, and infinitely beyond his reach. In danger of sinking into a morass of longing that she would certainly despise, he hauled himself out of it and tried to speak calmly.

'I'm sorry not to see Daniel now. Apart from liking him very much, we need to stay in touch with a generation that judges things differently from ours. They can accept as friends people we still think of as enemies, and they're right to do that – the future *requires* acceptance, not undying hatred.'

Jeanne tried to match his effort to talk of general things. 'You're a fine one to talk of acceptance, my friend. Is Britain not being carried into the Common Market, kicking and screaming every inch of the way?'

'Well, perhaps, but we weren't exactly made welcome: twice vetoed, I seem to remember, by the Great Man himself, who had *some* cause to feel grateful to us after all!'

'True,' she agreed soberly. 'Jacques admired de Gaulle of course, but in the end he came to believe that the General outstayed his welcome and did France much harm. My husband was a wise, good man. Daniel still misses him and so do I.'

She said it, he hoped, without any other intention than to do justice to Jacques Lescaut. But she had neatly reminded him of the fact that he'd met her a little while ago remembering her husband's anniversary. There was nothing for Robert Ashton to do except pull himself together, thank her for a pleasant half-hour, and leave her contentedly alone in the house that contained all the memories of her married life.

He stood up to go, holding out his hand. 'I'm sorry I badgered you about coming to see us. God knows I have no right to lecture you about anything at all, but sooner or later you and people like the Lamberts *will* have to make peace with each other.'

She didn't answer, and he went towards the front door thinking that they would part with nothing more said. Then, just as he was about to walk out, she found something to say.

'I'm very sorry, Robert . . . for Daniel; but even more so for Daisy if she was hurt.'

Had she ever used his name before? No, he'd have remembered if she had. He stored away the sound of it, but shook his head. 'You didn't ask us to come and settle down almost on your doorstep. William has a theory about life's patterns needing to complete themselves. In this one thing his judgement seems to be all to hell! The truth is that our patterns are never complete, because the gods who play such merry havoc with our lives see to it that happiness usually eludes us in the end.' Then he gave her a little salute and walked away, leaving her to remember another time when she'd had to watch him leave and then quietly close the door.

Fifteen

At supper that evening, occupied with trying to decide whether to report his conversation with Jeanne, it took Robert longer than it might have done to notice that William also was unusually quiet.

'Something bothering you?' he enquired.

'Puzzling me,' William amended. He smiled at his friend across the table. 'You can have the quiet Christmas you wanted after all. Giselle Lambert rang this morning. It seems their plans have changed. Instead of entertaining us at home in Foutances, they have to go away.'

'It sounds straightforward enough,' Robert pointed out. 'Why be puzzled?'

'Only because Giselle talked too much! She isn't a chatty woman as a rule – it's one of the things I like about her. This morning she went on and on, as people do who fear they're making an unconvincing job of lying.' William's rosy face looked troubled. 'Where we eat our Christmas dinner isn't important, but I can't help feeling that what lies behind Giselle's change of heart *does* matter.'

'I think I know what it is,' Robert answered slowly. 'The Lamberts' name cropped up in a conversation I had with Jeanne Lescaut today. She rather predicted what has just happened. Our friendship with Marcel Lambert wouldn't survive his knowing what you and I did in the war.'

'We fought on the same side, I thought.'

'We aided and abetted men like Pierre Darroze. On the way home I stopped at the war memorial. Among the names of those "*Morts pour la France*" was that of Philippe Lambert. My friend the boulanger saw me standing there and came out to explain – Philippe was the notaire's elder brother, shot in a reprisal raid.'

'So what are you thinking – that someone here has spread word of our puny efforts to help the Resistance movement?'

Robert gave a little shrug. 'Perhaps, but it doesn't follow as the night the day. Lambert might be acquainted with one of our Bordeaux friends. They're always happy to boast of knowing you!'

'What do we do now?' William asked miserably.

'Nothing, I'm afraid, except pretend that we believe Giselle's fib. Poor woman – she must have hated being told to offer it.'

A little silence fell until William risked a different question. 'Why don't we see Jeanne Lescaut nowadays? *She* can't resent our wartime activities; she was part of them.'

'Like Daniel, apparently, she's too busy.'

'Too busy for a friendly visit now and then? It's hard to believe.' William sounded so regretful that some explanation had to be given.

'It may well be true – she teaches music at a school for disturbed children. I've heard of the idea before; involving these children in playing an instrument makes them more tractable, more capable of learning other things.' In spite of himself almost, Robert went on. 'I recognised the old violin-case Jeanne still uses. She used to carry messages hidden in it when I first knew her!' He sipped his wine, and searched his mind for something less revealing to say. 'Jeanne gave me a piece of news, by the way: Daniel and Annette Darroze's daughter are marrying in the New Year.'

But this only served to plunge William into gloom again. 'Something went wrong *there*, too. It shouldn't have done; Daisy and Daniel looked so happy together.'

'He was already tied hand and foot to the Darroze family,'

Robert pointed out sharply. 'Daisy knew that, and understood what it would have cost him to tear himself free.'

'I feel sorry for Jacqueline,' William said unexpectedly. 'The poor girl will do her best, but Daniel won't forget Daisy in a hurry, if at all.'

The words echoed in the quiet room, spoken and uncancellable, calling to mind the failure of Robert's marriage to Christine. 'Take no notice,' William said hurriedly. 'An old fool of a bachelor like me knows nothing of the problems of holy wedlock.'

Robert smiled, understanding the cause of his embarrassment. 'What you really are is incurably romantic! You'd like Jeanne's son and my daughter to complete a pattern that was begun and couldn't be finished years ago. Daisy herself would tell you that we have to live in the harsh, real world, not in one beloved of old-fashioned lady-novelists!'

It was as close as he'd ever come to admitting that his wartime adventure had left its mark on him, but it still puzzled William. Christine had always identified Daisy's namesake, not her daughter, as the woman he hadn't been able to forget. But Robert, wondering what had possessed him to pursue William's damned patterns, now embarked on a topic that would sufficiently distract his friend.

'Jeanne was in church lighting a candle in memory of her husband, when I met her. She still misses him very much. Jacques Lescaut was a friend of Pierre's, and an admirer of de Gaulle to begin with. Admiration didn't last, though. Apparently he ended up believing that the General did France much harm; I'm sorry he's not still here for you to argue with.'

'I'd have to agree with him,' William admitted sadly. 'Great virtues aren't always accompanied by great flaws, but Charles de Gaulle had both, with knobs on, as children used to say!'

It was a subject to see them safely to bedtime, and at breakfast the next morning neither of them referred to the rest of the evening's conversation.

* * *

The days shortened into winter but the mild weather still held. For a man with a new vineyard to plant it was something to be thankful for. Even more welcome to Robert was a telephone call from Pierre Darroze one morning, when William was away in Paris, recommending a young man who was looking for work.

'His name's Jean Lecours. He's the son of a "*pied noir*" I used to know – a good man, even if he never got over having to leave Algeria and come back to France. We don't need more help at the moment or I'd take young Lecours on myself.'

The youth arrived on Pierre's ancient auto-cycle and shyly introduced himself. He understood, he said, that Monsieur had vines to plant. It was something he could do, having worked in a vineyard before.

'In this region of France?' Robert asked.

'No, in Algeria; my mother was Algerian.'

It explained his swarthy skin and very dark hair, but along with these things went a gentle manner and a smile that was likeable.

'You decided not to stay there?'

'I prefer to live in France; it's where I belong,' Jean Lecours insisted quietly. 'But I didn't understand that things have changed. I took a job with Monsieur Bonnard, but it wasn't what I wanted to do – just driving machines all day long, and pouring chemicals into the soil.'

'Not what we do here,' Robert said, smiling at him, 'but we aren't serious agriculturalists, just amateurs who enjoy growing things.'

'Could I help for as long as you need me?' There was pleading behind the question that Robert couldn't resist, and when William returned he was told that their labour force had been temporarily increased by someone who, being on the right side of thirty, could at least plant vines without torturing his back.

'I think you'll like him,' Robert said, 'because you like unusual people. He bought a horse and gypsy caravan because he felt sorry for the horse! He's living in the caravan now, parked in one of Pierre's meadows.'

'Pity Daisy's not here,' William said regretfully, '. . . *she'd* like him for sure.'

Two weeks later, with medal-winning vintages to be judged in Bordeaux, William had to set off again. By then their own new vineyard was becoming visible. Admittedly there wasn't much to admire yet, but Robert and his lieutenant smiled at one another, seeing not the neat rows of bare, black twigs now running over the hill behind the house, but the summer greenery to come and September's rich harvest of grapes.

Alone in the house that evening, Robert heard a knock on the kitchen door. He found the man he still thought of as Cheval standing there, bare-headed as usual despite the falling rain. Invited inside, Pierre shook himself as a wet dog might and accepted a glass of wine.

'My daughter would say I'm letting standards slide, entertaining you in the kitchen,' Robert explained with a grin. 'But it's almost my favourite room in the house. William's doing some wine-judging in Bordeaux, by the way.'

'Jean told me – he eats with us most evenings now.' Pierre shot a glance across the table at his host. 'I expect you miss your daughter.'

'We both do. Daisy has a happy gift of enhancing life for other people. She's had to go earlier than expected to New York – her mother's second husband is ill, and Christine needed shoring up.'

Pierre nodded, then seemed for once uncertain how to embark on what he wanted to say next. 'I didn't come just to keep you company. It seemed the moment, with William away, to tell you that something is going on in the town.'

'Something unpleasant?' Robert queried.

Pierre nodded again, then sprinkled raindrops as he ran his fingers through grizzled hair still thick as an animal's pelt. 'I know who's behind it – Michel Bonnard. He's seen the reservoir, and your new vineyard, not to mention Jean working in it. He understands now that you won't leave the Petit Manoir unless you and William are driven out.'

Robert stared at the lined face of the man watching him. It hadn't been handsome even in youth, rarely smiling or looking pleasantly relaxed. But it belonged to a man he'd still trust and fight beside if ever danger came.

'I've wondered who it was that upset our friendship with the Lamberts,' he admitted. '. . . Bonnard, you think?'

'Of course, and I'm afraid one of my own men helped him without meaning to. He was in the bar one evening when Bonnard's handyman was shooting his mouth off about you and William – under orders no doubt. I needn't spell out the sort of thing that was being said. Patrice warned him to watch his tongue, got sneered at, and knocked the fool down. Then he made him listen to the truth.'

'And the man took it back to his boss. Still, I'm afraid it doesn't prove that Bonnard's behind whatever's going on.'

Pierre took a gulp of wine before answering. 'I have friends here as well as enemies. They watch and listen; it isn't difficult in a small town. Bonnard's deliberately stirring up ill-feeling against you – among the shopkeepers and the other people who run Foutances. In the end, he reckons, you'll give up and leave. Then he'll have punished you for laughing at him, and got hold of his river frontage, and Yves Deschamps will have the house to sell again at the sort of price he knows I can't afford.'

Robert smiled a little ruefully. 'It isn't quite what we planned for our retirement – to have to sit out a siege! But we'll stay unless it becomes clear that we're never going to win against the barbarians. William loves this place too much for us to give up without a struggle, and so do I.'

'Good,' said Pierre, almost happily. 'That's what I wanted to hear.'

'But what you also have to understand is that it's *our* fight, not yours.' Robert's voice was suddenly very firm, and he didn't smile back when Pierre grinned at him. 'I know you for a true comrade, but I won't have the town torn in two over me and William.' A glimmer of amusement wiped the sternness from his face. 'Try remembering instead that *you* didn't want us here either not so long ago!'

Pierre gave his habitual shrug, pushing aside something that was of no account. 'Old prejudices die hard, that's all. We agreed the past was over and forgotten.' He finished his wine and stood up. 'I'd better get back. Annette and Jacqueline will still be arguing about the wedding, I expect. Jacqueline wants it simple, and I'm on her side.' On his way to the door he suddenly lobbed another question. 'How do you get on with Jean?'

'Very well. He's a thoroughly nice young man. William wants to set him on to renovating our lovely but dilapidated *pigeonnier* when I've run out of work for him. So far as I can see he'll be here as long as we are!'

Pierre nodded. 'My wife and step-daughter make a fuss of him, but Daniel likes him too, and he's even harder to please than I am.' Then, with a small farewell salute, he walked out into the rainy night.

Robert was still tossing over in his mind the dilemma of whether to report this latest disturbing conversation when, the following day, the telephone rang and Daisy's clear voice sounded along the line. Her shocking news was that instead of continuing to make progress after some serious surgery, Arnold Goldman had died suddenly the night before.

'My dear, I'm so sorry . . . so very sorry.' Robert paused for a moment, wondering how Christine would deal with her bereavement. Not doubting her affection for her second husband, he nevertheless reckoned that she would be beautiful and brave, a model of exquisite fortitude. Feeling ashamed of the thought, he was more truly concerned about Daisy. 'What about you, love – can you cope? Do you need any help?'

'No, we're managing very well. It's almost as if dear

Arnold knew . . . he left everything so neatly arranged. You needn't even think of rushing over. The Goldman family is large and influential, but Mum's being splendid too.'

'You'll stay there for a bit, I suppose, after the funeral. Your mother will be glad of your company.'

'Yes, but she hates the idea now of Christmas in New York. I couldn't think what to suggest, and then I had a brainwave. Could I bring her to the Petit Manoir? She won't want to stay for long, but you and Uncle Will making a fuss of her would be just what she needs, and she'd like to see the house.' After a brief pause Daisy spoke again sadly. 'I'm afraid you don't fancy the idea.'

Robert hurried to deny it as convincingly as he could. 'Of course you must both come. I hope I'd have thought of it myself if you hadn't. Just let me know when and where to pick you up – Toulouse airport, I should think, but you might have to change flights in Paris.'

Daisy promised to telephone again as soon as the funeral was behind them and there'd been time to think of their own arrangements. When she'd rung off Robert remembered his conversation of the previous evening. Now wasn't the time he'd have chosen for her to come back; but at least there was one thing to be said for Christine's visit: who better than his very noticeable ex-wife to scotch *one* of the lies that Bonnard was probably circulating about him?

William returned home that evening to the special dinner prepared for him by Madame Albert. She'd given up hope of her pâté de foie gras or magret de canard putting any flesh on Monsieur Ashton's long, lean body, but her other English gentleman was a different and altogether more rewarding patron to feed.

William did the duck justice and spoke of his Bordeaux friends, then asked for local news.

'American news first,' Robert answered. 'Arnold has died unexpectedly – Daisy rang to tell me. She suggested bringing

Christine here for Christmas. I said we'd both be very pleased.'

'Of course, of course,' said William, looking shocked. 'Poor Christine, what a terrible thing. It was a very successful marriage. Bound to have been when Arnold did everything she wanted, but she made *him* happy as well.' He looked across at Robert. 'I shall love to see her here, but there's no awkwardness for *you* in her coming?'

'None at all; in any case I want to share Daisy's sense of responsibility for her a bit.' He hesitated a moment, and then went on. 'As it happens, the timing of the visit may have its awkwardness. Pierre reckons that Bonnard is behind some local gossip about us, and behind Giselle Lambert's cancelled invitation!'

'He hopes we'll take fright and leave, I suppose. What did you say to Pierre?'

'That we shall sit tight, but *he*'s not to get involved. If we're not careful he'll be fighting the war all over again, with his fellow-citizens this time instead of Germans.'

A faint smile touched William's face. 'Life at Wapping was much more tame than this, don't you think?'

'You're supposed to be angry, or anxious, or upset,' Robert said after an astonished pause. 'Dammit, not *pleased*!'

'React in a way the enemy doesn't expect,' William advised gently, 'it unsettles him. If I meet Bonnard in Foutances I shall greet him like a long-lost and dearly-loved friend!'

'Hurrah for Machiavelli combined with the bulldog-breed,' Robert murmured, and grinned at him with great affection.

A week later Robert was waiting outside the arrivals lounge at the airport in Toulouse. Passengers off the flight from Paris came through quickly, and he spotted his two at once – Daisy, elegant in navy-blue, her overcoat tailored as precisely as a 'British Warm', Christine in dramatic black cape and wide-brimmed sombrero hat. Rather to his surprise he was glad to see her, and it was suddenly easy to offer the embrace she was expecting. Her face under the shadow of the extravagant hat was still beautiful, and probably always would be, even if a little artifice might be needed in later years.

'Dear Robert,' she said at once, 'thank you for letting us come. I had the feeling that Daisy was missing you and Uncle Will, and la belle France.'

'You've had a bad time,' he said gently. 'William's waiting at home, impatient to spoil you both rotten!'

She managed a brave smile, and allowed him to hug his daughter before he attended to her again. With her various pieces of luggage retrieved from the carousel, they headed for the car, and Christine announced unselfishly that she would sit in the back. It gave Daisy the chance, once they were out of the city traffic, to ask her father the question he was prepared for. 'All well at the Petit Manoir?'

'Very well, apart from some colder weather than usual that is threatening my beautiful new vines – they don't care for a run of frosty nights.'

'And . . . at the Ferme Darroze? Is dear, grumpy Pierre also complaining about the weather?'

Robert hesitated briefly. 'He's complaining about something else – Annette's plans for her daughter's wedding to Daniel. Much too extravagant, he thinks.'

'When is it to be?' Daisy asked, staring out of the window beside her.

'In the spring before the farm work gets too heavy.'

She said nothing more for a while, but finally added a quiet comment that he almost didn't hear. 'Jeanne Lescaut will be pleased – she seemed anxious to have Jacqueline as a daughter-in-law.' Then, as if that subject didn't interest her very much, she asked to be told about the new arrival, Jean Lecours.

Sixteen

The shops in Foutances were very busy; not only was it a Saturday morning but Christmas was no more than three days away. There was a crowd at the boucherie's delicatessen counter and, ahead of him, Daniel recognised the small round figure of William Harcourt. When his own turn came to be served William was still there, unattended to, seemingly ignored. Daniel was about to point this out to the butcher's wife behind the counter when a hand lightly touched his wrist. He looked down to see William shaking his head.

'I'm not in any hurry,' the Englishman said with a smile. 'When the shop empties for a moment Madame *will* notice me – she'd hate to miss making a sale!'

Daniel's expression said that he saw nothing amusing in the situation, but again he was forestalled. 'Please don't worry; just leave me to wear down the good lady's resistance in my own way.'

Reluctant, but obedient to the note of command now in William's voice, Daniel asked her curtly for what he wanted, slammed down money on the counter and, with a very courteous bow to William, walked out. Later, back at home, his face was still white and tense but Jeanne Lescaut didn't comment on the fact until she'd put coffee in front of him.

'I know you hate being asked to shop, and no doubt everywhere was crowded, but need you look as if you've just been having teeth drawn?'

He managed a faint smile, but it faded as he began to

describe the scene in the butcher's shop. 'It was prearranged,' he finished up, 'with the others there waiting to see what would happen. I thought Uncle Pierre was exaggerating, but he wasn't; something unpleasant *is* going on.'

Jeanne resisted the temptation to remind him that he hadn't believed *her* either in the past when she'd insisted that the war still wasn't forgotten. Instead, she tried to sound cheerful. 'I don't think you or Pierre need worry too much about William Harcourt; he may look soft and cuddly as a kitten but he's steel inside.' She glanced at her son's face, then spoke again. 'I think you're upset about something else as well.'

She expected him to shrug it aside but words suddenly seemed to be dragged out of him against his will. 'I saw Mr Harcourt again later on – he was getting into his car, but the driver was Daisy Ashton.'

'Is it so surprising?' Jeanne queried gently. 'Her father lives here.'

'I know, but he said she wouldn't be back before the spring. I . . . somehow counted on not seeing her again.' He spooned sugar into his coffee, then repeated the gesture, unaware of what he'd just done.

Unable to watch his face, Jeanne looked instead at the branches of an amelanchier tree tapping against the kitchen window. She'd meant to trim them in the autumn; now the task must wait another year. But she was still seeing the pain in her son's face and wondering if he would have recognised his fiancée at that moment had she walked into the room.

Daniel set down his coffee-cup and stood up. 'I've got some farm business to discuss with a man in Bassoues, don't wait lunch.' He forced himself to smile at his mother because she was looking anxious. 'It doesn't matter about Daisy. She won't be here long, and I don't suppose we shall coincide at all.'

But that afternoon, needing to check the level of water in the reservoir, he met first the exuberant black retriever that belonged to Jean Lecours and then, instead of its owner, the girl who'd abandoned him for a life in London. She was winter-pale now, with her strangely coloured hair bundled under a woollen hat because the afternoon was sharply cold. Her face was thinner than he remembered, and more schooled. The mouth he'd kissed now refused even to smile at him; for a moment he thought she was going to pass by with only her hand sketching a brief greeting.

'I was expecting Jean when I saw the dog, not you,' he managed to say.

'"The dog", which is all his owner calls him, seems to prefer us; I don't think he likes Jean's horse. I've christened him Nelson after one of my heroes and he seems to recognise the name already, clever chap that he is.'

To prove it, the clever chap came bounding up to lick her hand and wait for her to throw the stick she was holding. She flung it across the field and smiled as Nelson hurtled away after it. Now, she thought, it was Daniel's turn to say something, but he could only stare at her and know what he had lost.

'I didn't intend coming back for Christmas,' she finally muttered by way of an explanation, 'but my mother's husband died in New York instead of recovering from an operation. She needed looking after until she gets used to being without him, and I knew Daddy and Uncle Will would help.'

She could see them as cartoon figures in her mind's eye, with balloons coming out of their mouths – nothing in Daniel's balloon, far too many words in her own. Then suddenly he did speak, and asked the one question she couldn't answer with the truth.

'Why didn't you wait?'

In desperation she looked around the lovely, quiet landscape and found a sort of answer there. 'What I was to wait *for* didn't seem quite right,' she said at last. 'Farming here is what you've grown up always meaning to do; my ambition is different, and so is the place I belong to.'

Before he could find a reply Nelson trotted back and

dropped the stick at Daisy's feet with a bark of triumph and anticipation. Conversation was all very well, he seemed to say, but shouldn't be allowed to interfere with the afternoon's serious business. She bent down and picked up the stick. 'No more; it's time to go home, I'm afraid.'

With a brief smile for the man watching her, she'd turned away when he suddenly spoke again.

'You seemed to belong here that day in Auch; you seemed to belong with me. I thought *you* understood that too. Couldn't you have waited . . . just a little?'

She had to look at him and see the anguish in his face – anger would have helped her but there was none, only loss and sadness. Every detail of their day together was vivid in her mind. But so was every word that Jeanne Lescaut had said – yes, dear God, what a terrible pity it was that things once done couldn't be undone in later years. The Bible was right as usual: the sins of the fathers *were* 'visited upon the children unto the third and fourth generation'. She swallowed the nausea in her throat and finally answered.

'No . . . I couldn't wait,' she said. Then Nelson's black muzzle nudged her hand as a reminder that he was there and she clutched his collar like a lifeline, to make a final effort. 'My father mentioned your wedding soon. I wish you happy, Daniel.' *Now* she could walk away, and he had to let her go because there was nothing more to say. She found her way back towards the house and returned Nelson to his rightful owner.

'He's tired you out,' Jean said anxiously, looking at her drawn face. 'I'll keep him in the caravan in future.'

She could even smile and shake her head. 'No, don't – we like each other.'

But he watched her walk indoors and thought she didn't realise that her eyes had been full of tears.

They went on Christmas Eve to Midnight Mass in Foutances, William having checked beforehand with the curé that the presence of a clutch of Protestants was unlikely to inflame the rest of the congregation. The church was crowded, but Robert made out Jeanne and Daniel sitting with Jean Lecours and the household from the Ferme Darroze several pews ahead of them. Even Pierre was there, probably dragooned by Annette into making his one church visit of the year. The Cheval noticed them arrive and got up deliberately – to come and greet Daisy, he said, who was sitting next to her father. He smiled warmly, approving of her neat navy overcoat and the little pillbox of white fur sitting on the back of her head. Then his glance moved questioningly along the row to where Christine, introduced to the mayor by William, was now having her hand bowed over.

'Daisy's mother,' Robert explained, 'recently widowed in New York. She's here for a change of scene.'

'I hope she enjoys being stared at. Most of the women here, and probably all the men, have got their eye on her.'

'Christine won't mind that,' Robert confirmed. 'A professional actress feels obliged to attract attention!' He smiled at the man he could now think of as an ally. 'It's time you sat down, having shown the good people of Foutances that we're not entirely without friends!'

Pierre grinned, leaned down unexpectedly to kiss Daisy's cheek and then sauntered away. 'What was that about?' she whispered.

'Tell you later – we're here to celebrate the birth of Christ, are we not?'

She nodded and by dint of filling her mind with childhood's lovely images of a star-lit sky and a crib in a cattleshed, managed not to think of Daniel sharing the service with the girl he was going to marry.

Afterwards, as the crowd edged its way out, there was an unforeseen moment when Daniel and his mother were stationary beside the party from the Petit Manoir. Having introduced them, Robert had to turn away. Christine offered Jeanne Lescaut a dazzling smile. 'I'm glad to meet you after all these years. I can laugh about it with you now, but once upon a time it mattered to me very much that Robert adored the memory of your mother!'

Jeanne offered her own faint smile, wished the glamorous Madame Goldman a pleasant stay at the Petit Manoir, and then made the sharpness of the night air an excuse not to linger.

Back at the house, Daisy and her mother refused the offer of a warming glass of Armagnac, and chose to go to bed instead. William stirred the embers of the fire into life while Robert poured the brandy.

'Nice service, I thought,' William said. 'The Curé's the best kind of country priest – sincere and simple.'

'And brave as well, I'd say. There must have been plenty of people there who resented being reminded in the season of goodwill to forget old enmities and to welcome strangers in their midst! Who put him up to *that*, I wonder?'

William merely smiled, and ignored the question.

'I *did* call on the mayor,' he admitted instead, 'the day you went to the airport. He's a good man; I thought he deserved to know that we like his town very much.'

Robert eyed him severely. 'You're getting very devious in your old age.'

'I know,' William agreed, and sipped his brandy with relish.

Three days after Christmas, Christine announced that it was time she went home. 'I've loved being here,' she said to Robert, and he had the feeling that she meant it. 'I hope you'll let me come again, but now I must get used to managing without Arnold. There will be things to see to, and I don't mean to be a helpless widow, relying on lawyers and accountants to do them for me.'

'Shall you want to go back to the stage?' Robert asked. 'I'm assuming that you won't need to.'

Christine nodded. 'There'll be no need, but I should like to.

I know it's hard for anyone outside the theatre to understand, but it's where people like me come fully alive.' She pushed the subject aside with one of her graceful, practised gestures. 'What about you – are you going to stay here, despite the problems with your beastly neighbour?'

'William will get the better of Bonnard, by fair means or foul! I think the idea is to provoke him to some illegal action that will prove his undoing. Do you want Daisy to go back with you?'

'I can manage perfectly well now and I've told her that.' Then Christine smiled at him. 'I doubt if she'd come anyway at the moment; not while she thinks she might be needed here!' She hesitated, then spoke again. 'Our daughter is unhappy, but I expect you're aware of that. I haven't asked her whether the grief is here or in London.'

'Knowing Daisy, I'm sure she's grateful for that,' he said gently.

Christine left two days later, to catch a direct flight back to New York from Bordeaux. Her final triumph had been a farewell call from the mayor, who wished her to know that Foutances had felt itself honoured by her visit. Robert was still smiling at the thought of it when he waved them away, Christine sitting beside William in the back of the car and Daisy driving. He returned indoors to hear the telephone ringing, and then Jeanne's voice on the line.

'I need to talk to you. Could you drive over now if it isn't inconvenient?'

He agreed and replaced the telephone, surprised, until he realised that she was probably anxious about Pierre or Daniel stirring up trouble with Bonnard.

A holly wreath still decorated Jeanne's front door, reminding him that she was at home because of the school holiday. She greeted him calmly enough, but he thought she looked strained and tired, as if she'd been sleeping badly.

'Couldn't you work less hard?' he asked abruptly as she

led him, by habit he thought, to the kitchen overlooking Jacques' garden. 'Why not take a term off from teaching?' Having started, he suddenly found he couldn't stop. 'Why not come with me to some peaceful Greek island and sleep in the sun for a week or two? I've been waiting thirty years to take care of you.'

The words died in the silence of the room and he cursed himself for a fool. He was a middle-aged man, not an impulsive youth who could be forgiven for blurting out what was in his mind. He saw her mouth quiver – perhaps he'd almost made her laugh with the futility of what he'd said. But with the same gesture he'd frequently seen Pierre use, she pushed her hands through her short, dark hair and tried to answer calmly.

'It's kind of you, but I don't need a holiday. What I do need is for you to listen to me, without interruptions if you can manage it.' But then she fell silent, as if examining the words in her mind and wondering which of them she could bear to use.

'Daniel's been fighting a battle with himself since the summer,' she finally began, 'trying to prove that he could forget your daughter and marry Jacqueline instead. He might have won his battle if Daisy hadn't come back. But when I saw him catch sight of her in church on Christmas Eve I knew that the promise I made Jacques would have to be broken.'

There was a long pause until Robert prompted her. 'I'm still listening, my dear.'

She nodded and started again. 'Jacqueline understood what had happened between them – the *coup de foudre* that only true lovers know. Her way of dealing with it was to tell Daisy she must forget Daniel because in all probability he was her half-brother.'

'*What?*' The gasped, forbidden, interruption made her frown at him.

'It's what Pierre certainly believed, although he never told me so. I suppose Jacqueline overheard him one day, talking to

Annette. Soon after you left the farm I was obviously pregnant – who else was there to blame?'

'So *that's* why he could scarcely bear the sight of me when I came back after the war,' Robert murmured, almost to himself.

Jeanne nodded again. 'Jacques claimed the child as his, said we'd been lovers, and married me. Daniel grew up loving him and we were happy together.'

'Jacqueline told Daisy, you said,' Robert urged her on, forgetting again that he wasn't to interrupt. 'That's why she rushed back to London?'

'Yes, but she and I also had a conversation first. Daisy asked me, not quite in so many words, to confirm or deny what Jacqueline had said. I didn't lie, but I'm ashamed to say that I allowed her to believe what wasn't true because I couldn't bear Daniel to know who his real father was.'

'I'm *not* his father?' Robert asked hoarsely.

Jeanne spoke in a quiet voice that seemed to make what she said even more horrible. 'The man was a drunken German officer who caught me on my way home one evening. With my basket full of messages it seemed preferable to be raped than make a fight of it. I was thrown out of his car afterwards and left in the road. A month after that I was certain I was pregnant. I didn't dare tell Pierre – he'd have gone out to kill the first German he could find and got shot himself. I told Jacques instead, knowing that because he'd always loved me he would take care of me. I thought I'd hate my child, but came to adore him. He wasn't anything like the beast who'd fathered him; he grew up brave and gentle, just like my father and Jacques himself – like you, too, as a matter of fact.'

Robert leaned over to gently wipe away the tears that were now trickling down her face, no longer wondering why she'd kept him at arm's length and revered the memory of her husband.

She smiled a little at the gesture and came to the end of her story. 'I must tell Daniel the truth now, and it will be the hardest thing I could be asked to do – he loved Jacques and was rightly proud of him.'

'He'll be still *more* proud now,' Robert insisted gently, 'and he will love *you* more than ever. That I promise you.'

'It's how he will see himself that troubles me,' she murmured sadly. 'When you tell Daisy, please help her to understand why I treated her as I did. I don't know what difference the truth will make – perhaps it's too late now to make any at all.'

'I don't know either,' he agreed. '*They'll* have to make of it what they can, without any interference from us.'

Jeanne nodded, and he had the feeling that she now wanted him to leave; the emotional strain of telling her story had been exhausting and she needed to recover by herself. But she said one last thing. 'I shall tell Pierre the truth because it's only fair to you; but no one else.'

He stood up to leave, and as on other occasions she walked with him to the door. Her face was still damp with tears when he kissed her goodbye, but he went without saying anything.

She watched him walk away, thinking of how their conversation had begun. He hadn't repeated his offer to take her to a Greek island and she didn't expect he ever would. The girl whose idealised image had stayed with him over the years must look different now. Try as he might, he would never see her again without seeing a drunken German officer straddling her in the back of his car. Romantic wishful thinking couldn't survive that kind of brutal reality.

Seventeen

The travellers returned late from delivering Christine to Bordeaux, and after supper it was already bedtime. The next morning, after William had gone to his study to catch up on the previous day's news, Robert suggested driving Daisy to Larressingle, a hill-top, wall-encircled bastide that she had still to visit. She looked slightly surprised at the invitation on a cold day at the beginning of January, but no outing with her father was to be refused, and she set out with him very happily.

'You were right to choose today to come,' she said when they were back in the warmth of the car drinking thermos coffee, after walking round the almost deserted village. 'Imagine sitting out a winter here, looking down on the tents of the surrounding English barbarians below!'

'You've been listening to Pierre's version of local history,' Robert suggested, 'according to which our soldiery were a brutal, licentious lot, while the Gascons were "parfit gentle knights" to the last man!'

She grinned at him, then spoke in a different voice. 'Now confess why we came out today without Uncle Will.'

'So that I could talk to you alone,' he admitted. 'Listen, Daisy, love, while I tell you a story.'

Slowly and almost verbatim he repeated what Jeanne had told him, but with no need to warn against interruptions. Daisy still didn't say anything even when he stopped talking, and eventually he went on himself.

'I was to try to make you understand. To do that I must

say something else. Jeanne and I spent part of one short night together, always remembered on my part with love and gratitude: the very next day I had to leave the farm and set off for the coast. She hated misleading you, but it was only so that the truth shouldn't have to come out about Daniel's father.'

At last Daisy found something to say. 'I thought she was trying to preserve their neat "French" arrangement for Jacqueline's future and the future of the farm. Poor, poor Jeanne . . . It also explains why she was so sharp with me about my "highly coloured" fiction – I might have dreamed up the very nightmare she was involved in.'

'She will have told Daniel the truth by now. You must work out whether knowing it changes anything . . . for you, I mean.'

She turned to look at him, almost with disappointment. 'Are you afraid he might suddenly become a crop-headed Nazi with a nice line in raping defenceless women? Never in a million years. Until he dies he'll be the man he now is.'

'I agree with you,' Robert said gently. 'But now consider something else: could you really share the life of a Gascon farmer? That is what Daniel *is*, apart from being a very nice man.'

A sad little smile touched her mouth. 'I don't have to consider it because your question doesn't arise. The truth changes nothing because it comes too late, or might never have been able to change anything at all. Daniel is committed to Jacqueline. I knew it even before I ran away to London, but more than ever now, he'll do what he sees as right and necessary. I shan't hear from him again.'

She spoke with such quiet certainty that Robert said nothing more. He merely touched her hand, and started stowing away cups and thermos in the picnic-basket. Daisy spoke instead. 'You know, Mum always believed that the memory of Marguerite wrecked your marriage. That was wrong, wasn't it? It was Jeanne all the time?'

He gave a little nod, but it was Daisy who spoke again. 'Give her my love please, when you see her again.'

He leaned over to kiss her cheek, and then put the car in gear.

After lunch, as usual now, Daisy and Nelson set out on their afternoon expedition together, while Jean Lecours and William planned the renovation of the *pigeonnier*. She heard talk of ridge tiles and joists and rafters as she walked past them, but explained that Nelson's mind was much more concentrated on rabbits. Her own mind lingered on the morning's conversation with her father and it made her careless of the direction Nelson was taking. When she caught up with him at last she was aware that they were trespassing. An enticing scent had led the dog on to their neighbour's land, and by sheer ill-fortune the neighbour himself happened to be there, talking to a stranger.

She whistled to the dog but, certain that a rabbit was in the hole he was now glued to, Nelson refused to hear. There was nothing to be done but engage in an unseemly struggle with *him* and apologise as best she could to Michel Bonnard at the same time. She thought the man justified in pointing out the few young shoots of maize that had felt the retriever's large paws, but they scarcely merited the abusive tirade hurled at both her and the dog. Aware of being in the wrong, she promised that Nelson wouldn't be allowed to offend again, but added that dogs always chased rabbits when they got the chance; it was, she explained sweetly, their nature to do so.

'Well, keep him out in future or I shall do it myself. A farmer is entitled to protect his crops,' Bonnard shouted.

'Especially a farmer whose only interest in his land is the profit he can wring out of it,' Daisy agreed. 'Come, Nelson; we'll go home now.'

To her great relief he allowed himself to be led away this time before the man could think of a suitable insult with which to reply. She restored the dog to Jean, warning him that he was in disgrace for trespassing, and then went indoors to confess the sin to William and her father. The day was becoming quite an emotional strain, one way and another.

'So much for your charm offensive, Uncle Will,' she said apologetically. 'There's no doubt we were at fault, but Bonnard wanted to impress the man he was with – the arrogant English were to be shown who was boss. Nelson can't be allowed to stray again; that loathsome creature is quite capable of shooting him.'

'Provided he knows one end of a rifle from the other,' Robert pointed out. 'The chances are, I think, that he doesn't. Still, Jean must be careful.'

The following day, having promised to drive William to Auch, she didn't take the dog out at all. They got back after lunch with the floor tiles needed for the pigeon-house but found that Jean was not there. Robert emerged from the house instead to explain that he'd had to rush to the vet with Nelson, who'd been found ill behind the barn.

'Poisoned?' William queried quietly.

'Almost certainly, I think. There was a bit of meat still left that Jean took with him to be analysed. I feel sure it had been thrown there for Nelson to find.'

'Is he going to die?' This time it was Daisy who asked the question.

'I don't know, my love, but he looked very sick,' her father answered.

'Then I'm going to see Bonnard, *now*,' she muttered. 'It's deliberate wickedness, to punish *us*.'

'You're going to do nothing of the sort.' Robert's voice hauled her round to face him again. 'Stop a moment, Daisy, and *think*. Bonnard will simply laugh at you, ask for proof you haven't got, and then remind you of the law of slander.'

Seeing the rebellion in her face, William quickly chipped in. 'Your father's right, my dear. Leave the unpleasant fellow to us, please.'

'Then with your permission I'll go and join Jean at the vet's. I can cycle or take your car.'

'The car, of course, but for God's sake concentrate on driving it,' Robert said, 'not on murdering Bonnard.'

She offered them a little wave, half farewell, half apology, and roared away, leaving the two men looking at one another.

'Too much is happening all at once,' her father said. 'My darling Daisy has reason to be het up, but what has upset her most is not my story to tell.'

'Then I don't want to hear it,' William answered. 'I shall just pray instead that Jean's misbegotten hound *doesn't* die at the vet's.'

Nelson didn't die there, but when they brought him back later that evening he looked more dead than alive.

'The poison's out of his system, but so is everything else,' Daisy explained, white-faced with strain and tiredness. 'The poor fellow's so weak he can't stand up. I think the vet has rather given up on him, but we aren't going to.'

An hour later, having been persuaded to swallow a full bowl of bread crumbled up in warm milk that had been laced with William's best Armagnac, the dog had summoned up the energy to lick Daisy's hand.

'*He's* going to make it,' Robert said as they watched Jean take him back to the caravan. 'Now we'll think about *you*: I recommend a light snack and a restorative glass of wine.'

She smiled at last: 'Whatever the doctor prescribes!' And he knew what she was telling him: the discoveries of the day had been almost too much for her, but now she was herself again.

The following day, her afternoon walk took her to the farm to deliver Madame Albert's present for Nelson – his favourite biscuits, specially baked that morning. Jean Lecours' caravan, parked in a meadow near the farmhouse, was charming; painted in bright gypsy colours and as clean as a new pin, even its little brass carriage lamps gleamed with regular polishing. Daisy registered the fact that either Jean himself took pride in his house on wheels or the Darroze ladies did it for him.

She went to say hallo to the horse, quietly lipping at a bundle of hay, and then had an affectionate reunion with Nelson – not quite his exuberant self yet but clearly recovering. She was about to leave when the door was pushed open and Jacqueline walked in carrying a basket of freshly laundered linen. Her expression darkened immediately at the sight of Daisy, identifying her as an intruder. By contrast, her own familiarity with Jean's home was also made clear as she stowed away in drawers and cupboards the laundry she'd brought.

'I came to see Nelson,' Daisy felt obliged to explain, even though it must be obvious. 'I thought you worked at Cassaigne?'

'So I do, but not every day.' Jacqueline straightened the curtains at each little window with a proprietary air. 'A man on his own needs looking after. I keep things neat and tidy for Jean.'

'I'm sure he's very grateful,' Daisy risked saying in the hope of improving the tense atmosphere.

The olive-branch was ignored; Jacqueline wished it to be clear that she wasn't interested in anything Daisy Ashton was sure of. 'He's had a miserable life since his mother died . . . no one to care what becomes of him.'

'*We* care,' Daisy decided to insist. 'My father and my great-uncle value him very highly.'

The girl's fierce glance clashed with hers for a moment, suspecting patronage she would refuse. 'Jean won't always have to work for other people. He'll have a farm of his own one day; then no one will be able to despise him for being only half-French.'

'He *is* French,' Daisy corrected her sharply. 'His mother was as much a citizen of France as you are.' But she was tired of trying to communicate with a girl who was determined to dislike her; it was time to say goodbye and leave her with what she seemed to want – possession of Jean's home.

At any other time Daisy might have puzzled over Jacqueline's jealous concern for Pierre Darroze's protégé, but her mind was full of a different man instead. How would that conversation a moment ago have gone if the truth of Daniel's parentage could have been acknowledged between them? Would Jacqueline still be intent on marrying him, knowing that her own father had died of the treatment meted out to him by Germans? But she'd never know, of course; the truth was only to be shared with Pierre Darroze, Robert had said.

Deep in thought, Daisy was unaware of the man walking behind her until his shout made her turn round. It was Pierre himself, on his way to the Petit Manoir, he explained, as he caught up with her.

'You've brought us English weather,' he complained. 'We don't have these cold, miserable days as a rule.'

She smiled at the frown on his weatherbeaten face. 'Sorry! My father is worried about his precious vines. I think he and Jean walk up and down promising them that the frosts won't last!'

'Your father's a mad Englishman – what do you expect?'

'But you like him nevertheless, I think.'

'Yes, I like him,' Pierre agreed, 'and your uncle as well.'

Daisy frowned in her turn. 'We're grateful for that, but there are people here who don't like us, and it's hard to know what to do about them. We can't stand in the square with a placard round our necks saying that we love France as well as England.' She tried to make a joke of it but he heard the underlying note of anxiety in her voice.

'No need to worry, if that *is* what you're doing,' he insisted. 'Bonnard's nasty trick with the dog won't be repeated.'

'Perhaps not; all the same I have the unpleasant feeling that something else *will* happen. He's a man who expects to get what he wants; in his view my father and Uncle Will are stopping him.'

Pierre halted suddenly and, with his hands on her shoulders, turned her round to face him. 'They aren't fighting Bonnard alone, so there's no reason for *you* to get in a state. That's just being daft . . . but I somehow like you in spite of it!'

The clumsy, affectionate comfort made her smile. 'Well, you're not so bad yourself, Monsieur Cheval.'

He pondered the odd phrase, made even odder by being translated into French. 'Is that some sort of a compliment?'

'Almost our highest form of praise,' she answered gravely.

He didn't quite believe her, but a grin twitched his mouth nevertheless; then she was released and they walked on together.

At the house Pierre told his host that he'd come for a council of war, so they'd better have William Harcourt present and young Jean as well. 'I'd have brought Daniel but he's selling some of our livestock at Agen market.'

'The Curé happens to be here already,' Robert observed, 'though *he's* probably thinking more in terms of a peace-settlement.'

'It comes *after* the battle, not before,' Pierre pointed out, looking unhappy about having his usual style cramped by the presence of a man who would feel obliged to be law-abiding.

Madame Albert was asked to fetch Jean from the barn to join the others in William's study, and then surprised them by asking quietly if she also might stay. Generations of her family had lived in Foutances, she explained; she felt involved in the town's behaviour towards its newcomers. William smiled at her and, with his usual grace, led her to a comfortable chair.

'You know the situation,' he began when they were all settled. 'Michel Bonnard wants us out of the Petit Manoir. His plan is to make life so unpleasant for us that almost any offer will be acceptable. He can then keep the land, which he wants, and sell very profitably the house which he doesn't want. So far, apart from poisoning Jean's dog, he's relied on stirring up ill-feeling in Foutances – with some degree of success, I have to say.'

'Only among the people who were known collaborators,' Pierre said hotly, '. . . the fools who imagined that Vichy France would help to run Europe when Germany had won the war!'

'Not only collaborators,' the Curé corrected him gently. 'The Lambert family was never that, and there were other people like them who only wanted to survive, but suffered anyway.'

'There were also people *wrongly* branded as collaborators,' Madame Albert suddenly put in. 'I know why the butcher's wife listens to Monsieur Bonnard's slanders. She and I were children when our mothers were accused of sleeping with German soldiers, but we can't forget having to watch while their heads were shaved in the square. My mother was innocent, perhaps hers was too; but the committees running things at the end of the war only had time for revenge, not for justice.'

A little silence fell, and all over again Robert wondered how long it would take France to heal itself of the wounds the Occupation had inflicted. The evil was made worse by men like Michel Bonnard, ready to reopen the old scars for their own selfish purposes. It was Pierre Darroze who bravely put what he was thinking into words.

'We can't cancel out what happened thirty years ago. Terrible errors were made because terrible things had been done. Innocent people suffered while many collaborators escaped punishment and prospered; now they're very anxious for their wartime record *not* to be remembered. We live with these memories knowing that gradually they *will* fade. But Bonnard is deliberately keeping them alive. He is a bad man as well as a bad farmer. We must get rid of him.'

'But not by brute opposition,' Robert insisted. 'That strengthens people's attitudes; it doesn't weaken them.'

'Persuasion might change them, perhaps,' the Curé suggested. 'I had a visit from Marcel Lambert, which normally I would not mention to you, but now I will. *He* is not a bad man, my friends. He was unhappy and knew that his wife was also upset, about their discourtesy towards you – people whose acquaintance they had valued. But the past still overshadowed them,' the Curé's glance rested on Pierre for a moment, 'and as a result he felt he must still blame *you* for the death of a beloved brother. But I asked him to consider who it was that had actually shot Philippe – men like you, or the enemy you were fighting for the sake of France? I believe that he hadn't considered it in such simple terms before; now he is doing so.'

'The notaire is influential in Foutances,' William pointed out. 'So is the mayor, and he is already on our side. Between them they can undo most of the harm that Bonnard is doing.'

Pierre's large hands suddenly pounded the arms of his chair. 'Listen, my friends: it takes another Gascon to understand a man like this one. Bonnard tricked Gaston out of most of his land – lent him money on terms the poor fool didn't realise he could never meet. But Gaston foiled *him* in the end by hanging on to what Bonnard really wanted. He still wants it and thinks he can get the better of a couple of Englishmen unlikely to use his own dirty methods of fighting. After the Petit Manoir it will be the turn of the Ferme Darroze, because he wants yet more space for his bloody sunflowers and maize. But that isn't the sort of farming our land is meant for, and I'll shoot Bonnard before I let him take it away from me, or Daniel after me.'

Silent in a chair beside her father, Daisy suddenly got up and went to plant a kiss on Pierre's rough cheek.

'What was that for?' he muttered, confused by the gesture.

'For valour, past and present,' she answered, smiling at him. 'Monsieur le Curé's right – we have to reason people out of their prejudice against us. But a little extra ammunition would help. Can't we circulate something discreditable about Bonnard for a change, like the fact that he poisoned Nelson?'

'And that he's poisoning his land with chemicals,' Jean chipped in, surprised to find himself brave enough to say anything in front of these older men, but propelled into it by indignation. 'He's a profiteer, and not a true farmer at all.'

'He's any rotten thing we like to think, but we can't circulate rumours we can't prove,' Robert insisted. 'Still, it wouldn't hurt to look into the syndicate behind him – if it's fallen foul of the law somewhere else we should have a lever we *could* use.'

Pierre got up to go. 'Look all you want, but that sort of thing takes time. While you're doing it Bonnard will make another move, so watch your backs, my friends.'

The meeting broke up with his final words left hanging in the air but, taking note of Daisy's pale face when the visitors had gone, Robert smiled cheerfully at her.

'No need to look so troubled. The Cheval can't help thinking like the Resistance guerrilla he once was, but we aren't fighting an occupying army – only one tiresome man who's let "vaulting ambition o'er leap itself"!'

She nodded, accepting the offer of comfort, but her father knew that Bonnard was only a small part of the distress she tried to hide. He broached the rest of it after a moment's hesitation.

'I'm not trying to drive you away, love; it's the last thing I'd ever want to do. But wouldn't you be better off in London just now, getting back to work? I promise you that you can take Pierre's dire warning with a large pinch of salt.'

'I'll go soon,' she agreed, but she could have told him that it mattered very little where she was. Heartache didn't diminish with distance, according to some infallible mathematical law.

She was so careful now not to walk where she might bump into Daniel that it seemed the working of a Fate hell-bent on malice when they should coincide at the bank in Foutances the following morning. The day was cold but bright and the winter sunlight fell unsparingly on Daniel's face, making it look drawn and tired: the face of an unhappy man. But the unexpected sight of him at least answered a question in her mind. What she'd told her father was true: his parentage made no difference at all, either to the man he was or the way she felt about him, and the certainty produced in her a strange kind of contentment.

'You look half-frozen,' he said almost roughly. 'I suppose no one warned you that we occasionally get a hard winter. I'd better buy you a cup of coffee to warm you up.'

She didn't argue, understanding his intention: they were to re-establish neighbourly relations. That way there'd be no embarrassment whenever she came to visit her father. They went inside the café this time, and she found something to say that didn't concern themselves.

'I expect you heard about the meeting yesterday. We disappointed your great-uncle, I'm afraid; he wanted us to behave like the English of old and at least camp outside Bonnard's swanky villa chanting war-cries!'

'Strictly a fighter, my Uncle Pierre,' Daniel agreed, 'not a negotiator. I suspect him of finding peacetime life rather tame.' He paused while the waiter put coffee in front of them, then went on. 'Which brings us back to what we now know about the war.' His sombre expression caught at Daisy's heart, but she couldn't offer the comfort of her hand touching his, only whatever she could find to say to him.

'Don't blame anybody, please – certainly not your mother for what she felt obliged to do. Not even Jacqueline for the warning she thought I needed. I know that the truth doesn't change anything – it can't.'

'No, it can't,' Daniel agreed again, unsteadily. 'The Ferme Darroze will be mine when the time comes – Pierre's outright gift of his land, his house, and everything it contains. We've always understood that Jacqueline was included in that, the girl he brought up as his own. There was no difficulty about it. She seemed to want me, and I have always been very fond of her; in fact I once did make love to her. She isn't wanton, so from then on I accepted that she was mine. Then *you* came to the house next door, and my problems began. Now I know that I shall love you for as long as I live, but I shall pretend that loving can't hurt me. I'll ask Robert Ashton occasionally how you are, and smile when he tells me you're well and happy – so you must *be* happy, my love. The day might even come when I can see you walk towards me and not feel that my heart has suddenly stopped beating.'

She smeared away the tears that were trickling down her face and tried to smile at him. 'I'll promise to be happy if it helps.'

'You'll forget the odd French people you've met here,' Daniel insisted almost desperately. 'You'll certainly forget the one who turned out to be not properly French at all, because he had a drunken German pig for a father!'

The anguish in his face made her blind now to whoever else might see them and she stretched out her hands to him across the table. 'Your father could have been the Devil himself for all the rest of us care; you're the man you *are*, Daniel, loved by everyone who knows you, and we can't all be wrong.'

She fumbled in her pocket for a handkerchief to mop her cheeks and blow her nose – a prosaic little gesture that even made him smile. 'It's time I went home – back to London, I mean; but just for the moment I need to stay and see what happens here. I can't help feeling that Pierre Darroze understands the Bonnard mentality better than my father does. A man who can poison a beautiful, harmless dog is capable of anything.' She looked gravely at Daniel across the table. 'I'll have left before your wedding, but I shan't despair of happiness for the Ferme Darroze. Your mother's marriage achieved contentment in far worse circumstances; I think yours will too.' Then she suddenly stood up, courage exhausted for the moment. 'Don't come out with me – I'd rather just walk off by myself and hope we needn't meet again before I leave.'

Her hand touched his briefly, and then she was gone, with only a faint echo of the fragrance she wore to prove to him that she'd been there at all.

Eighteen

Daisy retrieved her bicycle, left outside the bank, and found some faint comfort in the fact that it hadn't been vandalised or run over. Even the little Union Jack flown from her handlebars – deliberate provocation, Robert said – was still intact.

She was about to climb on and pedal away when a quiet voice spoke behind her. When she turned it was the notaire's wife, smiling at her rather uncertainly. Was she, Madame Lambert suggested, by any chance free to lunch today with a small group of women friends, who met occasionally to air their views and complain that their menfolk had the running of Foutances!

Daisy managed to smile, wondering whether the effects of her meeting with Daniel were still visible. It wasn't the moment she'd have chosen for making another effort, but she accepted the invitation with what she hoped sounded like adequate pleasure and then cycled home. One of the morning's conversations at least could now be reported to her father.

She found him out in the barn, sawing timber for the new roof joists Jean was installing in the pigeon-house. When she announced that she was going out to lunch he smiled at her grim expression.

'You look as if you've been invited to an execution! Why go if it's as bad as that?'

'Giselle Lambert is making amends,' Daisy explained with an air of long-suffering resignation. 'I'm also to be shown that she and her friends are clever women who can talk about more intellectual things than Foutances gossip.'

Robert Ashton suddenly abandoned the saw and gave his full attention to her instead. 'I hope you don't really despise these ladies because, poor things, they're provincial and therefore not worth taking seriously?'

Her pale face coloured under the rebuke. 'Sorry – did I sound like a spoilt, big-city brat? I'm sure they're pleasant women, and I'll go along and smile and air my views with the best of them. But God help the first one who sneers at England or hints that you and Uncle Will shouldn't be here.'

'That's my girl,' her father said, now grinning at her. 'But my guess is that they'll be eating out of your fractious English hand, not trying to bite it!'

She smiled at last. 'I'll let you know when I get back.' But instead of walking away she still lingered there as if to enjoy the clean, sweet smell of the newly sawn wood.

'I've been too taken up with myself,' she said suddenly. 'What about you and Jeanne? After the little time you had together all those years ago she had to become someone else's wife and learn to love him. She's free again now, like you. Are you hoping that you can finally marry her?'

He couldn't help smiling at the question, so direct and typical of his daughter. 'I think Jeanne knows what I should like, but she's committed to the memory of Jacques Lescaut, quite as much as Daniel sees himself as committed to Jacqueline. So I suppose the answer to your question is that I have very little hope of marrying her.'

Daisy examined his face for a moment, resolved not to say that any woman who refused him as a husband must be half-way insane, however much she revered the memory of someone else. Instead, she heaved a long sigh. 'Our French romances haven't been a great success one way and another,' she pointed out sadly.

'I think we could safely say that they've been heartbreaking,' he agreed after a moment.

She leaned over to leave a little kiss on his cheek. 'I'd better go and make myself presentable; the town's ladies are sure to do better than trousers and a tired-looking sweater.'

When she'd driven off and Madame Albert had set out their own lunch on the table, Robert explained to William why she wasn't there. 'The Curé's little chat with Lambert is already having some effect it seems.'

William nodded, but so absent-mindedly that his attention was clearly elsewhere. 'You don't care whether our reputation gets reinstated or not,' Robert suggested with a faint smile. 'Quite right – why should it matter what the butcher and his friends think of us!'

William grinned apologetically. 'I *was* listening, but also thinking of the news I have to give you. The mail this morning brought an answer from my friends in Paris. They've been delving in the official records, probably illegally, and what they've found is interesting but also worrying.'

'Bonnard has a lurid past?' Robert suggested hopefully.

'No, but his father held a post in the Vichy Government and – wait for it! – was related to Pierre Laval. Not unnaturally, he decided to change his name to Bonnard after the war. Making a guess at our Bonnard's age, *he* must have been a schoolboy at the time.'

Robert was silent for a moment remembering the bloody aftermath of the war. The old Marshal had escaped the death-sentence, probably on the grounds of age, for betraying France; his Prime Minister, Pierre Laval, had not. 'The man *was* probably a traitor,' Robert commented slowly, 'but the manner of his execution was a disgrace – dragged out, already half-dead from his suicide attempt, to face a firing-squad. Is it some mad idea of revenge that is driving Michel Bonnard now, do you suppose?'

'I think so,' William agreed, looking for once very sober. 'I imagined that Pierre was getting paranoid about him, but now I can't help feeling that the Ferme Darroze *has* been Bonnard's objective all along; we're involved mainly because we just happen to be in the way, although Bonnard probably hates the English as well.'

'What happened to his father?'

'He died in prison before he could be brought to trial.'

Robert considered his next question. 'What happens next? We can't circulate this information, much as I'm sure Daisy would like us to.'

'I'm going to see the mayor this afternoon,' William replied. '*He* must know, in the strictest confidence, just in case serious trouble blows up.'

'It won't, I'm prepared to bet. Petty intimidation is one thing; serious trouble quite another because it would lead to the truth coming out – surely the *last* thing Bonnard must want.'

'Perhaps,' said William, sounding unconvinced. 'But I remember what Pierre said: it takes one Gascon to appreciate what another one is capable of. Still, we'll carry on in the calm English way that so irritates our dear firebrand at the Ferme!' Then William's face broke into a smile. 'I wonder how Daisy's getting on with the Foutances ladies. They little know that she'll be reorganising their lives for them in no time at all!'

But he missed her return, being already on his way to visit the mayor. Only Robert waited for her, hoping to be told that the lunch-party had gone smoothly. It was by no means certain; in her present frame of mind his daughter would meet rudeness with rudeness, and counter any provocation with a declaration of war.

'Well?' he asked after a glance at her tired face, 'or not well at all?'

'Not bad at least,' she admitted, then grinned at him. 'Rather pleasant in fact once we got over the initial stiffness. But the most interesting woman there – the wife of the head teacher – was the most hostile to begin with.'

'So naturally you asked her what *she* had against the English!'

Daisy nodded. 'She said that, stuck out on our safe little island, we couldn't understand what it meant to be part of continental Europe. We'd despised the French for their wartime armistice, not seeing that it was a beginning for them of something new: peaceful coexistence with Germany; a sign of what the future must hold in store.'

'She might have called it something else,' Robert suggested, 'their joint rule of Europe perhaps.'

'I called it that,' Daisy confessed, 'and she was honest enough to agree. The systems being set up in Brussels, she says, *are* to enable Germany and France together to rule Europe, without any interference from troublesome people like us! We avoided awkward subjects, you'll be glad to know. I didn't say what I thought of the Vichy Government, and she wasn't rude about you and Uncle Will helping the Resistance, so in the end we were getting on quite well.'

Robert smiled at her with great affection. 'Now I know why you look tired – you find it enough of a strain to guard your tongue in English; in French it must have been even worse!'

'Well, you *sound* tired,' she said, looking at him more closely. 'Where's Uncle Will, by the way?'

'Having one of his little chats with the mayor. Monsieur Martel is something of a bon viveur, and I suspect them of talking mostly about wine.'

She didn't, to his relief, pursue the subject of William's visit, and went away instead to change out of what she called her 'ladies who lunch' clothes.

That evening after supper, it was Robert who went out, dogged by a faint sense of unease he couldn't reason away and didn't wish to admit to. The night was fine, with a nearly full moon occasionally hidden by drifting banks of cloud. Memory suggested that it was the sort of night like long ago when he'd looked out from the cockpit of his Lysander, desperately searching the ground below for three small beams of light; the sort of night when men like Pierre Darroze had risked their lives to stand and wait for him. But now there was no engine-hum to hear, and nothing to be afraid of. The moonlit fields were peaceful, and he could return to the house ashamed of the edginess that had driven him outside.

The next day was serenely busy as usual. Daisy drove Madame Albert to Marciac, the only way to prove to her that its market was even better than the one in her home town. William emerged occasionally from writing in his study to inspect progress in the *pigeonnier*. Thanks to Jean Lecours' ability to turn his hand to almost any task, the once-derelict building was being turned into a charming annexe to the house – their bijou guest-wing, William amused himself by calling it.

Resting from their labours over mid-morning mugs of coffee, Robert and Jean talked at first of events mentioned in the day's news. Then Robert deliberately changed the subject by suggesting that it was Jean's future they should be considering. To his great dismay, the face of his fellow-worker was suddenly filled with aching regret.

'Forget I asked,' he said quickly. 'You'll be busy here for some time yet, and after that Monsieur Darroze might need you.'

'No, I shan't stay at the farm,' Jean said with quiet certainty. 'I shall harness my horse to the caravan and move on. That saddens me because I like it here . . . I like it very much; but I can't afford to dream dreams that won't come to anything.'

Robert offered all the comfort he could in the face of what had sounded like desolation. 'In our version of the Bible it's only the old men who dream dreams; the young men are required to see visions! Why shouldn't yours come true?'

'I think not, Monsieur, but I shall always remember the time I spent here.' Then he stood up to collect their empty mugs and the conversation was over.

For the rest of the day he was his usual self – a hard-working, pleasant companion; but Robert glanced at him from time to time, wondering what it was that could have caused him so much grief.

That evening the temptation to look round outside was firmly resisted. Instead, he stayed up to finish the book he was reading while the others went to bed. But before undressing he looked out of his window from sheer force of habit. With the moon now full, the sky was clear and scattered with stars so brilliant that another frost seemed likely. Then, as he turned away from the window, a different flash of light caught his eye, too low, surely, and too yellow to be a star; what's more, it had moved in a way no falling star ever dropped down the sky. He watched again and knew for certain what it was: someone carrying a lamp was outside on their hillside.

He crossed the passage and tapped gently on William's door; then as it opened, held a finger to his lips, warning him to make no noise. 'I think there's someone in the vineyard,' he murmured. 'I'm going out to have a look. You're to stay here, Will, please. But can you ring the farm without waking Daisy? We ought to warn Pierre that he might have trouble there.'

'I'll ring, then I'll get dressed. No heroics, please – if Bonnard's got a gang out there we must call the police.' But he was talking to himself; Robert was already half-way down the stairs.

He made for the back lobby where outdoor boots and coats were kept, and jumped when someone already there moved from shadow into a patch of moonlight. It was Daisy, zipping herself into a thick anorak.

'What the blazes are *you* doing?' he muttered, forgetting that everyone in the house was now awake and he could shout, not whisper.

'I saw something when I turned off my light; I thought I'd go and investigate.' Her mouth sketched a faint smile. 'Don't waste your breath – I'm coming with you.'

'I haven't got time to argue – come if you must, but keep quiet and do as you're told.'

She nodded and followed him outside. It was a cold and strangely beautiful world they walked into, a mixture of silver light and night-black shadow. Beyond the lawn, the vegetable garden and Robert's newly planted orchard, an archway cut in a wide yew hedge led them out on to the hillside. There were now four lanterns glowing, but only for a moment, then they were suddenly put out.

In the shadow of the hedge, Daisy whispered to her father, 'Why are they here?'

'To uproot our precious vines, I expect – then the frost will finish off the job of killing them.'

It was eerie and unpleasant, standing there. She thought suddenly of the men like Pierre and his friends, bent on sabotage against an occupying enemy – dangerous but necessary work. What *these* men were doing was simply the malevolent destruction of a neighbour's property. This was trespass and damage without any excuse at all.

Robert answered her next question before she put it into words. 'No, I can't stop four men by myself and in any case we need to catch them, not frighten them away. Hare back to William, tell him we need the police here fast.'

She turned at once, but he suddenly held her there. 'Too late, I think. The cavalry's arriving.' Daisy still saw nothing, but Robert with his sharper night vision had already moved away from her, keeping always in the shadow of the hedge. Then his dark shape coalesced with a larger patch of darkness – reinforcements coming from the direction of the Ferme Darroze. Straining her eyes, she thought she could make out four of them, equal odds now at least. A pitched battle wasn't quite her father's style, but she couldn't imagine the Cheval settling for anything less.

The huddle of figures broke up; two melted into the darkness and she lost sight of them, but her father and Pierre stepped into the brilliant moonlight, and the odd, ominous silence of the night was suddenly shattered.

The man who saw them first let out a warning shout, then threw down the tool in his hand and began to run down the hill towards the boundary with Bonnard's land. Daisy watched Pierre hurtle after him, while her father set off to head intruder number two away from taking the same escape route. The gap between them was too great, but at least the man was now coming towards *her*. Daisy stepped in front of him, heard him gasp, and put out her foot in the hope of tripping him up. He swerved sharply, shoved her to the ground, and rushed on. Winded, but on her feet again when Robert reached her, she pointed to a fight now going on fifty yards away in which two couples were embroiled; in one of them a man broke free and was promptly brought down again by a flying tackle. The other two struggled to and fro, but as steel flashed in the moonlight one of them sagged to the ground. The thud of running feet sounded on the frozen surface; then, as it faded, silence returned. The invasion was over.

Robert ran to that end of the field and found Daniel kneeling beside Jean Lecours. 'The swine must have hit him with a mattock – he's unconscious and his head is bleeding. I had to let the other one go.'

He sounded so angry and upset that Robert touched his shoulder by way of comfort. 'Of course you did; never mind, Pierre might have caught the one *he* was after.' Then, as Daisy struggled up to them, he spoke to her. 'Can you get back to the house, love? William must ring for an ambulance. Daniel and I will carry Jean down.'

She had blankets ready when they reached the kitchen with him. The wound on his head looked too ugly to touch, but she was wiping away the blood trickling down his face when the door opened and Pierre walked in. He seemed tired to the point of collapse, but the sight of their casualty brought him instantly beside Daisy.

'I know he looks awful,' she said quickly, 'but the ambulance is coming, and his pulse feels strong to me.'

Pierre's touch confirmed it, and then he listened to Daniel's brief account of the fight. 'It doesn't look like it now. But we *were* getting the better of them.'

Pierre's rare smile softened his face. 'At least you must have damaged them. I didn't even catch the bastard I was after. *Your* fault, partly,' he said to Robert. '. . . You will keep planting trees he could dodge behind! But the other reason is that I simply couldn't run fast enough.'

The admission was painful, and again Robert knew that comfort was needed. 'He was probably half your age, my friend; he's supposed to be able to run faster than you. But Bonnard chose fools to do his dirty work for him – without those needless lanterns we shouldn't have known they were there at all.'

'I've got the lanterns, and the tools,' Pierre said, cheering up a little. 'I went back and found them, just in case it occurred to Bonnard that *he* ought to get hold of them.' He looked up as a knock sounded at the door. William opened it and this time it was Annette who walked in, followed by her daughter.

'I was getting anxious after your telephone call,' she said briefly to William, '. . . thought you might need help.' But the one in need of help was suddenly Jacqueline, who had caught sight of Jean lying on the floor. With a little whimper of despair, she collapsed in the nearest chair, head slumped forward on her knees. While Annette bent over her, and William began pouring Armagnac into glasses, Daisy – still kneeling beside Jean – remembered Jacqueline's behaviour the day they'd met at his caravan. One more complication now seemed to be explained; she was going to marry Daniel, but there was no doubt that she was also deeply fond of Jean Lecours.

Annette allowed her daughter to recover and then spoke to the others as if she wasn't there. 'The child's overwrought,' she announced almost with irritation, as if it was somehow their fault. 'She's too emotional altogether at the moment, and this sort of upset doesn't help.'

It was Daniel who responded by going over to put an arm round Jacqueline's trembling shoulders. 'It's all right, *chérie*; Jean needs attention but he *isn't* going to die. When the ambulance comes I'll drop you and your mother off at the farm, and then follow it to the hospital. I promise I won't leave him alone.'

She nodded and managed a tremulous smile, while Daisy watched, with one thought overriding all the confusion in her mind: if living proof were needed of the power of upbringing over inherited genes, then it was in front of her now. Daniel *was* to all intents and purposes Jacques Lescaut's son – imbued with the same kindness and quiet strength that had made Jeanne's husband remarkable. There was immense comfort in the thought and, for herself, immense sadness as well.

Then another commotion outside heralded the arrival of the ambulance. To get Jean safely installed was the work of a minute or two. Then, as Pierre shepherded his wife and Jacqueline outside to where the farm jeep was parked, Daniel stopped beside Daisy, now standing white-faced by the door.

'Are *you* all right – not "overwrought and altogether emotional" as well?'

The question, asked so gently, made her want to burst into tears. She could only resist the temptation by answering almost without civility. 'I'm still in my right mind, I think. *You'd* better go; you're keeping Annette and Jacqueline waiting.'

He walked out without another word, and she told herself that the cause of her undoubted misery was simply the painful throbbing of her elbow, bruised when she'd landed on the ground.

There was one more duty that they left to William – a telephone call to report to the police the events of the night. He agreed with them that a visit before the morning would be pointless, and returned to the kitchen to find Daisy making coffee to offset the effects of the brandy. Pierre, looking deadly tired but far from sleepy, seemed in no hurry to go home; for the moment he just wanted the company of his friends, the true *copains* that they had now become.

'I had Daniel stay at the farm,' he explained tapping his beaky nose. '. . . I thought I could smell trouble coming. He saw the lanterns through a pair of binoculars; that's what made us set out.'

'The men were stupid to bring them,' Robert said, 'but I suppose they reckoned it was safe; most people here shutter their windows at nightfall. It's only odd creatures like us who leave them open.' He looked at William and gave a little nod; it was necessary now for Pierre to know what the records in Paris had revealed.

William described the contents of his letter, and his visit with it to the mayor. 'We agreed that no one else should know about it,' he finished up, 'and François Martel gave me his word. He's not a man to go back on it, but I *can't* believe tonight's attack was coincidental. Somehow Bonnard must have got wind of the letter.'

'I'll tell you how,' Pierre said grimly. 'The whey-faced secretary-creature the mayor hasn't yet been able to pension off has the run of his office. But she's the daughter of the man who ran the Milice in Auch during the war and turned in people like Marguerite and Alain to the Nazis. Ten years in prison afterwards wasn't nearly enough for the sod. She and I still hate each other. It would have been a pleasure for her to warn Bonnard about the letter. Incidentally, the man I was chasing *was* one of his – I saw him very clearly because he had to look round to see how close I was.'

At last, with a glance at Daisy, now nursing her throbbing arm, Pierre drained the cold dregs of his coffee and stood up. 'I must go home in case Daniel telephones. The lanterns and the tools are in your barn; with a bit of luck they'll be covered in fingerprints, but I'm sorry we didn't lay the enemy by the heels ourselves. I *am* getting old, it seems!'

Daisy leaned over to kiss his cheek. 'Not really . . . you'll always be the Cheval!' she said, and it summed up the view of all of them, Robert thought.

Nineteen

After falling at last into a heavy sleep it seemed much too soon to have to get up; but Daisy could sense that the house was astir and it was necessary to know what was going to happen next in their chequered life at the Petit Manoir.

Only Madame Albert was in the kitchen when she went downstairs, and it was obvious from the housekeeper's agitated air that rumours of the night's events had been brought in with her. Daisy no longer marvelled at the efficiency of the town's bush telegraph system; anyone nourishing the hope of secrecy in Foutances was doomed to die of disappointment.

'Poor young man,' Madame Albert began at once, '. . . such goings on, Mam'selle, when someone who does no harm is set on by villains.'

The story going the rounds was obviously incomplete, but Daisy decided to leave it as it was. Then she was stared at by the housekeeper, who at once reproved herself for running on when food and hot coffee were so badly needed. Daisy drank the coffee gratefully and was doing her best with the croissant put in front of her when her father walked in from outside.

'If you've been up for hours you should have woken me,' she said rather crossly.

He only smiled, shaking his head. 'I don't see why, but I'll bring you up to date now if you'll stop scowling at me! Daniel telephoned to say that Jean is all right – conscious again and head stitched – but they're keeping a check on him because the concussion knocked him out for a longish time. Pierre also telephoned: to offer help with replacing the vines that were pulled up, which may or may not survive. The last thing to report is that the police are here and William's conducting them round the premises.'

She stared at him as he reached for the coffee-pot, and poured out coffee for himself and refilled her cup. 'You sound very calm! Are you really calm . . . or angry . . . or just wondering whether we should go on trying to live here?'

He considered the questions before answering them. 'There's no point in getting agitated, though I'm afraid dear Madame Albert thinks we ought to be. I suppose I'm angry with Michel Bonnard, but I'd be more angry if I knew less about him. *He* thinks he has reason enough for what he's doing, and I can't help feeling rather sorry for him.'

'Which brings us to my last question,' she reminded him as he stopped talking. 'I know Uncle Will loves being here, and I think you do too now, even though it's not the place you would have chosen to come to. Pierre Darroze is a true friend at last, and you like Daniel very much. But it's horrible to be in such a state of war with our nearest neighbour, and shall we ever be anything else with Bonnard?'

'Probably not, I think,' Robert admitted. 'If William can't get the better of prejudice and entrenched distrust then I'm inclined to believe it can't be done.'

'So it means that Bonnard or we have to leave,' she persisted. 'That's what it comes down to.'

He nodded and stood up. 'Succinctly put, my love. But right now Will and I must go with the police to make a formal report. Don't stay here fretting yourself sick – do something useful, like getting on with your work!'

She agreed that it was sensible advice, and when they'd driven away even tried to follow it. But with no more than half a page written she was interrupted by the housekeeper, who announced that there was a visitor in the hall. It turned out to be Jeanne Lescaut, carrying a beautiful white azalea in an earthenware pot.

'A gift from my garden – quite tough, though it looks so fragile; you'll be able to plant it out,' she explained.

Daisy thanked her for it, saying that it would give them all great pleasure. 'I'm afraid my father and Uncle Will are at the gendarmerie at the moment – Daniel must have told you about last night's fracas.'

'It's the reason I'm here,' Jeanne confessed. 'Daniel came home for long enough to wash and shave before leaving for the farm again, but he was anxious about you – thought you'd got hurt in some way. I promised to come and enquire.'

Daisy's smile was rueful and sweet. 'It's kind of you both, but all I got was a bruised elbow from being pushed out of the way. It can't add up to much for someone with *your* sort of wartime adventures!'

She led her visitor to the main room of the house and, seeing it for the first time, Jeanne stared round appreciatively. 'Someone here – you, I expect – has excellent taste!'

'Well, the room itself was beautiful even before we put anything into it, but the nice discovery was that what we brought from our London house looked perfectly at home here. Uncle Will is the pianist, by the way,' Daisy said, pointing to a rosewood instrument that glowed in the sunlight pouring through one of the long windows. 'Unfortunately he refuses to play to an audience, so we have to listen by stealth.' She smiled at the idea but fidgeted – untypically, the woman watching her thought – with the bronze chrysanthemums that filled a copper jug.

'You look tired and strained,' Jeanne said with unexpected gentleness. 'It isn't to be wondered at, but if you're afraid that nothing's going to alter here I think you're being too pessimistic. God knows, we aren't easy people to persuade to change direction. That's true of all the French, but especially of us in this remote and backward corner, but things *are* changing nevertheless. The Anglais at the Petit Manoir have seriously undermined our idea that the English must be distrusted at all times! Foutances even discovers that it likes them, despite Bonnard's mischief-making.'

'It's a comfort, certainly, but we live here, not in Foutances,' Daisy had to point out, 'and we've failed spectacularly to convince Michel Bonnard that *he* likes us.'

'I don't know anyone that he likes, but having overreached himself very stupidly, he's about to discover that the town no longer likes him. The story of the poisoning of Jean's dog is known about, and the history of last night's events will be common knowledge before the day is out. It's enough to make even a stubborn Gascon change sides.'

Daisy found herself beginning to smile, hope returning in the company of this small, valiant and forthright woman whom she'd been foolish enough not to like at their first meeting. 'But the trouble's not just about us,' she remembered. 'The town has still remained divided within itself, my father says, after thirty years. Your uncle wanted the land we own here but he was deliberately baulked of getting it, and even the Curé must despair of teaching a resister and a collaborator to love each other.'

Jeanne's thin face was suddenly full of sparkling amusement. 'Even the Curé *needn't* despair! This morning I was greeted by three people who for a long time have managed never to notice me, and my final triumph was Madame Martinon, who crossed the street to ask if I would go and discuss with her the teaching of music in school!'

'I met her at lunch one day recently,' Daisy said. 'We agreed about almost nothing but still liked one another. I suppose that's encouraging too.' Then she smiled at her visitor. 'Will you stay to lunch? The session at the police-station will surely be over by then.'

She was disappointed to have the invitation firmly refused. New-found friendship and togetherness had their limits apparently. Foutances might now be learning to love them but Jeanne's intention to keep them at arm's length still hadn't been seriously undermined, whatever else had.

Left alone when she'd gone away, Daisy gave up the pretence of working, knowing that she must think about real people instead of the characters in her book. Were shared trust and affection still enough to marry on when Jacqueline could faint at the sight of Jean lying wounded on the floor? Had Daniel found her mother's explanation reasonable – that she was merely young and overwrought? Was anything but misery in store for all of them unless someone – Daisy unflinchingly saw that it might have to be her own role – was brave enough to sort the muddle out? On the whole she reckoned that she knew the answer to all those questions.

Madame Albert was clucking anxiously over her *tarte au saumon et épinards* by the time Robert's car was seen coming along the drive. She allowed them time to wash away the aroma of stale tobacco smoke and garlic picked up in the police inspector's office and then put lunch on the table. Daisy allowed her father and William a mouthful or two of tart before demanding to know what had happened.

'Pierre and Daniel have to give their report as well,' William replied, 'but all Bonnard's men have been questioned. The two older ones clearly weren't involved; the other two just as clearly were, helped by a couple of their friends. The damage to Jean, which could easily have killed him, was done by one of the friends; but faced with the charge themselves the men will hand over their names.'

'But it's Bonnard himself who's really to blame,' Daisy almost shouted. 'Don't the police understand that?'

'Not being fools, yes they do,' her father answered. 'The tools even come from his farm workshop – the old man admitted that – but Bonnard has so far said nothing, instructed by his lawyer, of course. Still, his men will expect him to help them, and if he doesn't, they'll drag him into it themselves.'

Daisy made a little grimace of distaste. 'It's all nasty, isn't it?' Then she glanced at her father. 'Do you still feel sorry for him?'

'Well, I still understand the compulsion he felt under,' Robert said quietly. 'The damned war has left these ulcers of hatred behind; another generation at least will be needed to get rid of them.'

'One nice thing happened this morning,' she said after a little pause. 'Jeanne Lescaut came, bringing a beautiful plant for the garden. Better still, she reckons that the ulcers you just spoke of may be subsiding. People like herself and Pierre are starting *not* to be ignored by those who didn't join them, and even the English are worming their way into the town's good opinion!'

'What more can we ask?' suggested her father politely.

'Oh, a lot more!' Daisy looked from him to William, who was happily contemplating the remains of the salmon tart. 'I've got a plan, as a matter of fact. You'll probably say it's pie-in-the-sky but you must promise to think about it at least.' They nodded, and she went on more slowly. 'I had a letter from Mum two days ago, enclosing a splendid cheque – a present from Arnold's rather indecently large estate. I was to enjoy it, she said, because that was what *he* would have wanted, and she still has masses left.'

'Your mother's right; good for her, and for Arnold,' Robert responded. 'So *how* will you enjoy it?'

'Well, I thought of buying some land, the rest of Gaston's land,' Daisy said in a rush, 'provided we can persuade or twist Bonnard's arm into parting with it. Then I'd ask Jean Lecours to manage it for me.'

A stunned silence fell, and she looked again from her father's face – expressionless now – to William's startled one. 'I don't hear any loud applause,' she said sadly. 'In fact, the hush is deafening; but I still think it's a beautiful plan.'

'You've thought *all* your plans were beautiful since you were five years old,' Robert pointed out. 'Mostly we've thought so too, but you have to be very careful when you start meddling in other people's lives.'

Thinking that his friend had sounded severe, William

offered the sweet voice of reason. 'Remember, my dear, that Bonnard wanted *more* land, not to dispose of what he'd already managed to secure.'

'I know, but perhaps he'll be lucky now not to finish up in prison. In any case he *can't* go on with his vendetta against us and Pierre Darroze. He might be thankful to sell and start again somewhere else if the town's people are turning against him.'

There were times, Robert reflected, and this was one of them, when his dearly loved daughter reminded him too much of her mother. Christine would have argued just so, convinced that no reasonable man could fail to see the rightness of what she asked for. But leaving Bonnard out of it altogether, there was another worrying aspect to Daisy's proposal. It was doubtful that she recognised it for what it was, and he could see that it would be his own unenviable task to point it out to her.

'Just assume for a moment that Bonnard agrees to sell,' Daisy pleaded. 'Wouldn't it be the best thing that could happen to Jean – a reasonable-sized farm to manage on his own? You've said yourself that he only needs a helping hand to get him started.'

'Of course, and he's excellent and worthy in every way. But he told me recently that his intention was to move on, rather than stay here and hanker for something he couldn't have; some*one* is nearer the truth, it's Pierre's seductive step-daughter that I suppose he has in mind.'

'Exactly!' Daisy agreed, smiling brilliantly at her father. 'And you must also admit that she was *boulversée* at the sight of Jean lying – dead, she thought – on our kitchen floor! Annette did her best to pretend that Jacqueline was no more than ordinarily upset, but the girl fainted, for Heaven's sake.'

'And from that you deduce that she's head over heels in love with *him* despite the fact that she's due to marry Daniel in a few weeks' time. My dear girl, this isn't a fairy-tale with the wicked step-mother – or mother in this case – forcing the heroine into a hateful marriage. Jacqueline gives not the slightest sign of being reluctant to become Daniel's wife, and why on earth should she? She'll be getting a delightful husband, and all that comes with him in due course – a large and prosperous farm, a comfortable home, and an undeniable standing in the district. My impression of Jacqueline is that she's very like her mother and that these things matter to her.' Robert stared at Daisy's pale face and spoke gently now. 'My love, you said yourself that Daniel would never renege on a promise. Don't you remember?'

She nodded, but said nothing, and he went on himself. 'Assume by all means that Bonnard is willing to sell, but consider also what you or we would do with Gaston's fields if Jean Lecours decides to leave rather than watch Jacqueline marry Daniel.'

There was a long silence in the room while Daisy confronted the truth she'd been offered, and Robert's heart ached for the sadness in her face. She was more honest and more intelligent than Christine had been; she would neither pretend nor misunderstand. At last she wiped a hand across her face and looked gravely at him.

'All right, it was a good idea that probably couldn't have been made to work; but at least I'll insist on one more thing: though far from wicked, Annette Darroze would be a difficult woman for a young girl to stand up to. She might reckon that a neat French arrangement would work well enough; but *you* could tell her the difference between that and true happiness in a marriage. Isn't that true?'

He didn't pretend either. 'Yes, it's true.'

Daisy nodded, accepting the admission. 'I should think our alarums and excursions are over now, wouldn't you? It ought to be safe enough to leave you, and my long-suffering editor must wonder if I've disappeared for good. I'll cheer her up by telephoning to say that I'm coming back to London.'

She managed a smile at the men watching her, and walked

away as if the conversation had concerned nothing more important than the way she spent her mother's gift. But Robert sat staring into space, and it was William who broke the silence.

'It *was* a nice idea,' he said sadly. '. . . A little short on practicality perhaps, but long on Daisy's usual brand of loving-kindness.' He waited for a comment, but none came. 'Would it hurt to sound Bonnard out with her idea? If Jean decides to hitch up horse and caravan, Pierre and Daniel might work the extra land themselves. *They'd* farm it properly again and we should lose a tiresome neighbour.'

'It's a very neat arrangement, except for one thing,' Robert at last pointed out. 'For the full beauty of Daisy's plan to work, Jean is needed to stay here and marry Jacqueline! Without that, Daniel isn't a free man.'

William turned it over in his mind and finally nodded his white head. 'Silly of me not to have understood,' he said quietly, 'but it *is* rather complicated. What do you imagine Daisy will do with her inheritance now?'

'Nothing simple. Being Daisy she'll find some other deserving cause that comes near to being impossible.' Then Robert abandoned the conversation by walking away, grateful that her opinion of his own failed marriage had at least been tactfully left alone.

Twenty

Jean was released from hospital two days later and allowed to return to the caravan, but not to go back to work. Daisy explained to Nelson, in temporary residence at the Petit Manoir, that it was time to go home, and set off with him across the fields. The caravan was empty but she met Pierre outside, who said the invalid was in the house, being treated like a hero instead of like a man fool enough to get hit on the head.

Daisy smiled at him. 'You sound so cross that I realise how delighted you are to have him home again!'

A grin transformed the grim expression on Pierre's face. He didn't know why it was, but the world always seemed a happier place when Daisy Ashton was anywhere around.

'Are you going in?' he asked. 'They're all there, even Daniel, who ought to be out in the barn mending a tractor for me.' He could have sworn she changed her mind while he was speaking.

'No, I won't stay, thank you. I only came to return Nelson. I've left him in the caravan wailing like a banshee – the poor fellow much prefers company to being on his own.'

'Silly damn dog,' said Pierre, glad to give the impression of a man whose only urgent ambition was to retire to a monastic cell. 'Still, he did lead Bonnard to make his first serious mistake. The man has no future here now, even though he's escaped facing charges. He should have been charged, of course; Robert and Jean were too soft on him.'

'I rather agree,' Daisy confessed, 'but my father says that

if we aren't magnanimous the evils of the war will never be forgotten. Uncle Will interprets things differently: he thinks we're being devious, not forgiving! Everyone in Foutances knows we aren't hounding Bonnard. If he can't stop hounding us, *they'll* find a way of persuading him to leave. I suppose it's quite a neat arrangement!'

'William's right – we aren't bad at guile ourselves, but we can't beat the English!' He said it now almost with pride, hostility long forgotten, and Daisy's answering smile was full of affection.

'You'll keep an eye on them for me, I hope, when I'm back in London. My flight leaves tomorrow.'

'Well, you'll have to come back for the wedding, girl. You can't miss that. It's going to be a fine affair Annette keeps telling me.'

With what she thought sounded like ghastly cheerfulness Daisy managed to reply. 'Not even a fine affair can tempt me back. I've spent too much time here already. You must wish Daniel and Jacqueline happy for me – there won't be time to see them before I leave.'

She kissed his cheek and turned away quite jauntily, she hoped, but Pierre watched her go, wondering why he should suddenly feel anxious about her. He wasn't thought to be an impressionable man, in fact his wife occasionally compared him to an insensitive ox; but even he could ask himself why a girl should smile so brightly at him when her eyes had suddenly filled with tears.

The following morning, when it was almost time to leave for the airport at Bordeaux, she waited with William while her father concluded some business on the telephone.

'I forgot something,' she said suddenly. 'When Jeanne Lescaut was here last we went into the drawing-room, and she noticed your piano. Why don't you ask her to come and play her violin with you? Wouldn't that be a pleasure for both of you?'

'For me more than for her, I dare say, but it's a nice idea.'

William was silent for a moment, thinking how to go on. 'I liked your other idea too, my dear. I know that it got rather heavily trodden on by Robert, but I learned years ago that good ideas often have a life of their own and spring up again long after they've been written off as dead.'

Daisy's smile thanked him for the comfort he was trying to offer, but she shook her head. 'I'm afraid life's extinct in that one, Uncle Will, and I did need to be told that I was overreaching myself. I'll shove the money in the bank for the time being, and forget about it.' Then it was *her* turn to hesitate. 'Don't forget to invite Jeanne, please. At the risk of meddling again, I want her to see how . . . how very *nice* she might find life here. You wouldn't mind, would you, if she did?'

He smiled at the suddenly anxious afterthought, and answered the question she hadn't put into words. 'I wouldn't mind at all; it wouldn't do for a curmudgeon, of course, but charmingly natured old bachelors like me rather favour having a woman in the house!'

He finished speaking just in time, as Robert came back to hurry her along. She kissed William goodbye, promised to come back for a summer holiday, and followed her father out to the car. He preferred his passengers not to talk and they said very little on the way to Bordeaux. At the airport she urged him not to wait, knowing that he planned to call on a sick friend for William.

Ill-feeling between them was out of the question but he *was* aware of an unfamiliar constraint, there since their disagreement about her proposal to buy what had been Gaston's land.

'I hurt you the other day,' he said abruptly. 'It was harsh to speak of meddling when you were suggesting something wonderfully generous for Jean.'

'I was suggesting something for myself as well,' she admitted honestly. 'You were rightly harsh about *that*. Shall you go to Daniel's wedding?'

'I expect so. Most of Foutances will also be there to prove that bygones can be bygones with the Darroze family.'

'So something good has come of it all,' Daisy said slowly. 'Hurrah for that at least.'

Then the expression on Robert's face made her shake her head – the small, firm gesture used since she was a child. 'You're not to look concerned about me. I'm not a Victorian maiden on the verge of a decline, and I doubt if the usual cause even then was disappointment in love.'

'Too-tight stay laces more likely?' Robert suggested gravely.

'Much more!' Then the gleam of amusement faded from her face. 'I shan't forget Daniel, or cease knowing that what I lost Jacqueline has got. But I shall manage well enough, and become a *very* celebrated lady novelist much given to airing my views on subjects I know nothing about!'

'And you won't stay away from us?'

'How could I when I love the Cheval so much! I'll see you in the summer, I promise.' Then she kissed his cheek and walked away, and he watched her until she was out of sight.

By the beginning of February the winter seemed to be over. The temperature still dropped quite sharply at night but they basked in the sun on the terrace at midday. Primroses and wild narcissus speckled the garden, and mimosa blossom scented the air.

The sight of the golden trees reminded Robert of a conversation with Daisy; almost a year ago at the Customs House he'd listened to her recommending that they should go and live in France. It had been the best idea she'd ever had. Gascony's benign climate suited William so much that he now looked a different man. They had a delightful new home, and a way of life that was very congenial. Even their troublesome neighbour's activities had been scotched, and Foutances had returned to being a pleasant place to visit.

It was probably much more than they deserved, Robert reflected, as he pruned roses one morning; in fact a beneficent deity had only let them down badly in the matter of Daisy's happiness. He asked nothing more now for himself – Jeanne Lescaut had made it clear that she was beyond his reach – but it seemed cruelly harsh that his own abortive love should be mirrored in Daisy's struggle to forget her son. Wasted love was the worst waste of all in a hatred-ridden world. He could do nothing to repair her broken contentment, but the matter they'd almost fallen out over kept troubling his mind. It was still there now, while he pretended that he was concentrating on the roses.

The task done, he put away his tools, noting that it wasn't quite warm enough yet to eat on the terrace; but it wouldn't be long before they could move outside. It was nearly lunch-time but, instead of being installed as usual in the dining-room, William was still in his study, hunched over some complicated sums.

'It looks as if you're working out how much your assets come to,' Robert suggested with a smile.

'I'm doing exactly that,' William agreed, frowning over the figure he'd arrived at.

'Then you'd better have a soothing glass of wine.' It was poured and given to him before Robert spoke again. 'Is there a problem I should know about?'

'No problem,' William said, laying down his pen. 'I was making sure I could offer to buy back Gaston's fields without landing myself in penury.'

The silence in the room unnerved him and he hurried on. 'Daisy's idea – you didn't think much of it, I remember, but I do.'

'Go on,' said Robert, not yet ready to admit to worrying at it himself.

'Well, it seems to me we're running out of time. The pigeon-house is nearly finished and soon now Jean will think he ought to hitch up his caravan. Perhaps he *has* made up his mind not to stay, but I'd like to offer him a worthwhile job and – with your agreement – the *pigeonnier* as a more comfortable home. He's survived hard times without bitterness, I'd like to see him prosper.'

'And if he refuses the offer?'

'Pierre and Daniel could work the extra fields, I'm sure.' William smiled at his friend. 'It's not such a quixotic idea! I *can* afford it unless I live another twenty-five years, which isn't very likely. And I'd like to see the Petit Manoir's farm back under its true ownership again.'

'All right, but it hinges on Bonnard himself. Is this wishful-thinking, or do you have grounds for believing that he'll sell?'

'Not exactly, but I bumped into Yves Deschamps the other day, and led the conversation round to the problems Bonnard might be facing. I reminded him – gently, I hope! – that we'd had a taste ourselves of being cold-shouldered by the community. It wouldn't be surprising, I suggested, if Michel wanted to distance himself from Foutances, perhaps even leave the neighbourhood altogether.'

'And Deschamps' ears pricked up, like Nelson's when he scents a rabbit?'

'There was a slight resemblance!' William said with a grin. 'So I dropped the smallest hint that I'd like to see Gaston's farm put together again. The good Deschamps was in a noticeable hurry to leave me after that.'

Robert refilled their glasses and carried them to the dining-room, where Madame Albert was calling that their soup was on the table. Sitting down again, he made his own confession. 'I've been thinking about those damned fields, too. I'd suggest that we shared the cost, but it was Daisy's idea. I think she ought to be in on it too if Bonnard agrees to sell.'

William clapped his hands with pleasure. 'Even better . . . quite perfect, in fact! How sure are you, by the way, that Jean Lecours won't stay?'

'I'm not sure at all, because he loves being here and he's too intelligent not to recognise a valuable offer if we can make it. But he's in thrall to Pierre's luscious step-daughter and he doesn't want to have to watch her marrying Daniel.'

'Poor fellow,' William said with feeling. 'Well, we shall have to wait and see.' He spooned croûtons into his soup and casually offered his next piece of news. 'Jeanne Lescaut is coming this evening, to see whether my piano-playing is good enough for her.'

'Someone else you happened to bump into?'

'Exactly! It comes of ambling through Foutances, as I frequently do.' William smiled guilelessly but his friend wasn't deceived.

'In Raymond Chandler's immortal phrase, you "have the candid, clear-eyed gaze of a second-hand car salesman", and I suspect a plot! But I've been waiting thirty years to hear Jeanne play. Am I allowed to listen outside the door?'

'Of course, dear boy. If she doesn't mind you can even come inside the room and watch as well.'

Robert smiled and abandoned the subject, refusing to say that he suspected his daughter's meddling fingers again. The irresistible force she represented was going to come up against an immovable object but this time, at least, her motives had been entirely unselfish.

He tried to await Jeanne's visit with the calmness required of a middle-aged, phlegmatic Anglais. In the event the evening was something they all enjoyed. At William's insistence she played for them some unaccompanied Bach – so beautifully that Robert found himself envying the children she taught – and then she and William tackled a lovely Fauré sonata for piano and violin. They needed more time and more practice together, but their shared pleasure was obvious already. Robert took no part other than to watch and listen, but he was content to know that two people he loved should be so richly enjoying themselves.

Jeanne was on the point of going home when she finally

turned her attention to him for a moment. 'No more trouble with your neighbour, I gather.'

'No, and I expect you also know Pierre's opinion that we've been too lenient with him!'

Jeanne's eyes sparkled with the sudden amusement he remembered. 'I wonder! The result of your leniency is that Foutances is *very* pleased with you, and there are rumours of Bonnard having been seen in the company of Yves Deschamps! We suspect that something is in the wind.'

'Who knows?' Robert suggested hopefully. Then his charming smile appeared. 'Will you please come again if I promise to understand that it's only for the music?'

'*Not* just for the music,' she corrected him quietly. 'I'd be a fool not to enjoy everything I'm offered here.'

He helped her on with her coat, and found himself wanting to button it for her as he would have done for a child. But she was a woman, not a child, and all he could allow himself was to smooth the coat's ruffled collar.

'How's Daisy?' she suddenly asked.

'Working very hard, but saying very little. I know a book is going well when she refuses to talk about it.'

Jeanne's dark eyes met his and he knew she shared his sadness about a girl she feared was lonely. It would have been a 'consummation devoutly to be wished', she seemed to be admitting, if Daniel could have freely loved his daughter. But she said nothing more and, with a light farewell kiss on his cheek, waited for him to open the door.

Twenty-One

The pigeon-house was unfurnished but otherwise ready for inspection, its beautiful brickwork cleaned and repointed, and the high, raftered space inside now made into two pleasant rooms. A kitchen and bathroom added on at the back completed the accommodation without spoiling its traditional appearance. Pierre and Annette, invited to admire the renovation, admitted that even dyed-in-the-wool Gascons like themselves could see no harm in transforming a derelict building into something so elegantly useful.

Pressed to say what would be done with it, William became vague – extra lodging for summer guests, he rather thought, since so many of their friends found the location of the Petit Manoir irresistible. He urgently required – and explained this to the Almighty he reported to each evening – to hear something from Yves Deschamps, but what he gratefully received the morning after the Darrozes' visit was a letter from Bonnard himself, offering to sell what had been the remainder of Gaston's land.

'Whom do we consult to know if the price is fair?' William asked.

'The notaire,' Robert answered after a moment's thought. 'He must have been involved in every land transaction around here since the war, and I'm sure his staff are discreet – unlike the vindictive lady in the mayor's office.'

'At least she's no longer there. Martel managed to get rid of her at last, which must have done a great deal for happy working relations at the Mairie!'

By the end of the day events were moving quickly. Marcel Lambert agreed that the asking price was reasonable, and their letter accepting the offer was immediately sent. Robert reported over the telephone to Daisy that evening and offered her a third-share in what was being bought. She agreed at once, without reminding him that it had been her idea, which showed, he said to her solemnly, a degree of self-restraint bordering on the heroic. Nor did she ask what had made him change his mind, or how the farm was to be managed, and he was grateful for that as well. Anxious to reciprocate such generosity, he told her about Jeanne's evening visit, which was soon to be repeated. Daisy's pleasure at the news confirmed what he thought he knew – she *had* had another idea, this time about what might help an ageing, laggard suitor!

Early next morning he set out to find Jean Lecours. Now entirely recovered, the young man was polishing his horse's harness.

'Getting ready to go?' Robert enquired casually.

For once Jean's usual courtesy was a little lacking. He answered without even looking up from his task. 'Yes, Monsieur. There's nothing left to do here. I shall go north – there'll be work in the vineyards there.'

'Well, first put down that rag, please, and listen to me.'

Half an hour later Robert walked home to report failure. 'Our young man was very grateful, rather overwhelmed in fact, but I couldn't make him change his mind. He's going to head for Cahors.'

'Sensible of him,' said William, momentarily distracted from the problem in hand. '. . . Very good vineyards up there.' Then he caught himself up and frowned. 'What a pity, though. He's too good for us to afford to lose, and *he* shouldn't be losing us.'

'I was to say his goodbyes – I think he was afraid of breaking down. He promised to keep in touch, and let us know where he ends up.'

William nodded, but hadn't begun to ask what they should do next, when Daniel arrived with the vegetables and eggs that Annette normally delivered. She was afflicted with a severe 'gripe', he explained, and keeping to her bed, and the Darroze household was further upset by the sudden departure of Jean Lecours.

'He's gone very abruptly,' Daniel said with regret, 'but you mustn't be offended by that. He was very upset at leaving, very emotional in fact.'

Robert nodded, hesitating over what to say next. 'I knew he was getting ready to go; I saw him early this morning. Now I need to talk to you and Pierre, if you'll come over later in the day when you've both finished working.'

Daniel looked a little surprised, but didn't ask why a talk was necessary. It was typical of the quiet, self-disciplined man he was, Robert reflected. There was something else to remember, too: if Jacqueline hadn't been in the way, Daniel Lescaut might have become his son-in-law. It was hard to credit an unknown, brutal father with any virtues at all, but he might have handed on something worth having – Germanic courage and determination perhaps. Otherwise, except for those unexpectedly blue eyes, he was Jeanne's son, and his sudden, sweet smile was hers, too.

'We'll see you this evening,' Daniel said, wondering what had caused him to be stared at. Robert agreed, and watched him walk away.

The morning was over when Daniel got back to the farm with his deliveries completed. Annette, still in dressing-gown and bedroom slippers, was sitting at the kitchen-table – white-faced, and held rigid by some attack of shock or anger.

He hurried across the room, alarmed by behaviour that was untypical. She was a strong, unemotional woman as a rule, not given to showing any kind of weakness.

'Annette, what's the matter?' he asked quickly. 'Pierre said you were staying in your room.'

'I *was*; I've had a busy morning instead,' she said bitterly. 'The Museum at Cassaigne rang to ask why Jacqueline wasn't at work; I told them she'd left home as usual. Then I rang the police and hospitals – no accidents reported. That was a formality. I'm quite sure I *know* what she's done – run off with Jean Lecours, the nice young man my husband thought so well of!'

'How can you know?' Daniel asked hoarsely. 'She could have been taken ill, had a puncture or a breakdown . . .'

He got no further before Annette's hand banged the table. 'I tell you she's *gone*, Daniel – bewitched by an itinerant odd-job man with a nice smile and a pretty little house on wheels.'

If only it were true! Daniel began to see in front of him a faint glimmer of hope almost too wonderful to believe in; he wouldn't believe in it yet – it was too precious and too perilous. 'You're thinking of the night Jean was hurt,' he said, forcing himself to speak calmly. 'Jacqueline was naturally upset, but that doesn't mean she wants to live with him for ever.'

'My stupid little daughter isn't thinking about "for ever",' Annette pointed out fiercely. 'It's *now* that counts, and for just as long as she likes the romantic idea of life in a caravan with a useless, soft creature like Jean Lecours – with not a penny to his name and no job to call his own. That isn't what I've planned for all these years.' It sounded even to her own ears something that could have been better said, and a faint flush of embarrassment touched her cheeks. 'You know what I mean, Daniel . . . I could be sure *you*'d take care of her . . . keep her safe for me.'

He nodded, afraid that if he looked at her she'd see that his mouth kept wanting to smile. Hope's glimmer was strengthening now into a steady flame, but he must keep it hidden, and try to feel sorry for a woman who had done the best she could for her daughter.

'You aren't right about Jean,' he said quietly. 'He's gentle but not soft. If Jacqueline is with him, he'll take care of her. There isn't any doubt about that.'

Annette swallowed a furious denial, remembering that Daniel had made a friend of Jean Lecours, and that *he* had more right than she did to feel angry and betrayed. 'I'm sorry,' she said belatedly. '. . . Jacqueline has treated you very badly, and let us all down. You'd better find Pierre and tell him; all I'm fit for is to drag myself back to bed.'

About to say that he would at least check again with the police, Daniel's heart suddenly faltered, then stumbled on unevenly. His eyes were now fixed on what he could see from the kitchen window – a gaily coloured caravan being pulled into the yard by an unmistakable piebald horse. Hope had lied after all. Jacqueline, sitting beside Jean Lecours, was being restored to the Ferme Darroze and to the man she was supposed to marry.

Daniel wiped a hand across his face, then turned to look at Annette. 'You'd better stay and greet your daughter before you return to bed. She's outside – the caravan is back.'

Speechless now as well as stony-faced, Annette simply waited for the kitchen door to open. When it did, Jean came in first, as if to protect Jacqueline from some expected attack. But it was she who spoke when it seemed to Daniel that the silence had become unbearable.

'I'm sorry I went when you were unwell, Maman, but I couldn't let Jean leave without me.'

'Then why are you back?' Annette asked harshly.

Jacqueline's eyes filled with tears but she answered for herself, not letting Jean speak for her. 'I wanted to stay with him for always; I thought he'd keep me with him. But when he saw me hidden in the back he turned round and brought me home.'

Annette's sunken eyes blazed at her daughter. 'He didn't want you after all, you mean. Do you suppose that your fiancé still wants you either?'

Jacqueline looked at Daniel, as if only just aware that he

was there. 'I'm sorry,' she whispered. 'You were kind to me, Daniel, but you didn't love me, did you? I thought you wouldn't really mind if I went.'

Before he could force his tongue to say anything at all, Jean Lecours entered the conversation, talking directly to Annette. 'You're wrong, Madame Darroze. Of course I want Jacqueline – I intend to love her for the rest of my life. But I couldn't allow what she was prepared for; we must be properly married, with your blessing. *Then* we shall live together.'

'In your painted box outside, no doubt,' Annette said bitterly. 'What will you live on when you can't get work?'

'I had the offer this morning of a job and a house at the Petit Manoir. I refused them, not able to watch Jacqueline living here married to Daniel. I believe that Monsieur Ashton will let me accept now if I say that things have changed.'

It was at this moment that the door burst open and Pierre Darroze walked in.

'First the caravan goes, now it's back! Will someone kindly tell me what's going on?' he demanded. His glance fell on his wife's white face, Jacqueline's tear-stained one, and then on Daniel, now standing beside Jean Lecours. 'No, don't bother – I think I can guess,' he suggested with ferocious quietness.

'No, you can't!' It was Daniel speaking now, with an authority that even the Cheval had to recognise. 'Jacqueline and I made a mistake – or, rather, we fell into the habit of thinking we should be man and wife. The truth is that she and Jean love each other – she enough to try to leave with him this morning, he enough to bring her back for your and Annette's blessing. You must let them be happy together, they deserve it.' Then he smiled at Jean, kissed Jacqueline's wet cheek, and walked out.

In the silence that followed, the others left behind stared at Pierre. He was the head of the household, he must speak first; and they waited for the expected outburst. But he walked across the room and touched Annette's cheek with a rare and gentle gesture.

'You were sick; now you've been upset as well, by this troublesome girl of yours, and a lad I thought I could trust. It's my fault for letting him stay here.'

'Of course it is, but he must go on staying now,' Annette said despairingly. 'We've lost Daniel as a son-in-law, but Jean wants to marry her.' She buried her face in her hands, and Pierre turned to Jacqueline.

'Help your mother to bed, girl. You can come back in here when I invite you to, not before.'

Jacqueline crossed the room and hesitated in front of her mother. 'I'll help if you'll let me . . . I want to, please.'

Annette slowly nodded, then allowed herself to be lifted up, and the two of them went out of the room.

While Pierre interrogated Jean Lecours, another unexpected conversation was taking place at the Petit Manoir. Robert was on his way back from inspecting the new young shoots on his precious vines when a vaguely familiar Land Rover bumped its way along the drive. He hadn't given any thought to the possibility of Bonnard coming in person to conclude their deal; now he realised that he should have done. After all, the man had come once before with negotiation in mind.

It was hard, nevertheless, to know how to deal with someone who'd sent underlings to do his dirty work, and then left them to face the consequences. A very brief '*Bonjour*' seemed to suffice as a beginning, and he then waited for Bonnard to find something to say.

'No doubt you expect me to start by apologising,' the man said at once. 'It wasn't part of my plan for the young man to get hurt – the fool my people used lost his head.'

'I think we realised that,' Robert agreed. Then, with a glance at Bonnard's strained face, he admitted something else that they had realised. 'We also understand why our arrival here and our friendship with a man you had a grudge against seemed worth punishing us for if you could. The war is a long time a-dying here, is it not?'

Bonnard nodded. 'Be thankful your own country didn't have to make a choice. We French brought Pétain back to power and, with him, Pierre Laval. We reckoned the old Marshal was a hero all over again for sparing us another dreadful war. Four years later, with Germany defeated, he and Pierre were denounced as traitors – breathtaking ingratitude, wouldn't you say?'

It was Robert's turn to nod. 'Perhaps, although you're ignoring quite a lot of other things that they encouraged to happen during those four years. But I agree with you that the end of two men who believed they'd served France well was terrible. I disagree that my own country didn't have a choice: it could have offered to capitulate; it chose not to. To that extent, perhaps, you can blame us for what happened afterwards and think you have cause to hate the English.'

Bonnard's mouth twisted in a faint, unamused smile. 'I *can't* quite do that, unfortunately. I have to acknowledge instead that you didn't share what you learned about me with the rest of Foutances; but it comes hard on a Frenchman to feel grateful, especially to an Anglo-Saxon! It's not the way we're made.'

Robert's answering smile *was* suddenly amused. 'I know,' he agreed sympathetically. 'What are you going to do now, apart from sell us back Gaston's fields?'

'Move altogether, I think,' Bonnard answered with a shrug. 'I've had enough of farming – it's a mug's game already, and will become more so. You may regret what you're doing.'

'We have very little to do with it.' Robert unblushingly bent the truth a little. 'It's my daughter who likes the idea of what she calls "land-owning" in France – probably because we didn't even possess a garden in London!'

Bonnard stared at him, then nodded. 'It's true what people say about the English – they *are* mad. But mad or not, the land is yours now. My lawyer will tie up all the details with Lambert tomorrow.'

About to climb into the Land Rover again, he was halted by the sight of Robert holding out his hand. After a moment's hesitation, with a tinge of colour in his face, he extended his own, smiled a wry smile, and drove away.

Robert walked back to the house, considering the unexpected thought that Michel Bonnard might have been a pleasant man if it hadn't been for a war and its terrible aftermath.

Twenty-Two

The first visitor the next morning was Pierre, trotting across the fields. Astride the mare he could look around and contemplate the state of his neighbour's meadows. Daisy would have guessed that he was feeling at peace with the world; hating cars, he never drove one just for pleasure. The morning was fine after overnight rain, and the mare's hooves threw up little prisms of light from the wet blades of grass. Pierre was content to accept that the whole of France was beautiful as nowhere else in the world was, but this corner of it – his corner – was the best that it could offer.

Robert was outside, raking gravel, when he arrived. Pierre knew his friend's age – seventeen years less than his own. That made Robert Ashton fifty-six now, but he was lean and fit and even his face, damn him, was still handsome!

'My mare comes here hoping to find Daisy,' Pierre pointed out, dismounting. 'You don't bring her sugar lumps.'

'I'll find some. Take a seat and I'll even bring you coffee as well.'

Pierre chose instead to wander about, comparing what he saw with the unkempt, disheartened place it had been twelve months before. His friends had spent money, of course, but they'd spent it with good sense – something he knew about – and with good taste that he could at least recognise. They'd even worked hard as well. He could find nothing to complain about by the time William Harcourt came out, smiling to find him there.

'Robert and the coffee are on the way,' William reported,

'and you and I shall sit and wait for them. What a lovely life this is!'

'You've made it so,' Pierre said unexpectedly. 'You've done a good job on the mess Gaston left behind.'

'A real compliment, I think – you don't deal in false ones.' William's smile thanked the visitor. 'The workmen, Daisy and I can take most of the credit for the house. Out here it's Robert who's done all the hard work. And now here he comes with the coffee.'

With a mug looking lost in his huge hands, Pierre stared at it considering what he'd come to say. 'Daniel mentioned that you had something to talk about, but we didn't come over last night.'

'I didn't expect you,' Robert said calmly. 'Daniel reported that Annette was unwell. How is she now?'

'Getting better; but other things happened yesterday, and it was Daniel's guess they might change what you'd been going to say.' He saw Robert about to interrupt, and shook his head. 'Let me talk first.' In a few graphic words he described the previous day's scene that he'd plunged into in the farmhouse kitchen. 'I was to blame – Annette still thinks so – for encouraging the boy to stay. But the damage is done now; all we can do is let Jacqueline marry *him*, instead of my great-nephew.'

'Is it so very bad?' Robert asked quietly. 'I wouldn't object to Jean Lecours as a son-in-law.'

Pierre chewed on this for a moment but finally acknowledged its truth. 'I don't really object either, seeing that you seem willing to give him the start he needs; if you're still willing, that is.'

'Of course we are,' William put in almost impatiently. 'We offered him the pigeon-house to live in, too.'

Pierre's mouth relaxed into a reluctant grin. 'I'm afraid he'll find that his bride insists on the caravan, at least until the winter comes! It serves him right; according to Annette, that's what attracted the silly child in the first place.' He paused, aware that for once he must struggle to go on putting thoughts into words. 'It always looked the perfect arrangement, Daniel marrying my step-daughter; even they seemed to think so, although there were times when I wondered if we'd made it too clear to Daniel what we wanted of him. Then Jean Lecours came along, twenty-two to Jacqueline's nineteen, instead of Daniel's thirty-two; a boy still, content to laugh and play with her, and strum his guitar. Daniel's a different sort of companion altogether; even I can see that.'

Robert remembered Jeanne's son whenever he was with Daisy – no lack of laughter then, and the unmistakable glow of awareness and contentment that had shone between them. 'I think we should applaud Jacqueline's courage in running away,' he said finally. 'It might turn out to have saved a lot of unhappiness in the end.' Then he smiled at Pierre. 'I'm afraid it means that we don't offer you Gaston's farm after all – it will have to be Jean's job now!'

'He'll work hard for you,' Pierre commented, but Daniel and I'll keep an eye on him. What's Bonnard going to do with the rest of his land?'

'I'm not sure, but he spoke of perhaps getting out of farming altogether.'

'Let's hope he does – I'm sick of his bloody sunflowers staring at me. We might get someone there who understands what real farming is.' Pierre smiled at the thought, and stood up to leave. 'Life's been quite exciting since you English arrived – it seems strange to remember that I didn't reckon I wanted you here!'

'Spoken so handsomely,' Robert observed, 'that I'll admit I was unhappy about us moving into the Petit Manoir. Fortunately for all concerned, William and my daughter knew better. Buying the farm was Daisy's idea too – she's having a share in it.'

'Good, it means she'll have to come and see us occasionally. Now I must go, my friends. *Au revoir!*'

* * *

Annette's 'fine affair' became, instead, her daughter's quietly celebrated wedding to Jean, attended by few people other than her family and the household at the Petit Manoir. Looking at Annette's resigned expression, Robert felt sorry for her; she was a tough, ambitious woman whose priorities didn't include the gentler aspects of life. But she'd tried to make for Jacqueline the choice she'd have made for herself, and even now couldn't properly understand why it had been rejected.

After the ceremony in Foutances they were invited to a lavish wedding lunch at the farm: salade quercynoise, salmon in champagne, and a perfect filet de boeuf in Périgueux sauce. In this, at least, Annette had been determined to show them the best that she could do.

William munched happily, deep in conversation with Jeanne between mouthfuls. Robert ventured, after a glance at his own neighbour at the table, to ask how *he* felt about what had happened. Daniel looked across at Jacqueline and Jean, eating the delicious food put in front of them but probably incapable of noticing what they ate.

'They're happy beyond words,' he said simply. 'How can I be anything but pleased for them?' Then his mouth twitched in a rueful grin. 'I'm not sure whether the female population of Foutances despises or feels sorry for me! Whichever it is, I'll be glad when they get over the nine-day wonder of it all and find something else to talk about.'

Robert thought it more likely that the town's unattached ladies were even now eyeing one another and weighing up the competition, but he was reckoning that it might be tasteless to say so when Daniel asked a sudden question.

'Do you keep Daisy up to date with all our goings-on?'

'Of course – she feels involved in them.' Then out of the kindness of his heart, Robert also answered the question Daniel hadn't steeled himself to ask. 'I hoped she'd be here today, not wait to come until the summer. She's too busy, she said. There's a moment in the writing of a book when an author *has* to bash on, apparently, regardless of everything else.'

Daniel borrowed Robert's words. 'Of course! Why should she interrupt her London life for us?' Then, as if he'd lost interest in the subject, he looked across the table. 'The musical soirées seem to be a great success. My mother's the hardest person in the world to please but she reckons that William is a natural musician.'

'A public performance is even in the offing, I gather!' Robert answered, obedient to the change of tack. 'My old friend can't help feeling it's late in the day to start a new career, but nothing that's happened to us here has given him more pleasure.' He watched Jeanne himself as he spoke, wondering if he would ever tire of noting the expressions that constantly changed her face. Probably not; perhaps he could make a new career of it, like William's music.

When luncheon was over bride and groom set off for a brief honeymoon in Jean's caravan. Nelson went to stay at the Petit Manoir, like Pierre's mare disappointed when he got there, Robert suspected, to find Daisy missing. Still, Madame Albert's biscuits *were* waiting for him and so were the rabbits, ready to be chased in fields normally out of bounds to him alongside the river.

By the time Jacqueline and Jean returned to begin their married life the transfer of Gaston's land back to the Petit Manoir had been completed, and the question of how it should be used had now to be decided. Too shy to put forward a suggestion himself, Jean asked Pierre to do it for him: would they consider the breeding of horses?

'Not farming as such,' Pierre pointed out before Robert could, 'but it still strikes me as a good idea; the land is suitable, and Jean Lecours loves and understands horses. I think he'd make a success of it.'

William applauded at once, enchanted with the picture leaping to his mind of beautiful, long-tailed creatures grazing in the meadows. More slowly, Robert agreed as well. That evening he reported to Daisy that the Petit Manoir stud-farm would be in operation as soon as Jean had converted the barn into stabling for horses. Replacing the telephone when the conversation ended, he was still smiling.

'If nothing else brings Daisy back, the thought of the stud-farm will. She'll never be able to resist the horses!' he explained happily to William.

But in the end she returned before the first horse had arrived. It was William's concert with Jeanne that she decided she couldn't miss, especially when it coincided with her father's birthday. She said nothing about coming, just made her plans, flew to Toulouse, and hired a self-drive car there. Well-meant surprises didn't always work, she recollected on the drive home, and the road to hell was said to be paved with good intentions; but she was certain of being loved and didn't really doubt her welcome.

The countryside was bathed in late-afternoon sunshine as she puttered along the drive. She'd missed the mimosas, but the orchard was full of blossom, and the vines that climbed the hillside behind the house were now a bright, singing green. It all looked beautiful, and she'd missed it every day she'd been away.

It also seemed very quiet when she cut the car engine and got out; if no one was at home it would be a little anti-climax that she deserved for coming unannounced. Then, even as she thought it, her father came round the side of the house. He stood rooted to the spot for a moment, and she was half-tempted to burst into tears at the sight of him.

'If you're not pleased to see me I'll go and call on my friend, the Cheval,' she suggested unsteadily.

Then he opened his arms and she ran into them, just as she'd done as a child. 'You're thin . . . too thin, and too pale,' he said holding her at arm's length to stare at her. 'But I'm so *glad* to see you, my love. I can't tell you how much you've been missed.'

She was smiling now, though rather misty-eyed. 'I burned some midnight oil and got my manuscript finished. I think it's all right, but don't ask! I wanted to be here for your birthday, and I *couldn't* miss Uncle Will's musical début; I seem to have missed too many other things as it is.'

'He's in Foutances practising with Jeanne at the moment. Go and see what Jean's doing in the barn, while I warn Madame Albert you're here. I expect this evening's ordinary menu will be instantly torn up and we shall now dine like kings on *foie gras* and her *confit de canard*!'

There was more rejoicing when William returned, although he modestly suggested that his own performance, unlike Jeanne's, would scarcely merit a journey of five hundred miles. 'Still, you'll increase the audience by one, Daisy, love, and at least *you'll* be lenient if I hit a wrong note!'

She promised that she would, and then asked to be told about their new venture, and about Jean's wedding. The state of her father's friendship with Jeanne she didn't ask about; she was prepared to wait and see that for herself.

The next morning she walked across the fields to the Ferme Darroze. Pierre, in the middle of moving cattle, shouted to her to stay where she was and prevent them straying into the wrong field. With the gates shut, and his beautiful Blondes safely settled, he advanced to catch her in a warm hug.

'You should always be here when I need you, Daisy, but I shall have a bone to pick with your father. He didn't say you were coming.'

'He didn't know – I couldn't stay away any longer! I'll call and say hello to Annette, but I've really come with a small wedding present for Jacqueline.'

'You'll find her in the caravan; she doesn't work at the Museum on Saturdays.'

From the tone of his voice Daisy deduced that the wedding had now been accepted as a *fait accompli* that might turn out well after all. But she decided to leave the thorny subject alone and asked instead if he was going to attend the evening's concert.

'With my niece and my friend William as the star performers, I shall certainly be there,' Pierre said with dignity. 'I'm to be dressed up for the occasion, apparently. I mention it in case you have a problem recognising me.'

She grinned and pointed out that sheer size alone would make him hard to miss, got a friendly whack for the impertinence, and went to call briefly at the farmhouse. At the caravan a few minutes later she found Jacqueline perched on a ladder outside, polishing windows. Not entirely sure of a welcome, Daisy smiled in her usual friendly fashion, and Jacqueline descended to ground level.

'Are you coming in for coffee?' Madame Lecours asked unexpectedly. 'It won't take a minute to make.'

Daisy was led up the little staircase to the front door and into the caravan. The space inside might be small, but it was skilfully made use of, and Jean's home clearly had a proud and loving mistress. Looking round while Jacqueline made coffee, Daisy was able to say sincerely that she felt rather envious.

There was a slight pause while the conversation faltered, and she thought it the moment to produce the present she'd brought – the small figure of a horse, standing on a wooden base; beautifully carved, the animal had ears pricked and head slightly turned, as if listening to a sound that it alone could hear. Daisy had fallen in love with it herself and in truth was parting with it rather sadly.

'I knew it had to be something small,' she explained '. . . but it seemed appropriate, in view of the stud-farm!'

'It's beautiful,' Jacqueline said, stroking the horse's flank. 'Jean will love it.'

There was another little pause and Daisy looked at her hostess. Marriage suited her; a little plumper than before, she looked prettier and more serene. Daisy also detected, in the inspection she was now receiving herself, a clear hint of pity. The Anglaise might be fashionably thin, and extremely chic, but she was a poor thing without a husband, perhaps without a man to love her at all!

Feeling that their small talk would soon be exhausted, Daisy plunged bravely into the middle of things. 'There have been changes since I was last here, but I don't need to ask if you're happy. My father and great-uncle both think you've done very well to keep Jean here!'

'Maman didn't think so,' Jacqueline suddenly decided to admit, 'and of course Daniel couldn't help being disappointed. Still, he understands now that I didn't realise until my dear Jean came along how *sérieux* he was, and how much older than me.'

She smiled gaily, presumably still confident that Daniel was safe from marriage with the House of Ashton. Daisy thought of Jean Lecours' sweetness, and hoped that he would have persistence and strength enough as well to teach his wife that she wouldn't be free in future to change her mind whenever she felt inclined.

'I've seen your step-father about this morning, but not Daniel,' Daisy said casually.

'Oh, he's got to look after Jeanne today; we don't expect him here.'

'Are you all coming this evening?'

Jacqueline's little moue said yes, but indicated that not much pleasure was expected. 'It's not our kind of music,' she explained, 'but Maman's right – we shan't be given another chance to see inside the Château de Chambray; *gens ordinaires* like us aren't normally invited there! The Vicomte comes to the Museum sometimes, and we're supposed to feel grateful that he bothers, but I don't see why we should.'

'Republicans one and all no doubt,' Daisy suggested, still trying to smile. She thanked Jacqueline for the coffee, and went away reflecting that she might always find it hard to like Annette's daughter, but it was a feeling that was almost certainly reciprocated.

William had already left when she got home. The Château where the concert was to be held was some distance from the town, and he and Jeanne were going there together.

'Why there?' Daisy asked her father over lunch.

'Because the de Chambray family support the work done at Jeanne's school, and that's what the evening is in aid of. In fact one of the Vicomte's grandchildren went there – it isn't only for society's rag-tag and bobtail unfortunates. Incidentally, we have to dress up a bit, I'm afraid – thanks to William, we're included in the supper afterwards. The chances are that my black tie is now green with age!'

But she told him solemnly when they set off that he looked lovely, a compliment he was solemnly able to return. Daisy might still look as if she'd been working too hard, but in her dark blue georgette blouse, frilled at neck and wrists, and matching organza skirt he reckoned she was beautiful. Red-gold hair, which she'd allowed to grow long, was intricately coiled, and he noticed that she'd made up her eyes more dramatically than usual. Altogether, he told her, she was doing the Petit Manoir proud.

'Well, we *gens ordinaires* – Jacqueline's phrase! – have to make an effort,' she agreed, grinning at him. 'Even Pierre is being coerced into a suit; he mentioned it in case we mistook him for someone else!'

They joined a procession of cars at the entrance to the Château, and drove along slowly, with ample time to admire the lovely, eighteenth-century elegance in front of them. Inside the ballroom at last with not too much time to spare, they were hastily led to the reserved seats waiting for them. Within a few minutes, introduced by their distinguished-looking host, Jeanne came out to begin the concert alone.

She played her favourite Bach, with the pure intensity demanded by the music, and seemed to match it perfectly herself, Daisy thought. A dress of dark red silk glimmered when she moved, as if silver threads were woven into it, but in her playing she was the least ostentatious of performers

– all they were required to do was listen, not admire the violinist. Next came William, to play two of Debussy's preludes, and then his enchanting 'Golliwog's Cake Walk' from the 'Children's Corner'. Daisy took hold of her father's hand while the pianist settled himself, but relaxed after the first half a dozen bars. This wasn't an ordeal and she needn't feel nervous, because her blessed Uncle Will was thoroughly enjoying himself! He made way for a dark-haired Spanish girl and her accompanist who performed a group of love-songs by Granados. Then Jeanne and William reappeared to perform the Fauré sonata that had been the first thing they ever played together. It sounded different now, Robert realised – practised, perfect, and heartbreakingly beautiful. There was silence when they ended, then shouts of applause. The Vicomte returned with a graceful speech of thanks and promised that an evening so enjoyable must certainly be repeated. The public part of it was over, and the audience began reluctantly to drift towards the doors. Daisy glimpsed Pierre, splendid in dark suit and tie, shepherding Annette out, but she could do no more than wave to him across the crowd.

'Why weren't they invited to the supper?' she wanted to know. 'They've as much right to be there as we have.'

'They *were* invited. Pierre refused, Jeanne said, because he didn't own a dinner jacket. He could have hired one easily enough, but she failed to persuade him.'

'Brave as a lion, but too shy for an occasion like this?'

'I think so,' her father agreed. 'Now we'd better go and curtsey to our hosts, or whatever it is we do to a Vicomtesse.'

A buffet supper was set out in the grand dining-room, and then the guests were encouraged to wander about – into their hostess's beautiful salon and music-room. Daisy was being questioned about life in London by the Vicomte's granddaughter when the words she was about to say died in her throat. Daniel, in evening clothes that certainly didn't look as if they'd been hired, had come to stand beside them. His blue glance skimmed over Daisy, before he bowed to her companion.

'Forgive the interruption, Mam'selle, but your grandmother says that she requires you for some chore or other!' His smile sympathised and charmed as well, and when a clearly reluctant Mam'selle de Chambray had left, Daisy managed to say so.

'You quite knocked her for six, poor girl, if that expression means anything translated into rather bad French.'

'Knock-'em-dead Lescaut,' he agreed in unexpected English. 'I do occasionally watch American films.' Then he took a gulp of wine. 'Your father didn't say you were coming.'

She explained again, wishing that he seemed a little more pleased that she was there. 'He didn't know. I just decided to turn up – for the concert, and for his birthday tomorrow.' She hoped she'd sounded like the globe-trotting Daisy Ashton, who thought nothing of indulging an expensive whim whenever she felt inclined. Anything would be better, no matter how misleading, than having him assume that because he was free of Jacqueline she now had expectations herself. He could have got in touch with her if he'd wanted to; he hadn't done, and his charming smile just now had been directed only at the Vicomte's blushing granddaughter.

Unhappy and unsure, but determined to die rather than mention the name of Jacqueline, she stared at her father, proudly escorting a radiant Jeanne. There, at least, was certainty to cling to; they looked so happy together. She gestured at them, managing to smile.

'Uncle Will's very keen on the idea of unfinished patterns completing themselves. *There's* one that seems as if it might be going to after thirty years!'

She expected to see Daniel smile but saw with a small shock of surprise that he was frowning instead.

'I think you're mistaken,' he said rather stiffly. 'My mother was devoted to Jacques. It's true that he died eighteen months ago but I doubt if she's forgotten him so quickly.'

'She doesn't have to forget him at all,' Daisy pointed out with more force than she meant to. 'Memories remain, but they needn't stifle hope of a fresh happiness. Surely your mother deserves that? I know that my father does.'

The disapproval in his face was now so clear and so hurtful that she was goaded into rushing on. 'I suppose you'd rather have a *French* stepfather—'

'After a German father?' he interrupted her. 'Yes, I believe I would.'

It was too late to explain what she'd been going to say – that English invaders hadn't always been welcome – the damage was done. Even so she might have tried, but Daniel was nodding to William, who'd come to stand beside them. He offered his congratulations civilly if without any warmth and walked away.

She smiled, because that was what she was there for – to smile and chatter and pretend that bitter tears weren't trickling down into the cold, sad depths of her heart. She was introduced by William to the mayor, and by him in turn to the rest of the town's notables, and wondered afterwards whether what she'd said to them had made any sense at all. But it was over at last; she could sit in the back of the car on the way home, staring at the moonlit countryside. Her surprise visit had been a mistake after all; she must be careful never to repeat it in future.

Twenty-Three

Robert's birthday dawned in a morning so fine that they decided to carry their breakfast out of doors. Sitting on the terrace, with green landscape unfolding to the horizon, William was blithely moved to quote the Song of Solomon: 'The rain is over and done, the time of the singing of birds is come, and the voice of the turtle is heard throughout the land.'

'Well, the voice of the cuckoo, anyway,' Robert suggested. 'I think he's hidden in the ash tree over there.'

'How shall we celebrate today – by throwing an informal party, or selfishly by ourselves?' William asked next.

He addressed the question to Daisy but, after a glance at her pale face, Robert answered before she could. 'Selfishly, I think – we did our social duty last night. In any case I have some work lined up for Daisy.'

'I've work lined up for myself,' she pointed out, 'but I'm willing to help you as long as it isn't something beastly like trapping moles.'

'Just a little gentle hoeing among the vines. We aren't supposed to use chemicals on the weeds for the first three years.'

She agreed to weed, and they set off after breakfast through the garden, leaving William to recover from his exertions of the night before. Hoeing a row parallel to her father's, Daisy felt her overstrung nerves relax; it was therapeutic work out on the sunlit hillside, with just enough breeze to temper the growing heat. If she was tempted to feel sorry for herself, she knew that she had only to look around to be reminded of how richly she was blessed. She put the thought into words when they stopped for a rest half-way through the morning.

'Why the sudden counting-up of treasure now?' Robert asked, smiling at her.

'Because I don't do it often enough. Like the rest of us, I'm more inclined to snivel over what I haven't got.'

He was silent for a moment, anxious not to intrude, but aware that talking might be a comfort to her. 'I saw you with Daniel last night. It didn't seem a happy conversation. Is that because you've decided that what you most want simply isn't here?'

She sat making a daisy chain, with the same concentration that she'd used on the task as a small child; an all-or-nothing girl altogether, he reflected, never any half-measures about her. It was a brave but dangerous way to live. Then suddenly she raised her head and looked at him. 'Oh, what *I* want is here, but I think I was mistaken about what Daniel wants.' She scattered the daisies in her lap and smiled almost convincingly. 'Never mind – my hopes of an Ashton/Lescaut alliance now rest on you! It might have been too much of a good thing in any case: father and daughter wedding mother and son. I dare say the Bible's Table of Consanguinity even prohibit it!' She got to her feet before he could reply. 'Back to work – I've got the terrace pots to fill this afternoon.'

He followed her, aware that if only one of them was to find complete happiness he'd have wanted with all his heart for it to be her, not himself. But he picked up his hoe instead of saying so, and they worked on in companionable silence until Madame Albert rang the bell that indicated lunch was ready.

Daisy devoted the afternoon to the task she'd set herself, only hampered by Nelson's determined efforts to dig up everything she planted.

'He's a retriever trying to be helpful,' Robert suggested with a dead-pan face as she salvaged a wilting petunia for the third time.

'He's everything that's delightful in a dog, but a plant-person's useful assistant he is *not*.' Then it occurred to Daisy to ask why he was there at all when the Petit Manoir wasn't his home.

'It is now,' her father said. 'Jean used to bring him every day and finally admitted that it was because Jacqueline reckoned a retriever growing to full size was taking up too much room in a caravan. The poor chap looked sad but relieved when I suggested that he might as well leave Nelson here.'

Feeling sorry for Jean, Daisy told herself to remember Jacqueline's touching pride in her home; but she stroked the dog's black head, and didn't reproach him for trying to bury her trowel in a flower-bed.

The following morning she offered him his favourite treat, a long walk beside the river. As usual, he soon found an excuse to get into the water, being convinced that he shouldn't go home dry as well as clean. She walked on, whistled because he wasn't following her, and turned round to see his head only just above water in mid-stream. She called and he answered with a strange yelping noise she hadn't heard him make before. She hurried back, wondering whether cramp was something dogs could get but, still calling, could now see that, whatever the cause, he was unable to swim or help himself.

She kicked off her sandals, waded in, and then found it easier to swim towards him. He wasn't close to a large clump of reeds, but she feared them all the same, knowing the extent to which their roots and stems spread under water. Alongside the terrified animal, she got her arms around him, but his coat was slippery, and his own struggles made it even harder to tug him free. With one hand needed to keep his head above water, she could only try to disentangle him with the other, but gradually she grew frightened herself, afraid of being unable to save him. The coldness of the water was weakening her as well; she would soon be in serious trouble herself. She could only pray that God in his mercy would send someone to help them before it was too late, and call out despairingly to the empty countryside.

The saviour they were sent she didn't even see arrive. One moment she and Nelson were alone in the river, the next Daniel was treading water beside her.

'He's caught underneath,' she gasped. 'I can go on holding him if you need to fetch a knife.'

The only answer she got was to see Daniel's head disappear under the water. She didn't know what he could do, or how he might do it; but panic had died at the sight of him. It would be all right now, simply because he was there. A moment or two later he re-emerged, shaking water out of his eyes and Nelson was pulled free.

'I'll come back for *you*, so don't go away!' he said – rather unnecessarily she thought.

'I can still swim by myself, thank you,' she said, with as much dignity as chattering teeth would allow.

She followed him as he propelled Nelson to the bank, clambered out, and forced her dripping feet into her sandals. The dog lay there looking spent, but at least with enough life left in him to pant and cough up water.

'He'd have drowned if you hadn't come,' Daisy said in a voice that wobbled on the edge of tears. 'That's his second life gone; he's using them up rather quickly.'

Daniel seemed to be concerned with taking off his shirt, wringing it out and putting it on again. Then he looked at Daisy, dripping and shivering in her soaked shirt and shorts, and sounded angry when he spoke. 'Well, leave him alone the next time he does some damn-fool thing. You could have got trapped out there yourself, trying to help him. Now I suppose we'd better get the stupid animal home.'

He lifted the dog in his arms and set off, with Daisy squelching along beside him. It was the noise they made, she thought, rather than the ridiculous sight they must present, that made a small bubble of mirth start to rise inside her. With fear over, she suddenly wanted to laugh. It wasn't advisable, of course, because it would irritate Daniel still more, but she couldn't help it; she had to laugh or burst. Helpless now, she stood still and looked at him – dripping wet himself, and clutching his large, sodden bundle of dog. Then, wonder of wonders, she saw him begin to laugh himself.

'Stop it, Daisy – I can't walk, laugh, *and* carry this damned dog!' he managed to say. 'What's more, you'll catch cold if you stay in those wet clothes much longer. *Move*, girl, please.'

Suddenly aware that she was as good as naked in the clinging garments, she got herself under control again, only asking in a quivering voice if she could help by carrying Nelson for a while.

'Just walk,' Daniel said briefly, 'and keep walking.'

In this way they arrived at the kitchen door, to be met by Madame Albert, shaken by the sight of them, but managing to stay calm. 'I shall see to the dog,' she announced. 'You, Mam'selle Daisy, must get into a hot bath; Monsieur also, in Monsieur Ashton's bathroom – and he must leave his clothes outside, I shall find him dry ones.'

Half an hour later Daisy went downstairs, warm again, and with her still-damp hair at least washed clean of river water. Daniel was sitting on the terrace, wearing trousers and a shirt she recognised as belonging to her father. Nelson lay stretched out at his feet, eyeing the delicacies Madame Albert had put in front of him, like an exhausted pasha making up his mind to sample a dish of sweetmeats. He wagged his tail at the sight of Daisy but decided not to make the effort to get up.

'I'm sorry no one else is here,' she said to Daniel. 'Uncle Will's gone back to the Château, having promised to survey the Vicomte's wine-cellar, and my father's in Auch. He'll be back by lunch-time.' She glanced briefly at Daniel, sitting with his hands enclosing the cup of coffee Madame Albert had brought him. 'Thank you for rescuing us,' she said quietly. 'I'm not sure what we've have done if you hadn't passed by.'

'I didn't "pass by",' he replied. 'I was on my way to see you when I heard you calling out.' He didn't mention, because it couldn't be put into words, the terror that had sent him headlong towards the river at the sound of her voice. But what he'd come to say seemed almost as difficult. 'I think

I distressed you last night – I'm sorry about that. What you suggested should have occurred to me as well, but it hadn't done and I was taken by surprise.'

'You still don't like the idea, though,' she stated, rather than asked. She thought he wouldn't like her to suggest that he had a rather Victorian view of widowhood, but the truth was that he was an old-fashioned man altogether; it was one of the things she valued him for most.

'Whether my mother marries again or not is her affair,' he said finally, and then smiled with Jeanne's sudden, sweet smile. 'We'll agree that your father isn't French, but I can't see much else wrong with him!'

The world, so sad and out-of-joint, was magically righting itself. The despair that had settled on her last night was drifting away, just as morning mist disappeared in the warmth of the sun. She didn't know how it had happened, but the stranger who'd frowned at her in the Vicomte's ballroom had become once again her dear companion of the day they'd spent in Auch. Perhaps the river had washed away some hurtful barrier of pride, or that shared gust of laughter on the way back had restored him to her.

'What happens now?' he asked, and she knew what he was asking: the question was about themselves, not about her father and Jeanne. If she said that she was going back to London, New York, or Timbuctoo, it would be the end for them. He wouldn't plead, just simply accept that what she'd claimed once before was always going to be true: she belonged somewhere else.

'My father offered the pigeon-house to Jean,' she said, apparently ignoring Daniel's question. 'I gather the offer wasn't accepted.'

'Jacqueline refused it, not Jean,' he answered, puzzled by the sudden switch. 'If they have a child she'll move back into the farmhouse, of course, but she has very clear ideas of what she wants and a *pigeonnier isn't*, I'm afraid, reckoned sufficiently "*comme il faut*"!'

The dryness would have been funny at any other time but Daisy couldn't smile now; they'd reached a point that she knew to be critical. 'I'm deeply thankful that Jacqueline *doesn't* want it – I'd like to live in it myself,' she said.

There was a little pause. 'Not . . . *not* London?' Daniel finally enquired. '*That* was what you said you wanted – big-city life and all that goes with it. How am I to know the truth if your English habit is never to say what you mean?' Torn between hope and despair, he reached out to grip her hands across the table. 'Tell me, and *mean* it, that you want to stay here!'

'Of course, I want to,' she answered simply. 'There wasn't a day in London when I didn't wish I was here . . . made myself work and work just so that I could come back. My dear love, I *hated* being there.'

She was released, but only for the moment it took him to reach her side of the table. Then she was pulled up into his arms, but she held him away with her hands against his chest. 'Listen, please, Daniel. I have to go on writing because that's what I can do. It's also true that I shall make a hopeless farmer's wife whether I write or not. Keeping that in the . . . the forefront of your mind, would the *pigeonnier* be *comme il faut* enough for you?'

She wanted to weep for the joy lighting up his face, but he managed to answer gravely. '*Exactly* what I'd choose, provided we can move into the Petit Manoir if . . . when . . . !' Her hand covered his mouth, but having kissed it he kissed her lips instead. Then he picked her up and returned to his chair with her cradled in his arms. Her flushed face smiled at him but he spoke with wonder in his voice. 'I managed not to fall in love with you that first day you stopped on the track – very hoity-toity I thought you! Resistance crumbled when that lout ran over your bicycle, and very soon became a rout!' His face sobered suddenly. 'Now I shall love you till I die, my English Daisy.'

She reached up to thank him with a kiss, unaware that

Nelson had observed the change in the seating arrangement and saw no reason not to join in. He was making a spirited attempt to climb into Daisy's lap when Robert Ashton walked out on to the terrace.

Still nearly helpless with laughter, she freed herself from the tangle of Daniel's arms and Nelson's paws, and went to meet her father. 'There's quite a lot to tell you,' she said.

'So I observe, my love.' He wrapped her in a warm hug and then went to shake Daniel's hand. '*You'd* better begin because I long to know first of all why you're wearing my best trousers!'

Daniel was persuaded to stay to lunch, but went back to the farm afterwards. Then Robert announced an errand in Foutances, but Daisy didn't quiz him about it. She was conscious of their conversation in the vineyard, but the Table of Consanguinity would have to lump it, that was all! She waved him on his way, and then went to sit in the empty pigeon-house, happily furnishing it in her mind's eye for the charming couple who were going to live in it.

In Foutances, Robert went to the bank, bought several things he didn't need and, after walking twice round the square, knocked at Jeanne's door. She wouldn't be there; she'd be at the school, at the hairdresser's, taking tea with a friend. But not one of these things he told himself was true – she opened the door. As once before, he was led straight into the garden, and he could see that she'd been working there. A music-score was open on the terrace table.

'I'm interrupting you,' he said, 'but there's a piece of news. When you hear it from Daniel this evening, try to look surprised – he'll want to tell you himself that he's resigned to becoming my son-in-law!'

Jeanne's brown face, serious until then, broke into a delighted smile. 'Oh, I'm glad – he and Daisy belong together.'

Robert nodded, then started again more diffidently. 'She

thinks that you and I do, too, but I take more credit for the idea because I've nursed it much longer than she has!'

Jeanne's smile had faded now, and he could read nothing in her face – not pleasure, not regret, not even the irritation she didn't normally bother to hide if that was what she happened to be feeling.

His own smile was rueful and sweet. '*Not* the best I can do, sweetheart, but I'm too nervous to make the sort of proposal of marriage you can't resist!'

She looked gravely at him and he still had no idea what she would say – other women behaved in ways he could usually predict; this one never had since he'd first known her. He had to prompt her gently.

'In case you didn't notice, I've just offered you my hand, my wealth such as it is, and all the love in my heart. Now it's your turn to say something.'

She did smile then, but only for a brief moment. Unusually, because she wasn't a woman who fidgeted with things, her fingers trembled on the pages of the score in front of her. 'I shall thank you, dear Robert, but not accept the offer,' she said at last.

His eyes were fixed on her face, a blue glance she remembered. 'You must tell me why not, please. I promise not to badger you, but there might be some objection that I *can* demolish.'

She stared back at him, aware that more than anyone she'd ever known, even more than Jacques, he'd remained the same – unchanged by altered times, altered fashions, and altered values. He was still the man who long ago had answered her with a smile when she scowled at him in the hayloft of her grandfather's barn. She'd been wrong to think he wouldn't repeat his offer to take care of her, because she'd not properly understood the extent to which she and her mother were still interwoven in his mind and heart. But Christine Goldman had confirmed what she knew – that his memory of Marguerite had never faded. *She* would always remain the woman who had come first with Alain Mayer, and then with Robert Ashton. For Robert now, Jeanne thought, her mother perhaps ranked behind Daisy in his affections. Jeanne Lescaut could count herself fortunate to come after that, but as it had been in her childhood, so it was even more now – she needed to come first, or manage on her own.

'There are no objections,' she answered finally, 'only instincts to go by. The truth is, I think, that you've stayed a little in love with the idea of finding me again. Having done so, you're kind enough to pretend that a drunken rape, an illegitimate child, and long years of marriage to another man have made no difference to the idealised picture you keep in your mind of young Jeanne Mayer, but she's no longer the same girl, my friend!'

He reached out to still her fingers with his own. 'It's not the remembered girl I love – although I do remember her – it's you, the woman you are now, all I could dream of in a wife.'

She released herself to blow him a little kiss of gratitude. 'My answer is still no, Robert. This house, and especially this garden, are precious and I can't imagine leaving them. I love my work at the school, and solitude here is something I've come to enjoy. Apart from playing music with William, knowing him is pure pleasure. My friendship with you is more precious still, but it *is* a friendship. We should be making a mistake if we tried to turn it into a love-affair after thirty years.'

He said nothing, while the memory of Daisy's wry comment echoed in his head – only one Ashton/Lescaut alliance was going to be allowed after all. 'Those things *aren't* objections I can demolish,' he agreed finally, 'and although I would very much like to try, I doubt if a macho demonstration of love-making would do anything but remind you unpleasantly of the brutality that men are capable of. I shall have to take my *congé* with what grace I can muster, but you must believe one thing: I'm not infatuated with some dream of the past; I'm the man who loves you now and always. I may remind you of the fact occasionally and – who knows? – when I'm a doddering eighty-six and you are rising eighty-one, you might even think it's time to accept my offer!'

She tried to smile, but he saw tears glistening in her dark eyes. 'We shall share our children in any case – isn't that a great deal to be glad about?'

'A very great deal,' he agreed, 'and so is everything else about the life we have here. It seemed almost impossible at the beginning that it would turn out like that – ingrained prejudice, entrenched mistrust, and wartime misunderstandings all seemed to add up to a scenario of unmitigated disaster. But we English and you French have somehow come to know each other, and thank God for that because it was high time we did.'

She nodded, but he thought her mind was occupied with the objection she *hadn't* mentioned; she couldn't leave simply because here were all her memories of Jacques Lescaut. To live with another man now would be a betrayal that loyalty and gratitude couldn't allow. Feeling that all he could do for her was to take his own sadness away, he stood up to leave but her hand stayed him.

'Wait there, Robert, while I fetch wine. We must drink to Daniel and Daisy, and also to the indispensable *Entente* that hasn't always been quite *Cordiale* enough!'

She went back into the house, there to weep tears that hadn't been shed even when Jacques had died. The house, the garden, her precious solitude – these things *could* have been left, but not for a man who offered himself to her simply out of the kindness of his idealistic, English heart. There'd been a moment just now when she'd wavered, almost ready to be convinced that he saw her as the woman she really was and loved what he saw; but it was wishful-thinking, of course.

She dried her wet face and, calm again, picked up her tray and went outside. She could even smile at Robert as he got to his feet, because what she'd said was true – they *did* have much to celebrate, even now.